The Grimm

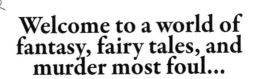

Welcome to a world of fantasy, fairy tales, and murder most foul...

My name's Elle. Princess Arielle, for those who know my history. Cursed by my own father and banished to Grimm, I'm a siren, a killer, and one of the best damned cold-case detectives in the hundred realms. I don't stop until I uncover the truth, no matter where that truth leads.

After discovering a bloodstained ribbon and a poison-tipped cat's claw at a cold-case crime scene at the Charmings's castle, I'm sent to Wonderland to investigate. Wonderland is a harrowing place full of madness and dark secrets. I'd rather be landlocked than step foot on that twisted soil, but I don't have a choice. My insatiable thirst for truth reveals a conspiracy that will not only rock the Grimm world but also my own.

No one ever walks away from Wonderland unscathed... no one.

Join me for a spellbinding tale you aren't soon to forget.

---

1. https://www.facebook.com/groups/hattersharem/

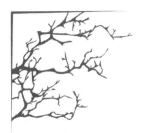

Prologue

G *rimm Reports*
 Cold Case File# 278: The Charmings's

Detail of Events

22nd of July. Hysterical female calls in to the Grimm PD. Two bodies reported as DOA. One male. Brown hair. Blue eyes. Goes by the moniker Groundskeeper. Dressed in skins. Partial decapitation of skull. Ten yards from his body, a Jane Doe. Blond hair. Pale blue eyes. Nude. Stomach has been mutilated, fingers and toes amputated. Bodies dumped close to a lake behind the estate of one Prince Charming and Snow White. No evidence of weapons on scene. Castle and grounds swept, nothing to indicate those within have any specific knowledge of the crime.

Actions Taken

New head of groundskeeping and head chambermaid taken in for questioning. Neither claims to have seen or heard anything, and everyone else in the Charmings's employ denies any knowledge of said event. Detectives Mulan and VanWinkle returned for a second sweep of grounds and keep. Neither Charming nor White willing to talk further, and none in their employ will either.

Summary

A year later, cold-case file remains. Will send one final inspector specialized in water rescue out to the scene to scour lake upon the grounds for any possible clues.

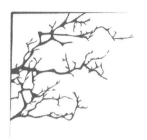

Chapter 1

Detective Elle

I took a final gulp of water as I stared up at the whitish-blue sliver of moon hanging in the sky amongst millions of glittering stars. There was nothing above me and no life swimming alongside me. It was just me in the cursed pool, alone. Cast out forever from my own kind. A pariah now, where once I'd been exalted, praised as the most beautiful jewel of them all.

But I did not mind the silence, not anymore. I was a long way away from the girl I'd once been—simple, silly, and naïve. I would never again be those things. My sins were terrible chains upon my soul. Every anguished cry, every tearful plea—I relived it all, night after long night, except now, in this finite sliver of time when my demons slept and I could breathe again, if only for a moment.

This was my favorite time of day, not quite night and not quite morning. *The witching hour*, we Grimmers called it. That point in the day where very little life stirred, and yet the world was expectant, pregnant with the possibility of what was yet to come.

The morning was calm and cool. Relaxing. But it wouldn't be for long. Today's assignment would take me far from my protected waters. It wasn't that I hated land, but staying out of my waters for too long made me twitchy. I'd learned to deal with the discomfort years ago, but it was never fun.

Snarling at the thought of just how long I'd be forced to stay in the above this time, I snatched a shell-pink pearl from the river floor with a little more force than necessary, kicking up layers of sediment and turning my normally clear waters murky.

With a final flick of my fiery-colored tail, I thrust my body through the deep water and, in one smooth motion, jumped clear of it, gills sealing shut and lungs adjusting to breathe air.

I landed gracefully on my feet upon the cold, wet stretch of sand, needing a second to acclimate myself to the sensation of air versus water. I shuddered but squared my shoulders after a third breath. I was ready.

A balmy breeze feathered across my naked flesh, causing me to break out in a wash of goose bumps. Clutching the pearl tightly, I raised two fingers to my mouth and released a piercing whistle, the likes of which only a siren could ever achieve. The high-pitched, tonal quality was enough to pierce through someone's skull and turn a brain to soup if I wished.

Giving myself a quick shake to dry off, I reached for my skintight black leather pants, which I kept tucked beneath the rocky overhang, and slipped them on. The tighter the better, and not because it showed off my body. I had shapely, athletic limbs that many *leggers* seemed to find admirable. But I couldn't care less what my legs looked like. I wore the things out of necessity.

I needed the tightness of the pants because it mimicked the pressure of water against my tail. The first twenty-four hours outside my water were never fun and usually more than a little disorienting and nauseating for me. I took a deep breath. You'd think, after being forced to wear the bloody things going on almost five decades, I'd have grown used to the queer sensation, but I doubted I ever would. I was a creature of the deep. It wasn't natural to live my life on land, but I had no choice in the matter.

Just then, a ball of golden light zigged and zagged through the air, acting drunk as it waltzed closer. The ball of light was actually a sea-dwelling sprite dressed in vines of sea kelp, with long black hair that trailed well past her ankles. It was Caytla, and I had to stifle a groan. Of all the sprites to heed my call, she was the one I dreaded dealing with most. The bitch with wings would just as soon stab me in the back as make a deal with me.

The miniature woman with pointed ears landed on a jagged edge of rock in front of me. She grinned, exposing razor-sharp teeth that could easily make mincemeat of man or beast.

"Ye gots the treasure?" Her double-lidded reptilian eyes blinked independently of each other, and her dragonfly wings buzzed ominously. She was in a mood. I hated it when she was in a mood.

I clenched my jaw, feeling the muscle in my cheek twitch, but I turned my palm over, showing her the pearl. "I've got it, you filthy creature."

If Caytla felt insulted, she didn't let on. A sprite's greatest weakness was her avarice for treasure. She reached her wee fingers out, but I yanked the pearl out of reach just before she could snatch it from me. She hissed, and her wings buzzed, sounding like the droning whir of a disturbed hornet's nest.

"Well?" I snipped. "Have we a deal?"

She swallowed, staring at the pearl with unwavering, greedy focus.

"Aye, we've a deal, fish." She spat out the slur with a nasty little snarl. The remarkably stunning water sprite thrust out her palm, exposing a ball of golden brilliance.

Sprites were evil, nasty little buggers, but they were part of the siren family tree, which meant they were as appealing to look upon as I was. Her skin was ivory-fair with not a single blemish upon it. Her hair was the color of a raven's feather glinting in the sunlight—black and green tinted with hints of darkest violet. She had a lush little mouth, full and bright pink. But in the Grimm universe, the most beguiling and beautiful amongst us often had the cruelest hearts.

I narrowed my eyes and clenched my fingers over the pearl.

Caytla's upper lip curled back, and a heated wash of fury burned through her blood-red pupils. I'd seen that look in her eyes before—determined greed. She might not want to heel for me, but she'd do it because, more than anything, she wanted the treasure. I grinned, and her wee nostrils flared.

"How many hours of water are in it?" I asked. My kind usually didn't need spelled trinkets to walk on land. But I wasn't like most sirens.

The last time the treacherous fae had sewn me a shirt with water from my pool, there'd only been enough water to last me ten hours. I'd nearly turned to stone before I made it back to my river. If I'd gone even a minute longer without returning, the effects could have been catastrophic and likely irreversible, and the tiny bitch knew it.

"Forty-eight hours' worth, just as demanded," Caytla spit. "Now give or I go."

Sprites were deadly, perfidious creatures, and I wouldn't normally bother with any of them, but desperate times and all that. Only the sprites were capable of weaving the sorts of enchantments I required.

"Give it to me. And I swear to the gods, if you screw me again, little sprite, I'll take you below water and drown your sorry hide."

Caytla zipped from her perch on the rocks toward my palm. The sprite made the transfer quickly, zooming out of my reach with such blinding speed that I'd not seen her move at all.

Wings buzzing furiously behind her as she hovered before me, Caytla took a tester bite out of the edge of the pearl. Her smile turned lascivious.

"Unlike some, I don't cheat," I hissed.

She just rolled her eyes. Satisfied I'd not cheated her, Caytla bowed and pocketed her prize, which had now shrunk down to the size of a penny. But there was no reverence in her bow, nothing but loathing irony.

"Ye ken where to find me, *princess*," she muttered with dripping sarcasm.

I ground my teeth together, clinging tight to the golden orb in my palm to stay my hand. I wished to the gods I didn't need to do scratch with the fae, but that was the price one paid for treason against one's king. I loathed the taste of humble pie.

The sky was already beginning to lighten with shades of peach and tangerine. The witching hour was nearly gone. Twirling, Caytla streaked like a ball of light back toward the haven of the sprite stronghold. The trail of her maniacal laughter grated harshly on my nerves. Only once I was sure the fae had gone did I sigh and glance down at the orb.

Sprites could not lie. It was their one fatal flaw. So I trusted that, at least this time, the demonic creature had given me what I needed. But having been a detective for years, I knew the precarious nature of my job and just how often things could change on a dime.

Turning, I picked up a shell from the sand and, using a bit of my own magick, called my water into it. The funnel of water settled inside the perfectly shaped seashell, which now glowed a deep blue.

Stringing a bit of cord through a natural hole in its end, I tied the shell around my neck and exhaled deeply, feeling more at ease with the comforting weight of it pressed against my breast. Should anything unforeseen arise, I had an additional day's worth of water at hand to see me through.

"Reveal yourself," I commanded the orb in my palm, and instantly, it transformed into its true form—that of a flowing teal-colored peasant top.

I dressed quickly, feeling calmer when the waters of my home encapsulated my form. Then, grabbing my badge, holster, and gun, I withdrew the enchanted key card that helped me slip between realms. Walking over to the key card reader set in the rocks, I swiped the card through, stepping back just as a black wrought-iron door materialized where I'd been standing moments ago.

I strode through and left the safety of my seaside home for the dusty, busy streets of Central Grimm, choking on the thick smog of the city with my first breath.

The city itself was a network of gothic-style architecture, with buildings that stretched like giant fingers toward the heavens. It always took me a moment to adapt to the smog, sights, and sounds of the city center.

Cobblers peddled their wares from every sidewalk corner. Food hawkers, with shouts of "Fresh fish ere!" or "Sweet buns! Come get your sweet buns!" or any other type of delicacy one could imagine, vied for the attention of the crowds moving with great urgency toward their individual destinations.

My feet guided me by instinct toward one particular peddler, one who specialized in foods and drinks of the sea. He grinned as he saw me near, and I nodded.

"Georgie Porgie," I said, dipping my chin once.

He was thick and pudgy around the middle just the way his name implied. He had a head of shockingly frizzy orange-red hair that he never tried to tame, a broad forehead, a bulbous nose, and a wide mouth with blunt, flat teeth. He showed signs of aging around the eyes and mouth, but considering he was a sea-cave dwarf and over four hundred years old, he looked pretty good.

"Elle, my favorite customer." His thick voice rumbled like a rockslide.

I snorted. "You say that to all the ladies, dwarf?"

"Aye." He agreed while whipping up my usual—a squid-ink latte, heavy on the ink. His movements were smooth and efficient as he whipped up some heated sea foam for the topper.

"But in this case, it happens to be true. So, what's on the docket for today, eh?"

Every morning he asked me the same. And almost always, I'd say, "None of your bloody business." But today was different.

Reaching into my pocket, I dug out a miniature diamond. Usually, I paid Georgie in sapphires, but at that moment, I had a bribe in mind.

Dwarves were generally silent, thoughtful creatures. Because of their small stature, they were also easily overlooked, which meant people got lazy and forgetful in their presence. Dwarves often had their thumb on the pulse of the city and were an easy source of information.

For the right price, of course.

Holding up the flawless, half-carat diamond, I pretended to study it. A spoon clattered to the cobblestone floor, and I smirked.

"What 'ave you there, siren?" Georgie swallowed hard, words sounding awed and rushed.

Raising a brow, I pursed my lips and acted as though I hadn't heard him. The only beautiful thing about Georgie was the color of his eyes. The deep, intense green of them reminded me of my father's ancient sea-kelp gardens.

His hands shook as he handed me my latte. I raised a brow, taking the drink from him. I noted the way his Adam's apple bobbed up and down with each desperate swallow.

"'Ew's that diamond for, there, miss?" he asked, voice growing thick with accent. I smirked and rubbed the already flawless diamond against my shirt.

"Well, Georgie, it's for you."

Greed twisted his thick lips as he started to reach for it, but I shook my head and took a step back. His thick brows pulled into a pitiful frown. "And what 'ave I got to do to earn that butter, copper?"

I smirked. "Funny you should ask that, Georgie. All I want to know is the answer to a question. You, with your hands on the pulse of the city, must know something about this, I think."

He swallowed again, and from the corner of my eye, I noticed a long line of customers starting to grow antsy behind me. I needed to be quick about this. "Tell me, my friend, what do you know of the Charming murders?"

The case was old now, over a year at this point. It was the perfect time for criminals to flap their gums, suspecting they'd beat the law and were now in the clear.

His wide nostrils flared. A heavy, furrowed line banded from one shaggy red brow to the next. Georgie topped my latte off with another dollop of blue-tinted foam.

"That's a year old, siren. What would I know of it?" he spat, sounding annoyed but also edgy. He knew something. I'd stake what was left of my soul on it.

I narrowed my eyes, squeezing the gem tight. "So you're saying you know nothing at all? That's too bad."

He fidgeted from one foot to the next, gripping my cup so tight that his knuckles blanched. Oh, he knew something all right.

"Aw, c'mon, Georgie." I rolled the diamond across my fingers like a magician would a gold coin. His eyes never stopped tracking the movement. "You really gonna turn down a diamond?" It wasn't truly a question because I already knew the answer.

He wet his lips as he handed me the latte, which shook so hard in his hand that the contents threatened to slosh over the sides.

Snatching it away from him, I took a satisfying gulp and sighed heavily. "Well, that's too bad. I really thought you might have heard something. Maybe next time, old chap." I went to deposit the gem back in my pocket.

"No, wait! Stop," he barked. "Stop." Squeezing his eyes shut, he shook his shaggy head.

Being called a rat in Grimm was a dangerous thing and tantamount to signing your own death certificate if the wrong people found out.

Still, a diamond was a diamond and equal to a year's worth of wages for Georgie.

Biting the corner of my lip, I gave him wide, innocent eyes and a winsome smile. "What's the matter, Georgie?" I asked innocently.

"Damn you to the two hells, siren," he sighed, defeated, and blew out a deep breath. "Gimme here."

Placing the diamond in his hand, I smiled when he shuddered. There was nothing in the world a dwarf loved more than a diamond.

Rubbing the top of it with his finger, he said, "'Eard rumor from a murder of crows that a cat were involved. 'Tis only rumor, mind you."

Taking another sip of my coffee, I gave him a disbelieving frown. "A cat? I hardly think a house cat could have done what—"

He shook his head. "I didn't say it were just any cat, siren. But rather *the* cat."

He tipped his head knowingly.

It took me a moment to understand all he was implying, and when I did, I was the one who jerked and lowered my voice to a tight hiss. "Cheshire? Are you saying that Cheshire was responsible for the murders?"

That was the first I'd ever heard of it. But it was also true that most of our solved cold cases could be traced back to a dwarf's help at some point. I mulled over my choices. I'd been working this tiresome case for two weeks now, and all my leads had hit dead ends. This was easily the most confusing and convoluted case I'd worked on in years, and I could see why it'd gone cold. None of the evidence made any sense.

But for him to claim Cheshire could have been a part of it made absolutely no sense either. Traveling between realms was not only extremely difficult, but near impossible for most. Only a rare few could do it, and only then by strong magick.

"I said it were rumor only, but it is one I've heard tell a few times so far."

There was a tap at my elbow.

I turned, looking into the weathered face of an old fisherman dressed in yellow rubbers.

"I heard the same, miss," he said in an excited whisper, curling and uncurling his fingers in a silent appeal for his own diamond.

I snorted and shook my head. He reeked of ten-day-old fish parts that'd been sitting out in the sun to rot. "Then file a report," I snapped before glancing back at Georgie and nodding. "Good coffee. See you around, dwarf."

"Yeah," he said with a thick drawl, lips flat and tight with irritation. Glancing over my shoulder he boomed, "Weel, 'ew's next!"

Half a block later, I walked through the doors of Grimm PD and sat at my stark desk.

Detective Ichabod Crane gave me a tired smile. He was a thin man, but not unattractively so, who habitually dressed in black and wore his chestnut hair in a severe queue. He had a long face and intelligently keen blue eyes that reminded me of home. It was easy to think him merely a pretty face until one got to talk to him for any length of time and realized he was a genius at decoding even the toughest of riddles.

"Talk to the chief yet?" he asked, drumming long fingers on his desktop as he leaned back in his padded leather chair.

The precinct was a buzz of activity. Fairies, both big and small, flitted through the long, winding halls, dropping the morning case files onto the detectives' desks. In the corner, a group of three ogres stood munching on marrow-filled donuts. A couple of unruly arseholes were being booked for petty theft and tossed into temporary holding cells, and I knew there was a dragon being detained somewhere inside these walls thanks to the constant thumping vibrations of its tail slamming against the floor. My feet tingled from the aftershocks.

"You mean about the Charmings finally consenting to a sweep? Bo gave me the heads up yesterday afternoon."

He nodded. "Yeah. Damn. I really wanted that case."

Snorting, I finished off the last of my latte with a gulp, belched, and then tossed the cup into the garbage bin beside his desk, clapping my hands together when it landed with a dull clang.

Ich hated when I used his bin instead of my own. With a terse growl, he reached inside the bin, whipped out the discarded cup, and flicked it into mine. I smirked. It was so easy to rile him up.

He dusted his hands off, giving me a look that said, "So there!" before settling back down.

"Yeah, well, I'd be happy to hand it off. I hate dealing with royalty. Bunch of too-good pricks who think the rest of the world is worthy only to lick the soles of their boots."

Raising a stern brow, he pinched his lips, but his eyes twinkled merrily. "Correct me if I'm wrong, *little mermaid*"—he stressed the moniker he knew I loathed with every fiber of my being—"but you're royalty."

Hissing at him, I reached forward and punched his arm. "Say that name again, and I'll shove a water pick through your head. You know I'm nothing like the rest of them."

The teasing laughter died from his tongue. Ichabod was one of the few who knew what'd happened to me. It was a secret I kept close to the vest, and one he'd discovered because he was brilliant and deduced the matter on his own. It was also a secret he'd vowed never to share with another.

"I'm sorry, Elle. That joke was in poor taste."

Thinning my lips, I shook my head. "Whatever."

I should have apologized in return, but the hurt of that day and everything that'd happened to me since was a can of worms I didn't dare open myself to. Just thinking about it made me feel raw and violent, and that was the last thing I needed to deal with on a day when I'd be expected to bow in the presence of the bastard and his loathsome queen.

Wetting my lips, I stood, adjusted my holster, and sighed. "I guess I can't keep dragging this out." I was just about to turn when I stopped myself. "Look, if you don't have anything else on your card, I'd be more than happy to have you tag along."

"You know." He stood and slipped on his woolen, knee-length jacket. "I think I might."

I eyed the coat. "It's not cold outside."

"I take chills," he said smoothly and, raising a dark brow, he gestured for me to precede him to the time portal located at the back of the precinct.

Swiping my key card, I punched in the coordinates to the Charming estate. A rift of time parted the veil between realms—a spiraling tunnel of blue that spun with a kaleidoscope of colors.

The first time I'd traveled this way, I'd retched the moment I'd stepped through. The shifting and dancing lights had caused my equilibrium to go haywire. Now, I knew to take a deep breath, close my eyes, and slowly count to ten.

There was no other way to travel between the realms. No roads or even waterways could do it. The world of Grimm was literally separated by time and dimension. A millennium ago, a high council of wizards opened the transdimensional roadways, called *the between*, that connected Grimm to other dimensions. But due to the high rate of crime committed by outsiders, it'd been ruled that only an elite few could use them anymore—royalty, Grimm PD, and of course, high wizards, but they were few and far between. The wizards were an honorable bunch more concerned with studying their arcane arts than becoming actively involved in the worlds around them.

Which was what made Georgie's assertions about Cheshire so boggling.

In moments, we were out of the between and standing in a forest full of towering trees. Just yards ahead sat a castle that seemed to gleam like gold in the sunlight. Birds swooped through the azure skies, and rodents scampered up trees. Deer walked elegantly on grassy paths. The smell of apples was everywhere.

Or rather, rotted apples. Snow White refused to let any be picked from the orchards. She had a fierce hatred of the fruit, and I wondered why the Queen continued to let them grow in the first place.

I spied a team of knights on horseback clomping through the castle gates in our direction. At their head was Prince Charming himself, blond hair billowing in the breeze like a silky banner. Ich bumped my shoulder and chuckled. "You look as though you've bitten into a lemon."

"Yeah, well the thought of dealing with the Charmings makes me feel that way."

The last time I'd come here had been three years ago, and the notorious Casanova had attempted to push his hand down the front of my shirt and grab my left breast. I'd bitten him hard, leaving behind a permanent reminder on that oh-so-regal hand of his that fish bit back.

Ichabod raised a brow as though waiting for me to finish. "Anything I should know?"

Giving him a swift smile, I turned on my heel and nodded. "Yeah. Don't leave me alone with him. If you do, I can't guarantee the safety of his family jewels, if you know what I mean."

Ichabod shivered, cupping the front of his pants. "I'm pretty sure I do."

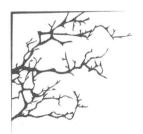

Chapter 2

Detective Elle

Charming sat astride his white mount, his blond hair shimmering like threads of gold in the early morning sun. He had a body made for sin and the face of an angel—square jaw, molten-amber eyes, sharp nose, and slashing cheekbones. He looked impressive, like a king. Clothed in the purple colors of royalty and bearing his coat of arms—a regal lion in repose—he'd actually made my heart flutter when I'd first met him.

That was until he'd opened his mouth.

"Hello, fish." His sensuous lips curled into a seductive grin.

I gritted my teeth, wishing like two hells I could punch him in the mouth. Ichabod cleared his throat.

The sound caused the king to turn and glance down at my partner for the day. "Oh, a commoner." Charming sniffed.

Ichabod parted his coat, revealing the Grimm PD badge. His face was calm and composed. Nothing ever fazed Ichabod. It was part of what made him such a bloody good detective.

I wished I had even a tenth of his composure.

"I'm sure you received notice from the precinct that we'd be arriving to-day." Ichabod was excellent at professional courtesy.

Giving a barely perceptible tilt of his head, Charming rolled his eyes. "Of course I did. And while I'm always happy to see you, girl—"

"Speak to my partner like that one more time," Ichabod growled, "and I'll see you cuffed for impeding the progress of a criminal case, king or no."

For just a moment, I allowed the façade of my face to change, showing Charming the monster hidden beneath the beautiful mask.

Sirens were gorgeous, but only if we wished to be. Behind the beauty was a mouth full of fangs and a thirst for blood.

Charming hissed as his horse reared back. I smirked, feeling petty and triumphant at the same time. I probably should care more or, at the very least, hate that I wasn't nearly as composed as Ichabod, but I didn't.

"Just take us to the lake," I snapped, my patience for faux niceties beginning to wear thin.

Without another word, the king turned his steed and led us toward the back of his estate. Thirty minutes later, we arrived at the edge of the lake.

The way the sunlight reflected off the surface of the water made it appear like glass. It was pretty, but I'd seen better. The lake was open, with no trees around for shade. It was an easy vantage point from which to see for miles around—and be seen from, as well. Not the best place to kill someone. But since the murders had taken place at twilight, the killer—or killers, as we'd not yet discounted that possibility—had benefited from the concealment of night.

I took a moment to stop and inhale. To a siren, the smell of water was like a fingerprint, distinct from one lake bed to the next. This one held a hint of sweetness from the apples rotted into the ground, a touch of earth from the heavy wash of disturbed mud from recent rains, and... sulfur? I sniffed harder, trying to understand the very faint but odd odor of sulfur that wasn't quite sulfur at all.

I wrinkled my nose. "Have you tested the levels of bacteria in this water?" I spared a glance for the king.

Charming shrugged, giving me a blank stare. "You would need to ask the groundskeeper. Why?" he snapped.

Reminding myself that I was a professional, I swallowed my growl and answered. "Because there is a smell of sulfide here, but it is not common to this region."

Ich hummed, a clear sign that he was already beginning to cogitate upon this riddle. Turning, he began a slow walk around the mile-wide body of water, eyeing the glassy surface of it like the academic he was.

Crossing my arms, I looked at the king, who stared at the water, dumbfounded. "And what has that to do with the murders?"

"I don't know," I answered honestly. "Maybe nothing. Maybe everything."

"Whatever." Shaking his head, he pointed at the lake. "As you can see, there is nothing here. Detectives have combed through these woods most thoroughly, to the aggravation of my Snow."

"Oh?" I cocked an eyebrow. "I would think you'd want this case solved. It doesn't exactly look good that a double homicide happened on castle grounds. Shouldn't it be your priority to see this case settled?"

He glowered. "You damn well know that is the only reason I allow you rats with badges to come scampering at my doorstep, you little bitch."

"Classy as ever, King. Why isn't Snow here?" I pressed harder.

Charming was as clueless as the day was bright. He was a pretty face with a title and nothing more. But Snow White was known to walk her gardens frequently. After reading the reports thoroughly, I knew Snow had claimed to know and see nothing, but sometimes, what seemed inconsequential at first began to make an impression over time. I'd hoped to question her once more, just to see if any new memory could be jogged loose.

"She is caring for our daughter."

Shocked, I shook my head. "Daughter?"

When had the Charmings gotten pregnant? To be fair, work often kept my mind preoccupied, but a royal child was a big event, one I should have heard about.

"Rosemary," he gruffed, and it seemed to me that a genuine smile crossed his lips. His eyes sparkled as he continued to speak of his daughter, so much so that I lost my words. It wasn't an act at all. The king was thoroughly smitten by his offspring. Perhaps the king had a soul after all. "She is almost a year and a half—"

Then he snarled, blinking himself back to the present. As though realizing who it was he spoke to, a transformation took hold of his features. "She is not coming, and I am only going to grant you both another ten minutes on these grounds before I kick you out. Do what you must and then leave us!"

With a flick of his crop against the horse's withers, Charming turned, racing at breakneck speed back toward the castle.

"Prick," I hissed just as Ichabod came trotting back to my side.

"What was that?" he asked, eyeing the guards left behind, who were now looking at us coldly.

Shaking my head, I dropped to my knees. "We've ten minutes to gather any evidence we can, and then we're to go."

We didn't have a warrant to search the grounds. We probably should have gotten one, but the Charmings had been more than willing to work with GPD up to this point. Had this case not involved royalty, there'd have been a search warrant, no doubt. But in Grimm, politics and rank smeared together into a messy, unwritten set of rules all adhered to. It was the good ol' boy system of "You scratch my back, and I'll make sure your precinct benefits."

Grimm was as crooked as the day was long, and there wasn't a thing I could do about it either. I'd tried once and nearly lost my badge for the effort.

"Did you find anything when you walked the perimeter?" I asked, still sniffing the breeze. The sulfide smell was faint, but it was definitely not from around here.

One of the most befuddling parts of the crime last year had been the complete lack of evidence. Normally, there was something—a stray hair, a bullet, fibers, footprints, something. But in this case, there'd been nothing other than the bodies themselves. But nowhere in the report had there been mention of the strange odor emanating from the waters.

Perhaps that was because the only beings who would have been capable of scenting such a minor anomaly were water elementals. And I was the only water elemental holding a badge. One prone to seeing conspiracies might wonder why I'd not been sent out immediately to investigate.

I inhaled deeply. "Something's not right with this water."

"They did a water drag and found nothing," Ichabod murmured, his eyes never leaving the rippling movements below.

"I'm sure they wouldn't have because what I'm smelling isn't actually in the water itself," I said and then ran my palm an inch above the surface of the lake. The complacent pool filled with ripples, then ripples turned into waves until, with a soft roaring sound, the waters parted, revealing the densely packed mud more than ten feet beneath.

I cocked my head, peering intently at the thick sludge and decomposing plant and animal life.

"Do you see something?" Ichabod asked a second later.

I shook my head. "No. But something is down there that shouldn't be in this realm."

Standing, I walked a slow circle around the lake, moving the water from one spot to the next as I studied the dense, wet earth. There was something encased below, I was absolutely sure. And when I got halfway around the pond, I finally spied what I'd been looking for—a ridged knot of earth, far different in coloration than the rest of the clay bed, which was a dull, rust red. This patch was black as tar, as though something had befouled the very soil itself.

Narrowing my eyes, I held out my palm and called for whatever was buried in the mud. A gentle swell of water latched on to the objects, suctioning them out of the muck before depositing them into my hand. I cringed at the wet glop dripping between my fingers. With a softly spoken command, the waters rolled back to where they belonged once again.

"Come here," Ich said and knelt, yanking me down beside him. Without asking for permission, he took the sludge from my hand, put it in the lake, and began gently shaking his fist. A moment later, a slow curl of a smile drew across his face as he withdrew his hand.

I stared at the brown-stained silk ribbon and the large, curved black object still caked in mud resting on his palm. "What is that?" I asked with a frown, unable to make heads or tails of what I was seeing.

Chuckling, he handed me the ribbon, which I promptly slipped into an evidence baggie before burying it in my pocket. Once again, he dipped his hand into the water, but this time, he was scraping his thumbs across the surface of the hooked object.

"Well, if I'm right," he murmured intently, "then you may have just found the murder weapon."

My brows rose. "What?" I asked, sounding shocked. But he didn't answer. He just continued swishing his hand in the water.

It took another minute or so to clean the object, and when he pulled it back out again, I was staring at a thumb-sized claw.

"A cat claw?" I hissed, recalling Georgie's words.

Ichabod frowned and glanced at me. "Of a sort, though not entirely. Do you see the banded striations upon it?"

He lifted the claw and turned it slightly, just enough so that a beam of sun could catch the onyx-colored band, causing it to shimmer like heated lava rock.

"I've read about claws like these," he said in that distracted voice that meant Ich was lost to the thoughts in his head. "The bands aren't merely decorative. They are a sign of poison sacks."

Very few cats possessed claws like these, and most of them came from one realm.

"This is from Wonderland," I said, as he handed it over to me.

The claw was aged and worn. I studied the smooth tip, noting the empty pocket where the poison had once flowed. I'd only ever met Cheshire once and wasn't certain he possessed poison-tipped claws, but Georgie's account was gaining more and more credibility.

Withdrawing an evidence bag from inside of his jacket pocket, Ichabod held it out to me. I dropped the claw into it.

"So, we know how this happened. Now, we need to figure out why and who," he said ominously, giving me arched brows.

Nodding, I knew exactly where the chief would be sending me once we reported back.

"I don't get paid enough for this job," I sighed.

Ich chuckled. "Says the princess with bottomless coffers."

I hissed at him, and he had the nerve to laugh.

CARRYING BOTH POUCHES, I made my way toward the chief's office. In the hour we'd been gone, the precinct had gotten even busier. Green and blue fairy light lit up the dash of the caller hotlines. Officers in uniform and in plain clothes were running around, bumping into one another in their haste to exit the building.

Frowning, but not terribly worried, as there was always some emergency or another in a city of this size, I continued heading toward Bo's closed office door. But after being bumped into for the third time by an officer, I growled, stopping the next uni I saw.

Tanner, a woodland satyr and beat cop for the past twenty years, with unassuming brown hair and eyes, glanced down at the hand gripping his elbow.

"Detective Elle?" he questioned with a slight bleat to his words.

He had his cap in his hand, and the top button of his shirt twisted into the wrong slot, causing him to look rumpled and harried. His normally neatly groomed black hooves clopped anxiously, dropping bits of dirt and grass on the polished floor as he glanced at the line of officers winding out the door.

Tanner often looked as though he'd just barely made it into work on time, but he'd never looked dirty. Today, he looked as though he'd taken a dirt bath. Considering he worked two jobs because his woodland nymph wife was heavily pregnant with their tenth kid, I spared his pride by giving his appearance little more than a passing glance.

"What the hell's going on out there today?" I asked, watching as a line of mystically issued crime-scene examiners—or MICE for short—followed close on the heels of several armed cops.

His nostrils flared as he grunted, and he struck his hoof down once more. "Robbery at the Bank of Grimm in progress. Chief thinks it could be the Slasher Gang."

Pursing my lips, I released his arm. The Slashers were actually a murder of shifter crows—a group of six men and women whose MO was to leave corpses slashed to bloody ribbons in their wake. They were dangerous and a top-priority capture.

Giving me a nod of farewell, Tanner rushed out the doors a moment later. Sirens began wailing down the streets as the cop cars rushed for the bank.

Ichabod walked around me, sat on the edge of a desk, and crossed his hands on his lap. "What's that about?"

"Possible Slasher sighting at Bank of Grimm."

Dark brows twitched high up on his forehead. "Rock orcs guard those vaults, so I'd say the Slashers are either desperate or stupid. Hope they catch those bastards for their sake, or there's bound to be blood filling our streets tonight." He chuckled. Ich was known for having a morbid sense of humor.

"Anyway, you ready to go speak with Bo, or what?" he asked.

Hugging the baggies to my breast, I gave him a knowing glare and a shake of my head. "Don't even try to horn in on my detail."

He held up his hands in a defenseless gesture. "I would never," he harrumphed, but his blue eyes twinkled merrily. "You think so little of me, fish."

Punching his bicep, I snapped my teeth at him. "Call me that again, and you'll be dinner."

Snorting, he pushed himself up off the desk. "Honestly, I've got mounds of paperwork to see to. But keep me up to date on your findings, at least."

Cold case was a small unit within the precinct. Just me, Ichabod, and one other officer worked the files. The case of the Charmings had been a source of irritation for Ichabod, who prided himself on being able to solve even the toughest of riddles.

"Of course." I jerked my head in the direction of the chief's white-tinted windows, ready to head back there and debrief, when I paused. "Ich?"

"Yeah?" He glanced up.

"When did the Charmings get pregnant? How did I not know?"

His eyes turned serious, and he glanced to the side looking uncomfortable. I shifted on my feet, getting a bad feeling. "It was during your stint in Neverland," he said quietly, then glanced off to the side.

We never spoke of Neverland. Working my jaw from side to side, I made a mental note to look through the royal archives for the banners announcing the birth of the princess.

"Gotcha. Well, okay then. I'll see you when I see you."

"Yup." With a flick of his wrist, Ichabod walked back to his desk through the nearly empty precinct.

Turning, I glided up to Bo's door, rapped once, and called out, "Chief!"

"Come in," a smoky female voice called out.

The chief—better known in certain circles as Little Bo Peep—was a middle-aged human with graying strands of hair in her once-blond curls. Her face was lined from years of stress and worry, but her brown eyes were hard and intelligent. She wore a sharply cut, light-blue shirt opened just a touch at the collar to reveal the silver shepherdess-staff pendant resting against the hollow of her throat. She was a trim, athletic woman with the ability to speak eloquently and have those around her follow faithfully.

Walking forward, I set the baggies of evidence down on her desk. Bo's office wasn't heavily decorated. There were pictures on the walls of her receiving medals and awards or posing for pictures with dignitaries and royalty. But none of those accomplishments ever seemed to faze Bo much. Her greatest pride was the framed picture of a gorgeous black-and-white-speckled lamb she called Ivony, a mix of Ivory and Ebony, sitting on her desk.

"What's that?" Bo raised a grayish-blond brow as she tapped the tip of her pen against the baggie containing the claw.

Sitting, I shrugged. "Not quite sure yet. But at first glance, Crane and I are pretty certain it's a poison-tipped claw."

"Hmm." Sliding it toward her, Bo opened the sack and tipped it over. The claw dropped into her palm.

For a woman who'd grown up a shepherdess, Bo had a finer mind than most. She had an uncanny way of understanding criminals' minds. Her insights often helped me approach a case from angles I may not have otherwise considered.

Bo also happened to hail from Wonderland, which meant she might know just what kind of creature this claw belonged to.

The chief said nothing as she slipped the claw back inside the baggie before turning her attention to the next object.

Ichabod and I had focused almost exclusively on the claw, whereas Bo seemed more interested in the brown-stained ribbon. She gave the ends several gentle tugs and rubbed her thumbs across it while muttering under her breath.

"Did you register these into evidence already?" She glanced up, still holding tight to the ribbon.

"Of course." I crossed my legs. "The second we returned. It's been sitting so long in the lake bed that there are no prints, and any traces of magick on them has worn off by now too." Curious, I asked, "Is there something interesting about the ribbon?"

"Yes. It's length and texture indicates it was made by Mr. Potts's Haberdashery and Ribbons. You'll want to go check them out first, see if they can recall to whom this particular ribbon was sold."

I looked askance at the scrap of evidence. How could anyone possibly remember, after all this time, who that ribbon was sold to? I must have asked that question out loud because Bo chuckled.

"You'd be surprised. Mr. Potts is quite the... eccentric, to put it kindly. As to your other statement about fingerprints, true enough." Nodding, Bo finally slipped the ribbon back into the baggie. "Elle, I'm going to give you special leave to carry these items with you to Wonderland."

My smile was thin. "I figured you'd say as much."

The thought of spending any time in Wonderland made me break out in hives. Without a guide through that twisted realm, it would be entirely too easy for anyone not of the realm to get lost and never find their way back. A cop with a key card was no exception.

Wild, unruly magick coursed through every inch of that twisted place, making it nearly impossible for an outsider to tell reality from illusion. I had enough water to last three days only, and that was in my shirt and seashell combined.

I fingered my shell pendant, and the feel of its coolness quieted the anxiety of my mind.

Bo's eyes narrowed. "How much water you got to last you?"

"I'll be fine so long as this doesn't take longer than three days, max."

The chief snorted. "Yeah, well, I wish I could say Wonderland was that predictable, but we both know that'd be a lie. Tell you what—make your way down to Thantor's dungeon. I'll send in a request for a temporary all-access key card, just in case."

I blew out a relieved breath. Thantor was an onsite gnome housed in the lowest parts of GPD. As a familiar to the High Wizard Balock, Thantor had access to small amounts of high wizard magick, meaning he could create for me a special key card that would allow access the transdimensional pathways without the need for a waystation.

"Thanks. I appreciate that."

"Course." Bo nodded. "I'll also ring the local constable to let him know you're coming."

I gripped the seat's armrests. The last time I'd been sent to Wonderland, my guide had been none other than Cheshire himself. He'd vanished and reappeared on me throughout the course of my investigation, causing me to panic every minute of the fifteen hours I was trapped in that realm. Needless to say, I wasn't much of a fan.

"Can you note that I'd rather not have the cat meet me this time?" I tapped the evidence baggie. "With this claw, he's definitely one of my persons of interest."

"Of course. But I don't think this belongs to Cheshire. Ruthless and slightly mad he might be, but he does not possess poison-tipped claws."

I'd suspected as much but hadn't wanted to rule him out just in case. "Then who does?"

Bo shrugged. "There are many in the realm who do. But still, question Cheshire. Because of his special abilities, the cat sees and knows most, if not all, of what's happening within the realm. I'm keen to read your report on this one."

Nodding, I stood.

"And, Elle." Bo tipped her head. "Good job. I'd feared we'd lost all viable leads at this point. I should have known a siren would sniff out the truth of things in that lake bed."

"Yeah. Well, I just wish it hadn't pointed in the direction of Wonder-land."

"Aw, c'mon. It's not all that bad." Bo chuckled.

"No, you're right. It's worse."

Bo's laughter followed me out the door.

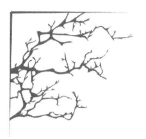

Chapter 3

Detective Elle

Thantor sat at a high desk, his tiny feet kicking back and forth languorously as he scribbled his quill across the roughened, cream-colored parchment unfurled before him. He was a wizened old gnome with few strands of gray hairs left on his liver-spotted head. He wore thick glasses that caused his pupils to appear twice as large as they actually were.

The dungeon he occupied was dank, cold, and very poorly lit, which was how the gnome liked it. He was used to living deep beneath ground and, like all gnomes, suffered from light sensitivity.

Dressed only in a long green woolen coat, he looked ridiculous, as most gnomes generally did. But it was to anyone's peril to believe them harmless.

Gnomes had no power of their own, but they were receptacles, which meant they were ideally suited to contain the excess power High Wizards couldn't or didn't wish to hold inside themselves any longer.

His long, pointed ears, which curled slightly inward and stretched several inches above his head, swiveled in my direction as soon as I walked through the door. No one could sneak up on a gnome. Nearly blind they all were, but their hearing more than made up for the loss.

"What do you need, siren?" Thantor's voice sounded like the low-rumbled cry of a demon in heat.

I tipped my chin at the golden key card sitting on the corner of his desk. "I've come for the card."

Taking it in hand, he held it out to me, and his curved black talon scraped against my palm as I took it. "It only has three days' worth of magick." He peered at me from over the top of his bottle-thick glasses.

"That should be enough."

He sniffed. "Should ye need more than that, there is a gnome in Wonder-land who goes by the name of Pillar. Find her. She'll be happy to oblige." Then he went back to scratching on his parchment and ignoring me completely.

"Okay then," I mouthed, and turning, I used my special key card for the first time, smiling as I swiped it through the air right where I stood. A time portal opened swiftly. "I could get used to this."

I stepped inside, closing my eyes as time sped by in a dizzying blur. Before I knew it, I'd crossed dimensions into yet another world.

Wonderland was like no other place in the existence of Grimm. Where it'd been only midmorning in the city, here there was darkness. The sky was ablaze with pinpricks of gem-colored starlight. A red moon hung suspended above me. Large, skeletal-shaped tree trunks twisted like spires into the air. Shadows breathed and danced all around.

I clenched my jaw, trying to catch my bearings. Right was right in Won-derland, but sometimes right was also left. One wrong move, and I'd wind up gods-knew-where.

It must be quite late at night. There was a deep sort of silence to the place, the kind that only happened during the witching hour.

Then I recalled something I'd forgotten 'til just now.

Glancing down, I breathed a sigh of relief when all I spied beneath my feet was a beaten-dirt path. Flowers in Wonderland were far from just decorative. In fact, most were very deadly. Some were carnivorous, and others emitted toxic fumes. It was perilous to get too close to any of them. The majority of flowers had been burned down in the Great Wonderlandian Blaze of '34, though there were still isolated incidents of the unwary being killed after wandering deep into the wilds of the untamed forests where a few flowers still thrived despite all odds.

The key should have deposited me close to my destination. Unlike Alice, I wasn't ignorant enough to go traipsing off on my own. If I had to wait here for my guide until the sun came up, I'd do it. But no sooner had I thought it than a buttery-yellow light flickered to life inside a thatched-roof hut a few yards ahead, beckoning to me like a beacon in the night.

Because sirens lived and played in the deepest parts of the ocean, we'd adapted to seeing in even the darkest of environments, which made it easy enough to spy the small wooden placard swaying gently above the doorway. It read *Home of Constables Mad Hatter and March Hare.*

I frowned. Already, I sensed this assignment was about to get far more complicated than it already was.

There'd been a recent change in the guard. The previous constable had been the White Knight. The knight might have been a little rigid and inflexible in his belief system, but he'd been good people.

I knew the reputations of the hare and the hatter only by gossip. The hare was said to be hyperactive and inattentive at the best of times, and Hatter was completely off his rocker, neither of which inspired confidence that this matter would be resolved quickly and efficiently.

"Dammit to the two hells," I muttered, wishing I'd been apprised of the change in constables earlier.

A flash of movement snared my attention. A red glow—like the light from the tip of a cigarette—blinked in and then out of focus. Turning, I glanced into the darkness and realized there was a form I'd not seen earlier leaning against a tree and watching me—a brown-skinned man dressed in jeans and a loose-fitting green shirt. The exposed bits of his flesh were covered in light fuzz from the tips of his ears to his toes. His eyes and hair were a warm brown color, almost like roasted chestnuts.

He took a drag from his cigarette, and I noticed the jerky shaking of his movements. I'd bet a golden pearl he was cranked out on some form of hallucinogen. And this being Wonderland, with a ready supply of spelled mushrooms at hand, I knew I'd win the bet.

"Ye be that detective lady hailing from Grimm, by any chance?" He spoke with the deep-throated trace of a Wonderland accent, and as he spoke, his nose twitched like a rabbit's. The front two teeth holding the cigarette reminded me of white, blocky cinders.

No doubt this was the March Hare.

"Yes." I walked over to him and shook his outstretched hand. His touch was warm, his palm slightly calloused. "And you are?"

"Harry."

"Are you my guide?" I asked once he'd released me. If he was, I'd be phoning in a complaint to GPD headquarters in a nanosecond.

"I was s'posed to be, but I fell into a patch of halo-shrooms not an hour past. I'm seeing man-eating dinghbats crawling everywhere." He gulped. "I don't think ye'd be safe with me as I am."

As he said it, the whites of his bloodshot eyes expanded in fear, and the vein in the side of his neck pulsed like the beat of a hummingbird. Now I understood the shakiness that coursed down every inch of him. He slapped at the air, and I took a step back.

"Right. Then is Hatter around?"

"Aye." He nodded at least four times. "Back there." He pointed before quickly turning his attention back to puffing on his cigarette.

Twirling on my heel, I jogged toward the constable's hut and knocked once on the door.

"Come in!" a thunderous voice boomed. "And by the devil, if that's you again, Hare, screaming of dinghbats, I'll choke you myself."

Swallowing my grin, I stepped inside.

The interior of the hut was not at all what I expected from looking at the outside. It wasn't a rustic one-room cabin that I'd walked into, but a warmly lit garden that glowed with the flames of thousands of floating candles. Lightning bugs danced and zipped to and fro, their green glow discharging at uneven intervals and casting a hazy pallor on the thick vines of ivy sliding up the trellis-covered walls.

A man dressed in a burgundy velvet jacket and with a shaggy head of thick black hair sat behind a desk with a cup of steaming tea on his left and a stack of papers that seemed to pile as high as eternity on his right.

He wore a black cravat with white dots, which tied neatly around his long, muscular neck. Not nearly as shabby in appearance as the Hare was, Hatter sported a trimmed goatee, had a large—but not too large—nose that was centered evenly on his angular face. Medium-sized lips were currently tugging down at the edges into a puzzled frown. His brows rose to a peak, which added a slightly devilish appearance to him. But all of that was forgotten upon witnessing the peculiarities of his eyes—one a rich green and the other a vibrant, almost neon blue.

I wet my lips.

"Who are you?" he snapped in a terse growl.

Spine going stiff, I snatched my badge out of my pocket and flashed it at him. "Grimm PD."

I might have lit into him for acting like such an ass if the attitude hadn't immediately dissipated.

He sighed, pinched his brow, and then shook his head. "I'm sorry. This has been a day from hells. A body was discovered face down behind the Queen's pub in a patch of spelled mushrooms. We've been fielding complaints all day." He stood and walked around to the front of the desk. "But not your problem. Forgive me."

Still prickly but understanding what it was like to have a crap day, I shook his hand. Long, strong fingers latched across my wrist.

His gaze was lucid, his eyes clear. In no way did he resemble the mad man of gossip. Grunting, I quickly dropped his hand.

"Yes. Well. I've had days like that."

A body had been found behind the Queen's pub in yet another realm of Grimm? Murder wasn't uncommon in our realms. Great evil lived and walked amongst us, but it did seem odd that on the day I was investigating the twin murders on the Charmings's lawn, yet another high-profile murder had been committed. I wasn't sure if the Queen's pub was on the Queen's property or just a nickname the locals had given it, but still... strange.

Shoving his fingers through his hair and causing the edges of it to poke up stiffly in many directions, Hatter twirled on his leather shoes, glancing around.

"Where is that bloody teapot? Care for a drink?" he asked, shoving at another stack of papers behind his desk, which caused them to tumble down around his feet like an avalanche. Hatter bent over to peer beneath his desk, presumably for the missing teapot.

I frowned. "No. I'm fine. But I am in a hurry to get things going, if you don't mind."

He stood abruptly, causing another flurry of paperwork to scatter around him.

The chief would throw a conniption at the way these two ran things. There had to be a backlog of several years' worth of form-filling to do. I cringed as Hatter sloppily gathered a few stacks of paper together then peered at the pile still scattered at his feet. He gave a resigned shrug before tossing himself down onto his chair, obviously giving it up as a lost cause.

"Forgive the mess," he muttered.

Try as I might, that wouldn't be happening any time soon. Tidiness was next to godliness in my eyes, and this was just a nightmare. Giving him a weak nod of assent, I pinched my lips shut and pretended that the stack of papers I sat on was actually a chair.

"You know, you really need a secretary."

He growled. "Aye. We do. Unfortunately, there are few in Wonderland sane enough to do the job adequately, and none of them are willing."

"Wasn't like this when the Knight ran things," I couldn't help murmuring.

"No, indeed. I've gotten us caught up on at least two years' worth of backlog at this point." He shot back.

I snorted. "Touché."

I'd never had a problem admitting it when I was wrong. That was partly the reason I found myself in my current predicament. He shrugged off my apology.

Lifting his cup of tea, he took a measured sip before setting it back down. "We'll leave at first light."

Hatter turned back to his paperwork, and from one minute to the next, was completely lost to his work, muttering beneath his breath as he scratched and scribbled things down, acting for all the world as though I were no longer even present. What the ever-loving hells?

I scowled and tapped my foot. This bastard had another think coming if he thought I was just going to sit here like a meek little mouse and continue to be ignored.

After another minute, I lost my composure completely and thwacked my palm down on the desk, startling him. He looked at me like I'd lost my mind.

"Listen, I don't have days to drag this out, Constable Hatter."

"Friends call me Maddox," he mumbled by rote.

I flailed my wrist. "Whatever you say. Look, I'm here to work and get home. Now, let's go."

He held up his palm, his lips pinched tight in a frown as he said, "I don't know how things work in Grimm, Detective Arielle—"

"It's Elle," I hissed, digging my claws into my knees at the sound of that goddess-awful name slipping from his tongue. Arielle had died years ago in a past life I wanted nothing to do with.

"Whatever." He threw my words back at me. "You don't want to be friendly, that's fine. But around here, we do things differently."

I chuckled, but the sound was anything but cordial. The bastard had me hamstrung, and I damned well knew it, but I wasn't going down without a fight. "You know I can't walk through Wonderland without a guide."

"And I can assure you that has no bearing on why we're not leaving tonight. You want your answers, then you must play by this realm's rules."

Seething with anger at this unexpected delay, I bit down on my tongue. He couldn't know I only had three days of water to see me through, and he was right that it was currently the dead of night. But working in a city meant keeping odd hours. Here in the country, that obviously wasn't so.

"I have just enough water to last me three days here, Constable."

He sighed and looked back up at me, his eyes clearly conveying his exasperation with this conversation. "I see. And should we need to return to your waters, I can assure you that I shall oblige you that journey. Our realm will remain open to you however long you have need of it, have no fear."

At least he sounded sincere. One thing Ichabod had always stressed was that using honey and not vinegar was the way to keep those around you helpful. Counting to three in my head, I forced myself to a calm I didn't feel.

"I'm sorry. I'm only anxious to get things underway. As I'm sure you understand."

Nodding, he stood and gestured toward the gardens. "There is a brook not fifty yards back should you like a swim in it. The waters run in from fairy."

They weren't my waters, but fairy water would help alleviate some of the pressure from being on land too long.

"Thank you."

Standing, I dipped my head one last time, but Constable Maddox Hatter was already back to work on his mounds of paperwork and lost to the thoughts in his head.

Speckled mushroom caps lit the way toward the brook. The garden contained a neatly trimmed set of topiaries—butterflies in flight, blooming roses, and even a thinking man. There were no flowers, but considering how deadly most of them were here, it was no wonder they'd decided against adding them.

In moments, I smelled the sweetness of fairy water. My fingers trembled as I lifted off my top and tossed it to the ground. Immediately it grew harder to breathe—not impossible, but far from pleasant. In two seconds, I had my pants undone and was kicking them into the pile of already-discarded clothing.

Turning, I faced the impossibly clear waters that glowed a deep-blue through the piercing darkness. This might be a garden within a home of sorts, but I heard the telltale song of predatory night birds somewhere off in the distance.

I dove into the deepest section of the brook, smiling the moment the chilly cold came into contact with my flesh and the burning sizzle of legs gave way to my golden tail. The rush of that transformation moved through my blood like a drug.

I swam several yards through the waters before turning back. Normally, I wouldn't have cared about the land while I was swimming, but Wonderland had an intrigue to it that had always made me curious, despite my misgivings.

Gliding easily against the swift current, I studied my odd surroundings. Trees here seemed unable to decide whether it was winter or spring, like someone had drawn a line straight down each of their middles so that half a tree bloomed with the rich green of budding leaves, and the other half was nothing more than spindly branches reaching like witches' fingers toward the sky.

Similarly, the landscape, too, seemed confused. On one side of the brook, it was deep winter with snow piling as high as my head in some places, and on the other, a balmy spring night with a plethora of lightning bugs zipping in and around bushes.

Animals I'd not noticed earlier came scampering out from between topiaries, shadowy creatures with eyes as big as my palm and bodies half that size.

The water I swam in tasted sweet and rich, pumped full of fairy magic so that each inhale of it reminded me of something fragrant and sugary. But the water itself was barren of life. There were no odd fish or unusual plant life in it, just rocks that gleamed like cut opal.

Turning onto my back, I allowed my fingers to trail languorously through the gentle swells as memories of a happier time crowded my thoughts. I thought of a time when, on a night, much like this one, I sealed my fate to a Prince of Thieves.

"What do you smile about, Detective?" Hatter's deep voice shivered across my flesh, making me gasp.

Frowning, I glared at him, hiding my tail beneath the water.

"I am sorry." He bowed. "I did not mean to startle you. I only came to tell you that supper is ready, should you wish to join us and discuss our course of action come morning."

His hands flicked impatiently along the sides of his dark trousers.

Angry—but only because the ghost of my past, which never seemed to stay gone long, lingered still—I shook my head. "I'm fine. And yes, thank you. I'm starving."

Before Maddox had a chance to turn away, I was shoving out of the water, calling the change instantly and suffering a moment of vertigo as my tail flashed once more into legs.

He averted his gaze quickly as a dark blush rose high on his cheeks. "I should leave you—"

"Oh, c'mon, Constable." I rolled my eyes, squeezing the excess water from my hair as best I could. "As a siren, nudity is nothing."

Marching over to my stack of clothes, I reached not for the pants, which donning might stop Maddox's blushing, but my shirt. I was gasping and shaking by the time I slipped the final button into place.

He frowned. "Does it pain you to be outside your waters that much?"

Glancing up, I'd not even realized he'd been watching me. Feeling infinitely better now that I felt my waters rub against my chest, I nodded.

"You have no idea."

Constable Maddox

MADDOX SWALLOWED HARD when Elle bent over once more to grab her leather pants. An honorable man would have turned on his heel, marched back the way he'd come, and not looked back. But Maddox hadn't been able to make his feet move.

When Detective Elle had first appeared at his door, he'd been instantly aware of her exotic beauty. There were few creatures in all of Grimm quite as lovely as a siren, and Elle was no exception. Her face was so flawless that it seemed carved of marble. She had high cheekbones, a pert nose, a heart-shaped jawline, and golden eyes. Robin's-egg-blue hair fell past her hips in a loose braid, and her long legs made his mouth water.

Her tail was equally as attractive—long and golden with perfectly shaped flukes. Her scales gleamed like coins in flame. She'd swum on her back in his brook, her eyes closed, an angelic smile on her face, her peach-tipped nipples poking out of the water and budded up tight. He'd lost himself then. She'd looked so innocent that he'd forgotten she was the same hard, demanding woman who'd snarled and snapped at him earlier.

Beneath the attractive exterior of any siren lay a darkness quite unparalleled in all of Grimm. As beautiful as they were, they were equally as deadly, if not more so. Many a wanderer had lost their souls to the briny depths of Davy Jones's locker to sirens such as her. And though he didn't know Detective Elle personally, her reputation was fierce. She was a man-eater.

Literally.

By all rights, she should have lost her badge for what she'd done—or had been alleged to have done. In truth, most of Detective Arielle Trident's life was shrouded in mystery.

She slipped on her leather pants, gave her hair one final twist, then twirled on him, raising a dark brow.

"Well?" she snapped.

Clearing his throat, Maddox stepped to the side and swept his arm out. "After you."

After several moments of thick silence, she glanced at him. "I honestly do not care that you caught me nude or wearing my tail."

He dipped his head. "I thank you for that. It's been many years since I've had a woman around for any amount of time. I fear my manners have eroded completely."

Elle nibbled the corner of her lusciously pink lips. "What do you know of me, Constable?"

Crossing his arms behind his back, he was content to walk at their meandering pace. This day had been hells on him—he'd not exaggerated that truth to her. And having only Harry for company for so long was exhausting.

"The truth?" he asked cautiously.

Her look said it all. "Of course."

"That you have killed many men in your lifetime. That you are prickly at the best of times, hard to get along with at the worst, and quite moody. Not to mention the cannibalism."

He'd halfway expected an outburst or a denial at the very least. But she gave none. Instead, she sighed.

"I'm not surprised. Seems to be all anyone knows of me these days. And I'd only be a cannibal if I'd eaten other sirens. Humans, no matter how similar on the surface we might appear, are nothing at all like me."

She'd not shied away from the most shocking of the allegations, which he supposed he had to give her credit for. Nor had she really explained anything, though he'd not failed to note the swift glint of fiery anger in her eyes when he'd said it. Whatever was in her past, he knew it was bad. It had to have been to get her exiled by her own father.

"These days?" he asked as he brushed his fingers along a topiary of a prancing horse whose leaves were starting to get a little unruly. He'd need to come out and clip them in the morning. "Was it once so different?"

She snorted. "I wasn't always such a bitch, if that's what you're asking. I was a sweet little siren once upon a time."

"I didn't mean to imply—"

"I didn't say you did."

Adjusting his cravat—it was perfectly tied, but he no longer seemed to know what to do with his hands—he nodded. "And so, what have you heard of me?"

"You?" She grinned.

The sight of her smile stole the breath from his lungs just as it had when he'd spotted her smiling in his brook. The woman had a way of making him feel hot beneath the collar.

Clearing his throat, he shrugged. "You make that sound ominous."

"Ominous, no. But you are infamous, Constable Hatter. You are said to be mad. Some say you belong in a padded cell. But..."

His brows twitched. "But?"

They were just about out of the garden. The scent of wild-onion stew and crusty bread had his stomach growling.

"You don't seem mad to me. Eccentric and bizarre, yes. But not mad."

It was his turn to chuckle. "Give it time, Detective Elle. I can assure you I'm quite mad. See my eyes?" He pointed to the vivid blue one. "Blue sees the past, green the future. I am full of madness, haunted by visions, and can never tell from one moment to the next when the apparitions will grip me."

She didn't say much to that revelation, but then, what was there to say, really?

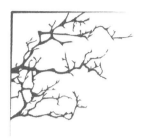

Chapter 4

Detective Elle

I thanked Harry, who'd handed me a bowl of soup and a chunk of warm grain bread fresh from the oven. I didn't enjoy much land food, but the stew was warm and full of tasty herbs and bits of onion, and the bread practically melted in my mouth.

"Thank you. It's delicious," I said after my fourth spoonful.

Harry shrugged. "Weren't I that made it, Detective."

I glanced at Hatter, who stared broodingly at his bowl with an unflinching gaze. The moment we'd sat, the man who'd been so cordial just moments ago on the walk through the gardens had up and vanished. He'd not said more than three words strung together since.

"You, then?" I asked him.

"Huh?" He finally glanced up, and I noted that his blue eye blazed like a jewel.

Blinking several times, he rubbed at his temple. "What? Oh, the soup. Yes, well." He shrugged but didn't say more.

Constable Hatter was clearly distracted again, a tight frown marred his otherwise unblemished forehead.

"Don't mind 'em," Harry said around a slurp of soup. "It'll pass soon enough."

I couldn't help but watch Hatter, his long scowl only seemed to grow longer as the seconds ticked past. But then, just as Harry had predicted, it did indeed pass. Hatter's shoulders visibly slumped.

"What did ye see this time, Maddox?" Harry asked, seeming unconcerned and unaffected by his partner's mercurial mood.

Hatter scrubbed his jaw with long, tapered fingers several times before sighing loudly. "Nothing of much help, I'm afraid."

I frowned, a spoonful of soup held close to my lips. "These visions you told me about, what are they exactly?"

"Oh, you know," Harry interjected, "a lil bit 'o this and a lil bit 'o that."

It was clear to me that the hare was still suffering side effects from the mushrooms. Every so often, his hand would jerk, causing the spoon to tip over and plop hot soup onto his thighs. But Harry didn't bat an eyelash. Although he did occasionally swat at the invisible dinghbats.

I raised a brow. "Right."

Hatter had taken a couple bites of his soup before answering, "As I've said, I see the future, the past, and even sometimes both at once."

"What?" I'd been about to place the spoon in my mouth, but instead, dropped it with a loud clatter into my bowl, much more interested in Hatter's abilities than my meal. "What do you mean exactly?"

"I've been this way my whole life, Detective Elle. I can be doing one thing, when suddenly my head fills with images. Rarely does it make sense to me at the time. Only once I have time to analyze what I've seen am I able to make the connections."

"But you said you can see the past and future at the same time. How's that possible?"

He shrugged. "A quirk of fate. I'm not really certain. Once, I saw an image of a dead blonde with an apple in one hand and a snake in the other. I learned over the course of several days that the woman had been a seamstress in the local village. She'd bought an apple from a grocer a few days past—"

Harry took over the telling of the story. "She'd set it aside 'cause she weren't planning to bake 'til the weekend. Only once she got to making her pies, out popped a venomous apple garter. It nipped her in the finger, and she were dead not ten minutes later."

Hatter didn't seem put off by his partner's constant interruptions. If Ichabod had done that to me, I'd have punched him square in the nose for it.

Lips stretching into a tight scowl, Constable Hatter spread his hands. "If I'd made the connection sooner, I might have saved her."

"Nah." Harry, who'd been eating like he'd not touched food in years, finally set his spoon aside and dipped the bread into the bottom of his bowl to get every last droplet sopped up. "That's the curse, ye see, Detective. Maddox can sometimes see the ending and the beginning, but the middle don't make no sense so as to offer us any guidance."

Setting his half-eaten stew and bread aside, Hatter kicked his left leg from beneath the table and rested his jaw on his fist, staring off into space once more.

"Are you having another one?" I asked.

"No." He rolled the one word on his tongue. "I am simply preoccupied."

"Then maybe ye should share it, Maddox. Best to talk these things out. Are ye done, by the by?" Harry pointed to my bowl.

"Oh, um. I guess." I blinked, startled when he snatched up my bowl and remaining bread, tearing into it with his big, blocky teeth.

"Makes very little sense to me," Hatter muttered. "There was a curl of ribbon. Brown. But perhaps blue. I couldn't honestly tell."

"That it?" Harry's face screwed up tight. "That don't tell us nothing."

"No. There was more. But it's all muddled in my head at present. There was a woman with strange eyes. A horse, perhaps? And silver shears."

I reached into my pocket, extracting the baggies I'd kept tucked inside. "I can't help you with the last three. But the ribbon wouldn't happen to look like this, would it?" I tipped the baggie over. The dirt-stained ribbon fluttered gracefully to the tabletop, and Hatter snatched it up instantly.

A deep frown marked his features once again, but instead of looking confused, he reminded me somewhat of Ichabod when he was analyzing a cryptic riddle. He brought the ribbon up to his nose, sniffed it once, twice, and then asked tersely, "Where did you get this?"

When I'd first met Hatter, I'd found his demeanor lax. But that man was not this man. This man was a detective through and through.

"I found it in the lake bed behind the Charming estate. That and"—I tipped over the second baggie, and the claw thudded hollowly upon the table—"this."

Harry reached for the claw, raising it to his eyes and peering at it casually before setting it down once more.

"I know this ribbon," Hatter said tersely, jaw clenched tight and looking aggrieved.

My heart raced. Could it really be that easy? He turned his strangely colored eyes on me and relaxed his jaw muscles just a little.

"Or rather, I know its maker. It is most assuredly of Mr. Potts's making."

The muted glow from lanterns hanging upon the walls cast a sickly yellowish pallor over everything, causing Hatter to appear more sinister than usual and Harry far less human. If I squinted, he almost looked like the hare he'd so often been compared to.

Hatter dropped his hand to the table and began drumming an idle rhythm with his fingers. His posture was stiff as he leaned back into his seat.

I nodded, getting the queerest sensation that I was missing something. He was acting strange, even for him, and that was saying something, considering his reputation.

"That's what my chief told me," I said slowly, trying my best to affect a nonchalant attitude. "What she couldn't say was who it belonged to."

"I've a hunch." Hatter continued to trace the edge of the mud-stained ribbon with his thumb, much like Bo had. Then, sniffing it one final time, he shoved it toward me.

I frowned as I gently extricated it from his lax fingers. "Why are you sniffing it, and whose is it?"

"The edges of the ribbon are smoother but tapered. As to why I sniffed it, the woman to whom I'm sure it belongs often wears these threaded through her curls, and she wears a very unique and particular brand of perfume."

"Blood-orange poppy," Harry finished. "Aye. It do look like Alice's style. Bloody damn dinghbats," he growled then shot to his feet so fast that the chair in which he'd been sitting toppled over.

I startled at the sudden, jarring thud of heavy oak hitting the floor. Harry did a strange histrionic dance, a movement of arms and legs, as he screamed at the wee devils to get gone.

I looked at Hatter, silently hoping he'd handle this awkward situation. He had his fingers steepled beneath his chin, looking at his partner with obvious puzzlement. A full minute ticked by as Harry continued his strange and wild dance before Hatter finally said with a heavy sigh, "Forgive me one moment."

"Of course."

Scooting off his chair, Hatter walked over to his partner, latched his hand into Harry's collar, and with a stiff jerk, walked the man out of the room.

The slamming of a door heralded his arrival only a couple of seconds later. Hatter brushed down his sleeves while giving me an apologetic look.

"How long will it take for that to wear off?" I asked, glancing over my shoulder to where Harry had disappeared.

"Days, if we're lucky. Although, Harry's developed a tolerance for halo-shrooms through the years, so who can say. I doubt very much it was the accident he claimed it to be, though." Sitting, he adjusted his cravat once more.

The man was as proper and tidy as his partner was not. And I couldn't help but wonder what it would take to make him look less proper and put together.

"Harry is not a constable, you see."

My brows twitched. "But his name is stenciled alongside yours."

"Yes, he is a figurehead only and quite gets in the way."

"If you don't mind my asking, why is he here, then?"

He shrugged. "The people willed it so. Harry has deep connections throughout all of Wonderland. And it is better to work with the devil you know than the one you don't. But he's harmless, for all that."

I grinned. "You do run things very differently out here. Harry wouldn't last two minutes at GPD."

He frowned. "I've often wished to apply for a position there."

I crossed my legs. I'd questioned his competence in the beginning, but it was becoming clearer to me that "mad eyes" or not, Constable Hatter had a very keen mind. "So why haven't you?"

"I'm not sure really. Fear, perhaps?" He shrugged.

It struck me as odd that he'd be so forthcoming about his feelings. "What could you possibly have to be afraid of? You seem smart and able-bodied."

"Aye." He snorted and pointed at his cheekbone. "But my eyes are a great source of vexation for me. I cannot control when and where it grips me. Grimm PD is the shining pearl between all the realms, the highest heights of sleuthing. I would simply be a nuisance."

I bit my tongue. I had no idea what to say to him about that. He was right—the eyes would always be a problem, especially in a crisis, where every second mattered. But it seemed such a waste for him to remain a constable when he was clearly smart enough for more.

He pursed his lips. "Anyway, that is more personal than I'd intended to be. Tomorrow, at first light, we'll make our way to Potts's." He stood and once more adjusted his cravat.

Was it wrong that I wanted to reach over and skew it just a little? That was an odd feeling coming from me, considering how very neat and tidy my own life was now.

"You can take a bed or the stream, whichever you're most comfortable in."

"Is the bed yours?" I asked.

He dipped his head. "It is. But as I've got no plans to sleep this eve, you are more than welcome to have it. I've mounds of paperwork to catch up on, as you no doubt have noticed."

The bed was tempting. Sirens lived in the water, but I was a siren who'd grown accustomed to many land dwelling indulgences, of which beds ranked very highly.

I was just about to nod my acquiescence when my conscience pricked me. "I could help, if you want."

He turned, and for a split second, I regretted the offer because the stacks of paperwork seemed to climb toward the heavens. Also, this wasn't my precinct, and I couldn't just take half the stack and he the other half. I'd be in his way, asking him how to file this or that.

Clearly, he thought the same thing, because he shook his head a minute later. "I'll be fine."

Shoving my hands into my pockets, I gave him a swift nod. "Then I'll take the bed, if you're sure you don't mind."

His answering grin—though swift—made my legs feel weak. The man was broody, strange, and undeniably attractive.

It would be a great thing when this assignment was finished and I could go home.

"My room has a clock face for a doorway. You can't miss it."

"You are a strange man, Constable Hatter."

"That's what they tell me, Detective Elle."

BREAKFAST THE FOLLOWING morning was a quick meal of tea and fish cakes. It was a tasty yet simple delicacy. I didn't usually enjoy cooked meals, preferring my food as fresh as possible. But Hatter was two for two with me.

He said not a word as he wiped his mouth with his napkin and pushed his chair back from the table.

"Are you ready, then?" he asked, reaching for a black top hat and planting it on his head with an absentminded flourish.

"Are we leaving Harry behind?"

"Yes. Upon waking, he'll be headed to the morgue."

"About the murder that happened yesterday?" I asked.

"Mmm." He nodded. "The very one."

Then, dusting off his burgundy pea coat, he glanced at me and said, "It will be cool where we're headed. Have you a jacket?"

Glancing at my peasant top, I tweaked the diaphanous sprite silk and shrugged. "I don't."

"You look about Harry's size. Hold on a moment."

Turning, he made his way to his partner's bedroom. I reached for another fish cake. I wasn't hungry, but it was good.

The gardens were awash in early morning sunlight. The snow from last night had melted, giving way to a beautiful spring day. Butterflies of varied shapes, sizes, and colors flitted lazily amongst the topiaries.

I nibbled on the delicious cake, trying not to think about getting barely more than two hours sleep last night thanks to Harry's loud snoring.

Hatter's bed had been one of the most comfortable things I'd ever lain on, like sleeping on mounds of thick clouds. But more than just Harry's snoring had kept me awake last night. There'd been a very distracting scent laced throughout the sheets, pillows, and mattress itself. Every time I turned, I'd smelled it. What had bothered me was that rather than irritating me, as most leggers' scents did, Hatter's hadn't.

"Here you go." The man himself came back a moment later, holding a patchwork cardigan.

Clearing my throat as heat slid up my cheeks, I nodded a jerky thank you, snatched the sweater from him, and slid it on. It was looser than I liked but fit adequately enough.

"It will take us several hours to walk to Potts's. How much water have you left?" he asked.

"One day trapped within the shirt, another day inside this shell." I feathered my fingers along my pendant. "But I thought maybe we could take the transdimensional pathway or, as I like to call it, the between." I snatched the gold key card from my pocket and waved it.

His devilish brows rose. "How do you set the coordinates?"

"You don't." I grinned broadly. "You just have to think about where you want to go."

"Indeed. That is most fascinating." Walking toward his office desk, he pulled open a drawer and riffled through it, taking out fistfuls of something and cramming it into his pockets. He did it twice before he finally nodded. "Let us be off, then."

I frowned, wondering what it was he'd shoved in his pocket. Unfortunately, it was none of my concern.

I swiped the air with the card, and I couldn't help but grin again when he inhaled deeply and a look of surprise twisted his brows.

"Have you never traveled between, Constable?" I asked him.

He reached a finger toward the swirling tunnel of chaotic lights. "Never. I've seen it a time or two when one of you Grimmers show up here, but I've never actually traveled by one."

I snorted. "Close your eyes and try not to breathe too hard, then."

I stepped in first, feeling the air snatched from my lungs from the initial rush of moving at lightning speed. In seconds, a doorway ripped through the strands of time, revealing a cobbled and busy section of Wonderland I'd visited once before.

Stepping out quickly, I shuffled to the side and waited for Hatter. I expected he might vomit, the way I had the first time I'd traveled through dimensions. But he came out not a second later, wearing a broad grin.

He didn't move until the sliver of light vanished, and then he shook his head.

"Astonishing. Are we to travel that way all the time?"

Chuckling, I slipped the key card back into my pocket. "You make it sound like fun."

Waggling his expressive brows, he nodded. "Better than falling into a halo-shroom patch."

"I'm going to pretend you didn't just admit to bumping, considering you're a constable and all."

He shrugged. "It's Wonderland."

And as though that were answer enough, he marched ahead of me, heading down the alleyway and out into the busy street.

This part of Wonderland was no different than downtown Grimm—grimy, seedy, and busy.

The buildings were leaning towers built of deep-red-and-brown brick and mortar. A light but constant drizzle of rain fell from the gray clouds above. The air smelled of fresh-cooked foods and sewage. Rats the size of house cats scurried from one set of gutters to another.

A woman with broad hips, blond hair pinned up tight to her head, and a plain wine-colored dress swung a large straw basket overflowing with fruits, vegetables, and a shank of tea-cloth-covered meat. She was followed by a gaggle of squawking children. Her screeched command for them to follow was louder than the cries of the vendors who lined the streets.

I shook my head, losing track of just how many children there actually were after number twenty-three sauntered by.

"Mother Goose, we call her." Hatter leaned into my side, his warm breath fanning the shell of my ear as his voice rumbled with a thread of laughter.

As he murmured her name, Mother Goose turned, and her eyes immediately caught Hatter's. Her face wasn't pretty. It was hardy, strong, though not unpleasant.

Setting her jaw, she changed direction and headed toward us with the single-minded diligence of one on a quest. My hand went immediately to my Glock.

"Constable Maddox!" Goose screeched, causing me to grimace in sympathy. I relaxed my hand on the grip. She was no threat.

Hatter merely tipped his head in acknowledgement. "Mother, how are you this morning?"

"Not well!" she snapped once she'd stopped just a few feet in front of us. Her blue eyes turned in my direction, scanning down my body as if assessing me. Then, with a turn of her nose, she turned her gaze back to Hatter. "A goat tore through my gardens this morn. Thus, my need to trek down to the city for provisions."

Her face turned red as she thrust the basket of goods up for his inspection.

Just then, the first of Goose's many children came circling around us, like sharks sensing blood in the water. I edged closer to Hatter's side, frowning as their singsong, high-pitched squeals grated on my sensitive hearing.

I waved at one getting too close. "Shoo."

The child stuck his finger in his nose and grinned.

My lip curled in disgust.

"And how certain are you that it was a goat?" Hatter asked, his tone and manner just as respectful as before.

A pair of sticky fingers tried to latch on to my wrist. Several sets of hands were doing the same to Hatter. A few of the bolder children dug into his pockets, their small mouths tipping up in delight when they came away with a treat. After that, the line of kids left me to go rummage through his pockets.

I thought about the fistfuls of stuff he'd shoved into his pockets before we'd left and knew it had been the treats. But how had he known? Had he had a vision of this? I looked at him from the corner of my eye, a little in awe of his talent.

Goose's face contorted into a frightful mask of lines and scowls. "How sure am I?" she snapped, "How sure am I?" Each time she asked it, her pitch grew just a little louder and more ear splitting. "I'm quite certain! That dastardly Farmer John has let loose one of his furry devils, and I'm telling you now, Constable, if that beast lays waste to another one of my azalea patches, I'll shoot it. Damned right, I will."

"Damn wight she will," said a boy no older than three, with hair the same dirty blond as his mum's.

Goose cuffed the back of his head. "You mind that potty mouth of yours, Charles."

The other children began snickering, and the whole lot of them grew increasingly louder, causing several sets of eyes to turn in our direction. I shifted on my heels. It wasn't that I hated children, but I wasn't exactly the maternal type either. They were sort of like window dressing to me—nice to look at from a distance.

"Aye, well, I vow to speak with John at my earliest opportunity," Hatter said, tone respectful.

"See that you do," she huffed. "You know how frightfully hard it is to grow flowers around here that don't wish you ill?" Then, with a stiff jerk of her head, she flounced off, her little goslings following behind.

"Holy hells," I gasped the moment they were well out of earshot. "I can't even," I sputtered. "How do you deal with her?"

He snorted. "Goose is harmless, as are her little ducklings. Not fond of children, are you?"

Hatter gestured for me to precede him, pointing in the direction of the busiest street crowded thick with vendors and Wonderland natives alike.

I shrugged. "I don't hate them, I just..."

I let the words trail off. I didn't give children much thought until I came across one during an investigation, and even then, only the most cursory reflection. Ichabod had once told me that fate had failed to gift me with the motherly gene. After today, I was inclined to believe it.

"They are rather a lot to handle, especially a pack of fifty beasties, to be sure." He crossed his arms behind his back.

"And how in the hells did you have so many candies in your pocket?"

Rather than answer, he pointed to his eye.

"Ah. Of course." I'd been right. He'd seen it. Quite a talent he had. Maybe there were some uses to his curse after all.

Thankfully, the rest of our stroll toward Potts's was uneventful. Mr. Potts's Haberdashery and Ribbons wasn't much to look at from the outside. It was a small, plain structure built of pale bricks, with wide, front-facing glass windows showcasing the current trend in men's and ladies' headwear.

There were several top hats like the one Hatter favored. But whereas Hatter's was plain and unadorned—except for the simple ribbon of black silk tied around it—these were almost theatrical in style, unfashionably large and so colorful as to be gauche.

One was cerulean with red ribbons and large glass beads around the brim. Another was lime green with blazing orange ribbons and an ornate beaded cockade. The women's hats were even more bizarre, some of them in the shape of a swan or other types of birds. There was even one that resembled a tarantula.

I shuddered.

"Don't knock them until you've tried them on, Detective." Hatter grinned, opening the door for me.

"Those will never go on my head. And I can open my own doors, thank you very much," I snapped, feeling more waspish than normal, though not really sure why.

The sparkling light of laughter in his bi-colored eyes died. "Of course."

I blew out a deep breath. I was beginning to suspect I was hells bent on making things as awkward as possible between us. It wasn't my intention, but Constable Hatter didn't act like most detectives I worked with. He was trying to be my friend, and I really wished he wouldn't. This was work, not friendship. The worst thing a cop could ever do was get attached. That was why I was so good at my job—I was cold.

The inside of the store was as radically decorated as the outside was plain. A large mountain of crystal chandelier hung suspended from the rough-hewn beams above. Ribbons of every color of the rainbow and many shades in between dangled like fluttering garter snakes from rafters above.

Thick rugs of Perisinous and Turkinish design lay scattered across the black marble floors. Standing behind rows upon rows of white display counters were women dressed in gowns that buttoned all the way up to their throats. The fabrics were the deep jewel tones of amethyst, emerald, sapphire, and ruby, with rich brocaded filigree.

The women were as equally stunning as the dresses they wore. All of them had high cheekbones, soft, sloping eyes, and wide, friendly smiles. Some were brunettes, others blondes, with a nice range of hair colors in-between, but they each had their hair pulled back into a loose chignon with one thick curl draped across their left breast.

I shoved my hands into the cardigan's pockets.

Many different realms comprised the Grimm universe. Where I came from, the predominant style leaned heavily toward contemporary sensibility. Women wore almost nothing, rarely dresses or skirts, except on very specific occasions. Hair styles varied from pixie length to more eclectic styles like mohawks and cuts where half the hair was shorn nearly to its roots while the other half hung long and loose down the back.

I'd never taken a set of clippers to my own hair. No siren had. The length of one's hair announced our age and determined the strength of our power. The two went hand in hand.

But here in Wonderland, that was not the case. There was a very Victorian air that'd adapted overtime but had never entirely gone out of vogue. Lace, ribbons, and silks still ruled the fashions here.

Hatter rubbed at a ruby-red spool of fabric tucked into a section of wall that was lined with more types and colors of fabrics than I'd ever seen in my life. This place dripped a certain type of femininity that made me increasingly uncomfortable.

"Ah, Constable Maddox," a male voice chirped delightedly. "To what does my humble shop owe this great honor?"

I twirled in time to see a mouse of a man, no taller than the base of my neck, come scurrying out from the back room. He wore a freshly pressed navy-blue suit that hugged his slim physique. A large green paisley bow tie bobbed up and down as he spoke. I couldn't exactly tell what he looked like. He had mousy-brown hair, a small upturned nose, and a chipped front tooth, but most of his features were hidden behind a small black filigree mask, the type one might see on a prince at a ball, worn around his eyes.

"I am well, Potts. Thank you." Hatter shook the small man's hand.

"We've just received a most enchanting order of to-die-for cravats in the very latest Wonderland style." Potts snapped his finger at the nearest counter girl, who ducked out of site, clearly searching for said cravats.

"This is not a social call, Potts." Hatter shook his head.

"Oh, no?" Potts's nose wiggled. Then he turned to look at me. "Oh, my dear. Who dresses you?"

I frowned, rubbing at the cardigan. "Myself."

"Mmm." Potts's lips thinned with obvious distaste.

Hatter cleared his throat. "This is Detective Elle from Grimm PD."

Instantly, Potts straightened his shoulders, and this time when he glanced at me, all traces of disgust had vanished.

"Indeed. Forgive me, mademoiselle. I did not know." Reaching for my hand, he took it, and before I realized what he was about to do, he kissed my knuckles. "I adore all Grimmers."

Grimmers was the name given to those who lived and worked inside of Grimm City proper.

I snatched my hand back, more than ready to get out of this flowery, stinky den of hell. Slipping the dirt-stained, worn ribbon from my pocket, I handed it to Potts.

"Ever seen this?" I asked without preamble, expecting an immediate denial. I'd come only on Bo's insistence, not because I thought it likely that, after so long, any man, let alone this little eccentric fellow, would remember the ribbon.

But the moment he picked it up, he gasped. "Of course I do."

I frowned. "You do? Whose is it?"

Potts didn't make a show of rubbing or smelling it, he simply looked at it quickly, then shoved it back at me. "That belongs to Alice Blue."

"As I suspected," Hatter murmured.

"Are you sure?" I squinted at the little man, doubtful.

"Oh, quite." Potts nodded vigorously. "She is the only one of my clients that demands her ribbons be made with a mystic cross-stitch."

"A mystic cross what?" I asked.

Taking the ribbon out of my hand once more, he flipped it over and whipped out a magnifying glass. "Look." He held the glass over the ribbon. "Do you see the x-style stitching at the edges?"

Bending over, I was able to make it out, a small x-shaped stitching pattern. But more than that, I also noted a soft white glow at its edges that I'd not noticed before.

"What's the glow?"

He nodded before burying the glass back into his pocket. "That is the mystic portion of the cross-stitch."

"What's so special about it?" Hatter asked.

Potts shrugged. "Nothing much. It's a very antiquated style, to be honest. There are now ribbons that can make the wearer's hair glow like flame. Alice, however, prefers the softer glow this style provides, as she says it adds an air of elegance and grace to her countenance."

"And you're sure she's the only one with this style of ribbon?" I asked once more.

"I know my ribbons, Detective Elle. This is hers and can be no other's," he said, voice quivering and lips thinned, obviously insulted. I was pretty sure I'd heard a hint of a growl at the end of his sentence.

Hatter smiled and held out his hand to the mousy man once again, who was now glaring openly at me. "Always good to see you, Potts." Hatter said, causing the little man to look back at him.

Potts nodded slowly. "Yes, and you as well, Maddox. Stop by any time."

Then, without looking at me again, he turned and disappeared back through the door he'd first come through.

Hatter didn't speak again until we were back outside on the busy, rainy street.

"Did I do something to offend him?" I asked, glancing once more over my shoulder.

At first, I thought he wouldn't answer, but finally, he glanced down at me. "Detective Elle, I told you last night we do things differently out here. Questioning Potts after he'd already told you that ribbon belonged to Alice was a serious breach in etiquette."

I could hardly believe my ears. "Excuse me? You do realize this is a murder investigation. I will question a suspect as I see fit."

"Potts was not a suspect, and if you want Wonderland's continued help, you'd do well to familiarize yourself with the customs of our realm."

He looked genuinely upset, and I hated that it bothered me. When he gave his head a tiny shake of disappointment before turning on his heel and walking off without me, I honestly felt like a child that'd just displeased a normally proud parent.

I wrinkled my nose. The feeling was not a comfortable one for me. But we detectives had been trained to understand that, though we might do things one way in Central Grimm, that didn't mean we were always free to do and act as we pleased in other parts of the realms. There were rules and customs. I knew this and was usually good at remembering it. So why was I failing so spectacularly right now? I suspected I knew why, and the truth did me no favors.

I frowned and shoved my hands into my pockets. I wanted to retort, insist I'd done nothing wrong and that Potts owed *me* an apology, not the other way around. But that was my bloody pride talking, and I knew it. Solving this case depended on continued assistance from Wonderland. I knew I could ill afford to have rumors spread that I was not to be trusted.

If Wonderland brought their pitchforks against me, then goddess help me, this case would go nowhere, and I'd be dead in the water before I'd ever even begun.

I sighed, realizing I would have to apologize.

I watched Hatter marching down the sidewalk, hands clenched and spine taut. He was put out.

"Argh," I muttered inarticulately. Goddess, I really despised Wonderland sometimes.

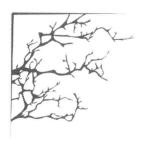

Chapter 5

Detective Elle

"When in Wonderland," I muttered beneath my breath, remembered Ichabod's admonishments of honey, and caught up to the constable.

Bloody hell. Was I really about to do this? Clenching my teeth tight, I zipped through the painful words.

"I do not make a habit of apologizing," I said, shoving my hands into my pockets to keep from fidgeting.

He kept silent for several heartbeats, hands clasped behind his back, staring broodily ahead as we walked through what felt like a maze of streets. Finally though, his lips twitched.

"As far as apologies go, Detective, that was a rather poor one."

I pursed my lips and rolled a wrist. "I call things as I see them."

He raised a brow.

"But"—I popped my tongue on the roof of my mouth to punctuate the word—"maybe I was a little too aggressive with Potts. Maybe."

Truthfully, I hardly thought I'd gotten aggressive with the man at all. I'd done far worse to others and had rarely received the reaction Potts had given me.

Stopping so suddenly that I stumbled over his left shoe, Hatter locked eyes with me as he latched a hand on to my wrist.

The touch surged like a riptide through my veins, making me feel dizzy. Frowning, I disentangled quickly, clearing my throat and nodding in thanks.

"You've been to Wonderland only once before, so far as your report states," he said, and I couldn't help but wonder if he'd stayed up late into the night to study up on me instead of working on his files.

"That's right."

"Then you should know"—he paused as a surly looking man dressed in a cap and threadbare work clothes walked between us without sparing either of us a passing glance—"that out here, a gentleman's or gentlewoman's word is never refuted."

"Oh, goddess," I groaned, wanting to slap my palm to my forehead. I was so sick of the high and mighty toff who thought they were above the law simply because of their status in life, which was often due more to chance than true worth.

"But," he whispered and leaned in so close that I drowned in the scent of his earthy cologne, "that is not to say we should blithely just believe."

His green eye winked.

"Constable Hatter, have you something in your eye?" I asked innocently, with just a hint of acerbic laughter.

He chuckled, the sound big and thunderous, calling attention to the both of us.

Fighting my own grin, I turned up my nose and sniffed. "Fine. I will only question a toff once and then make a note to fact check those lies once they've turned their backs."

"Now you're learning, Detective."

I rolled my eyes. After several more minutes of walking, I looked up at him. "So Alice was the original keeper of the bauble?"

"Mmm." He nodded. "And she's also who we're headed to see."

I frowned, taking a quick minute to study our surroundings. We weren't headed toward residences, but rather deeper into the business district. The structures were mostly ramshackle things that looked like they'd been built a century ago and never updated. Many of the buildings were lopsided, leaning too far to the left or right, with doorways built of brick that looked ready to crumble at our feet with one too-strong gust of wind.

Most of the shoppes around here were of the food variety—cupcakes and tea shoppes, candy shoppes, cupcake and cake shoppes—sugar, basically—though there were a few potions stores along the way as well.

One in particular caught my eye. Green fog swirled from the door of the Crypt. The wooden placard hanging above the door was etched with the design of a coffin with a single thorny rose lying atop it. The door opened, and a man dressed in tweed from head to toe and wearing a leather mask around his eyes walked out, carrying a black leather crop in his hands. Aware that he was being watched, he looked up and smirked lasciviously at me, licking his upper lip in a clear invitation for sex.

My lip curled. "The hells kind of place is this?"

"Why, Alice's shoppe, of course." Hatter sighed, and the sound of it made me think he wasn't near as enthused to enter the place as crop man had been.

Crossing the cobblestone street full of brackish puddles of water, I said, "Something tells me this isn't your first time in this place."

His jaw clenched, and his shoulders gathered. Anger clearly palpable in his words, he said, "No, it's not. And if I were you, Detective, I'd keep my breathing shallow in there."

That wasn't cryptic at all. I had many more questions, but now was not the time to ask them.

Squaring my shoulders, I yanked open the door, pointedly ignoring tweed boy as I sailed in. My nostrils were immediately assaulted by the thick, cloying stench of patchouli incense. Coughing the choking cloud of it out of my lungs, I waved a hand across my nose. "Holy balls, that stings."

Hatter said nothing but merely stepped to the side and extended an arm for me to proceed him to the counter.

Gagging had prevented me from taking in the full glory of the place, though as I did so, I really wished I hadn't.

A man in a horse-head costume was corralled inside of a padded leather pen. He hung over a wooden post, with his lily-white arse on full display, while another person dressed in black leathers from head to toe landed one swat after another on it. With each crack of the whip to his ass, the horse-headed man neighed. He didn't moan, groan, or cry out. No, he really *neigh-hhhhhed* for all he was worth and wiggled his bum faster after each strike, and it didn't seem to me that it was because he was in pain.

I wished I could say that was the strangest thing in the shoppe, but there was a long, dark corridor behind the horse fetishist, and blood-curdling screams echoed out from beneath its many closed doors.

I instantly recalled Hatter's premonition of a horse's head and was now more convinced than ever that what he had wasn't a curse at all. This had to be what he'd seen, which told me we were on the right track.

Hanging from the ceiling were many chains of varying length, some thin and delicate and connected to swings, others fatter and broader, supporting flat beds that looked capable of holding a ton of weight, if not more.

That green fog was everywhere in here, swirling around our ankles like charmed cobras, and I felt the tingle of its magick whip through my bones as the smoky stuff made contact with my skin.

Hatter had told me not to breathe too deeply in here, but I couldn't keep myself from dragging heavy whiffs of the stuff deep into my lungs. My siren's true nature made this place an intoxicating experience to my already sensually heightened nerves. I inhaled again and trembled as need moved like claws through every inch of me, making my skin prickle right up to the crown of my head and down to the soles of my feet.

I clenched my hands into fists, trying hard to shake off the languorous stupor of want and desire now crowding my insides.

I looked at Constable Hatter, who had his lips pursed and was very slowly breathing in and out with deliberation and care.

This was going to be so much fun. I could just see it—panting and sweating and moaning during my interrogation. How wonderful.

The door behind us opened again, and a gaggle of women—clearly woodland nymphs judging by their bark-like skin and twiggish hair—came barreling in, laughing and clinging to one another's necks as they kissed and fondled each other. They headed in the direction of the swings.

"Alice has been a naughty girl," I finally said in a kittenish and husky drawl. Dammit all to hells, I'd be happy to leave this place ASAP. It was hard enough being a female detective in a man's world. It would be doubly so with this dark magick making me act like the nymph I truly was. It'd taken me years to tone down the sexual predator that always lurked inside of me.

I nibbled my bottom lip, counting slowly to ten in my head. I could do this. I was no youngster, unable to control her baser instincts.

Hatter, who'd remained stoic 'til now, gave me a heated look. But not of desire. Whatever this sex magick was, he seemed completely unaffected by it. "You have no idea."

Then, fisting his hands by his sides, he walked in the opposite direction of the nymphs and horseboy, heading to the left, where the sex shoppe turned into more of a potions shoppe. I followed, and we passed row after row of wooden shelves lined with vials of glittering, glowing substances.

Most of the stuff I didn't recognize. The black anemone and labulum coral I absolutely recognized.

Picking up the glowing teal coral trapped inside glass, I tapped a finger against it. Hatter glanced at me askance, a question marring his brow.

"This is some hardcore stuff," I said. "I once gave this to a sailor who'd come too close to my home."

I couldn't help but shiver when Hatter moved into my space, leaning in so close that I could feel the heat of his words brush against the shell of my ear as he asked, "And what happened to him?"

If he had leaned in any closer, I'd have done what I'd been wanting to do to him from the moment I met him. I wet my lips provocatively, curling them into a dangerous smirk when his eyes widened. The predator in me wanted to play with the prey in him.

But I was no longer that woman. *He'd* shown me another way. *He'd* saved me from my own demons.

Holding tight to the memory of my dead lover, I clamped down on the beast inside of me. I would not suck Hatter dry. My siren days were behind me.

Labulum coral was harmless to merfolk but deadly to leggers. Just a shaving of the stuff on the tongue was enough to make humans experience many hours' worth of sexual high. But if too much of it was ingested, it could cause explosion of rapture that one could actually perish from. It would stop the heart cold.

I drew a breath, and that terrible magick swirled through every inch of me again, obliterating my newly born resolve to be good.

Digging my nails into my palms, I willed my pulse to calm by biting my tongue. Hard. I was trying. By the goddess, I was trying to control the madness, the desire to latch my nails into his starched collar, drag him to my mouth, and suck the very soul out of him.

My smirk was wicked as I said, "He died, of course."

Hatter's hot gaze traveled the length of my face, and I wondered how it was that he couldn't sense my being on a razor's edge.

My heart hammered hard in my chest. I'd consumed so many men, pulled them down into the depths of Davy Jones's locker, clung tight to their bodies as their lungs screamed for air and they shook and quivered in my preternaturally strong grasp until they were forced to take that last and final breath that sealed their doom.

That death's rattle was a drug to a siren. It was our entire reason for being. We lured men to their deaths to get our next hit, to feel the power of that final breath course through our body like pure, uncut devil powder. I'd cared not a whit for the desecrated frames I'd left behind. It'd only ever been about that final kiss.

Without thinking, I raised a hand and gently feathered my fingers along Hatter's sharp cheeks, using the tinniest taste of my power—the call, the siren's touch that turned men to putty in my hands.

Hatter trembled, eyelids fluttering as he leaned into me.

Just one kiss... one little taste to take the edge off.

A feminine clearing of a throat hooked our attention, forcing us to look up.

Freaking out, I jumped back from Hatter as though scalded. I hadn't had thoughts like those in decades, hadn't craved the feel of that final kiss, hadn't wanted what I'd wanted just now.

I needed to get the hells out of the shoppe.

I swallowed hard, breathing shallow and ragged as I hugged my arms to my chest and stared at the source of the timely interruption. Hatter shook his head as though shaking off a stupor. His palm landed on his chest, and his jaw clenched. He refused to look at me.

And well that he didn't. I didn't trust myself right now.

Standing in front of us was the woman of legend herself.

Alice hadn't aged much since the last time I'd seen her. She was still just as stunning as she'd been then, with her dusky colored skin and impossibly deep-blue and kohl-rimmed eyes. She wore a navy-colored dress with slits up both sides of her legs that didn't stop until they came to her waist. Even so, the bottom of the gown was far more conservative than the top, which had a plunging neckline that also ended at her waist. Her wild halo of icy-blond curls fell in silky waves down her bare arms to where the dress's neckline met the side slits. Threaded through those curls were ice blue ribbons, in the exact style of the one tucked in a baggie in my back pocket.

She gave us both a red-lipsticked smile. "Detective. Constable," she said in the smooth, sultry drawl of a woman confidant in her own skin. Then her gaze shifted to Hatter, and she smirked. "Back so soon? And with a female. What games are we to play tonight, lover?"

Lover? What the hells? And here I'd thought Constable Hatter was a buttoned up, stuffy, vanilla kind of guy.

His jaw clenched as his nostrils flared. "I'm here on business today. Nothing else."

"Oh." She crossed her arms, looking innocent and lovely. How that was possible, dressed as she was and surrounded by the sounds of sex and the sensual play of music streaming in from who knew where, I wasn't sure. But Alice had always been a study in dichotomy to me.

"Well, I'm happy to help. Come to my study for some tea?" She blinked innocent, beguiling eyes back at us. The woman could give even a siren a run for her money with the skill and ease of her sensuality.

Again, the sweep of fog curled around my flesh, and again, I felt the call of sex resonate through my bones. My legs felt unsteady, and my pulse quickened a little. Hatter's clean scent of soap and man was doing a number on my senses. Wetting my lips, I wished I could beg off and let Hatter handle this interrogation alone, but there was no way.

The man in question clamped down on my elbow, gripping it tight, and nodded once. "Aye. But clear the magick from the room before we do."

His thumb traced a hot, circular trail on my elbow. It was all I could do not to shove him up against one of the shelves and see just what kind of kink he was really into. I blew out a heavy breath, rolling my shoulders. If I had to stay here much longer, bad things were gonna happen.

Pouting prettily, Alice nodded. "Well, all right then. Just make yourselves comfortable until my return. I'll be back in two shakes of a tail feather."

The moment she'd gone, I turned on Hatter. "You could have bloody warned me about this place, Constable."

I rubbed my brow so hard that I felt like I was scraping my skin off.

He finally dropped his hand, and it sucked so hard that I totally didn't want him to. I knew this was just the side effect of whatever crap was being pumped through the ventilation system, but it'd been so long since I'd released my inner siren.

Not since the day my lover had died.

My heart clenched in agony as the hated memories tried to resurface. I clamped down on them desperately. But in my mind, I saw his sea-blue eyes, saw the flare of pain in them, and then the blood. The blood was everywhere, too much to stem, too much to fix. In one day, I'd lost him.

And in a fit of anger, I shoved Hatter back. He blinked, looking shocked, but not terribly surprised by my outburst either, which made me feel a fool. I pinched the bridge of my nose and shuddered, feeling the call surging like a wave through me, making even my bones tingle and ache.

"Don't touch me," I hissed, fighting to keep myself together.

"As you wish," he said steadily, and I hated myself.

I would not lose it in front of him, would not sink into the darkness of depression again. I'd lost everything that day—my life, my hope, the beat of my heart. It'd been a year and a half since it'd happened. I should have been over it. But losing part of one's soul wasn't something you could get over in a day, a year, or even a lifetime.

But none of that was Hatter's fault. Blowing out a heavy breath, I shook my head. "I'm sorry, okay. Dammit, why do I keep needing to apologize to you? Just..." I raised a hand slowly. "Please, don't touch me while we're here. I can't explain to you why. Just trust me."

His thrust out his jaw, and after a minute, he again said, "As you wish, Detective."

Detective. I knew why he'd used my title rather than my name, and though I should be glad of it, I wasn't. At all.

Alice returned seconds later. With a flick of her fingers, she bade us follow.

I trembled with relief when we walked through the door of her study and I no longer smelled the enchantment of sex weaving through the air. Plopping into a seat, I crossed my legs, gripping my shell tight in my fist as I breathed slowly in and out. I needed a swim in my waters, desperately.

Hatter took the seat beside me, his movements elegant and refined as he reached for the teacup and saucer Alice handed him.

I shook my head when Alice offered me a drink as well.

Getting straight to business, because that was the only way I had found to avoid the demons that constantly plagued my thoughts, I reached into my pocket and withdrew both sets of baggies.

Sliding them across the desk, I asked, "Do you know what these are, Alice?"

The beautiful woman glanced down, sparing neither baggie much of her time. Shrugging a gracefully sloped, dusky-brown shoulder, she said, "Of course. The ribbon is mine. The other is a claw."

"They were found at the scene of a murder," Hatter interjected.

Alice's eyes widened, looking startled for a half of a second. But then her calm façade smoothed back into place.

I thinned my lips, my "weird-dar" going off with bells and klaxons.

"I hope you're not implying I had anything to do with that messy affair?" She pouted her pretty red lips.

"Baiting a client with sex isn't going to get you off the hook, lady," I snapped, catching Hatter's frown from the corner of my eye.

Whatever. If he got pissed yet again because I was "harassing" the witnesses, he could just take a flying leap off the nearest cliff. I didn't trust Alice, and this was my case to solve. He was just here to guide me through this nonsensical world.

Something felt off. I'd been working the beat long enough to know when something wasn't right. And something was definitely not right. Alice's shock had felt too practiced, too fake.

"Why was your ribbon found at my crime scene?" I pressed harder, refusing to let the woman off easily.

Alice turned those intelligent eyes back on me and smiled grimly. "I don't know."

My eyes narrowed to thin slits. "So that's it. You don't know," I scoffed, not buying it for a second.

Alice's jaw clenched.

Hatter cleared his throat, snagging Alice's attention. Setting his tea and saucer down, he asked, "And the claw? Do you recognize it?"

"Why should I?" she snapped.

And just as I was about to yell from exasperation because I knew he'd let her off as easy as he'd let off Potts, Hatter snorted with derision.

"You and I both know, Alice," he chewed out, "the kinds of characters that float through these doors. Don't play coy with me. I saw the way you glanced at it. You know whose it is, so tell me now, or I'll sit here all day until you do." His voice was low, his words a hot, hard shiver of authority.

Well, hmm... So Hatter had a backbone after all. Not quite so prickly anymore, I settled back on my chair, awaiting Alice's answer.

She glowered at us both. "Ask Cheshire."

"It doesn't belong to him," I said. "I have that on good authority."

"No. It doesn't." Alice agreed with a raised brow. "But if anyone in this goddessforsaken realm would know, it would be him. Now, if you have nothing better to do, I would ask you to leave. And don't return unless you've decided to stop wasting my time. Good day to you both."

Standing, she gave Hatter a look full of hidden meaning.

Hatter didn't even flinch. Jaw clenching mightily, he inclined his head in a gesture of farewell, then stood and gestured to the door.

"After you, Detective."

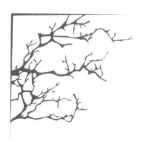

Chapter 6

Detective Elle

I rushed out the door, heading to goddess only knew where. All I knew was I needed to get out of the place ASAP.

Hatter was close on my heels. The second we were on the streets, he latched onto my elbow. "Wait," he said.

"What?" I snapped, knowing I was acting like the hothead I was always accused of being, but that place had been pure torture for me.

If he only knew...

"What is your problem?" he asked in a rush. "You wish my help, I help, and then you run from the place like the hounds of hells are at your feet. Do you want my help or not, Detective Elle?"

When calm, Hatter was an attractive man. But full of fire and brimstone and with those dual-colored eyes practically glowing from fury at my brusque behavior, I had to admit that my visceral reaction to him in there had stemmed from more than just the drugs pumping through the walls.

Deciding just to be blunt because that was my personality, I stepped into him so closely that we practically shared breath. I fisted his immaculately pressed jacket in my hands, jerked his face to mine, and said in a heated whisper, "Do you know who I am, Constable? What I really am?"

Startled, he glanced down at my hands. But he didn't look terrified by me, as any sane male should. I'd killed hundreds, if not thousands in my time.

"You're a siren."

"I'm not just any siren, male. I am *the* siren. The one who sunk countless vessels, the one who lived in a garden of bones fashioned from my many victims. The one cast from my home and my people because my lust was too great a power to contain."

He brushed my hands off his jacket, but continued to share my space, looking deep into my eyes as he said, "Yes. You're also the siren who reformed

65

her ways, who fought to show the world you've changed, who's responsible for taking down some of Grimm's most ruthless criminals. Your power doesn't terrify me, Detective. Your power is your greatest asset. So use it, but not against me. I am not your enemy."

Shocked, I felt as though I'd just been smacked in the face, because with just a few simple, honest words, he'd shredded the protective shell I'd fashioned for myself through the years. It was easy to snap and bite first when that was what people expected of me. But when someone could see past the rumors, past the legend, to the real and insecure woman beneath, well... that made me vulnerable. And being vulnerable made me uneasy.

Taking a step away from him, I wrapped my arms around myself. I hadn't just changed out of the blue. There'd been a reason for it.

A person.

A man.

Hook.

My lover. My everything. He'd taught me I could be more than the monster within. And now he was gone, and I was finding it harder and harder to hang on to that good woman. My work for Grimm PD was the only thing holding my sanity together, the only place I could find any solace from the constant and crippling pain. I could not have my safe place tarnished.

I shook my head. "You don't know what you're talking about."

"I know more than you think."

My spine went taut. "Did you see it? Have a vision of what happened?" I growled, angry all over again.

Working the wrinkles out of his jacket, he shrugged his shoulders. "I didn't need to *see* anything to *see* it. You may think you and I have nothing in common, but we are more alike than you'd imagine. Now, if you're ready to work, let's work."

There was literally nothing more to say to that. Grinding my molars, I debated on what I should do next as we resumed walking.

Alice hadn't exactly been helpful. Following up with Cheshire seemed like the logical next step. I doubted he'd be much more helpful than Alice had been, but leads were scarce.

"I don't trust Alice," I said simply, letting Hatter decide where to take my olive branch.

I was tired of apologizing for feeling like hells. But Hatter was right, I needed to grow up already. From now on, I was going to think with my head and not my heart. Hearts were messy, stupid organs that got one into trouble more often than they were worth.

He glanced down at me. "Neither do I. She knows something."

Glad that he wasn't going to make a big deal about what'd happened, I blew out a tiny breath of relief. "You sensed that too. When she looked at the ribbon, that's when my gut said—"

"She knows much more than she's letting on. Yes, I know. Though I honestly don't believe she knows how her ribbon ended up on the Charming estate."

I frowned, grabbed his elbow, and turned him around so that he could look at me. "Really? And you're not just saying this because you're personally involved with—"

"What you think you know about us, you don't, Detective. Trust me. I know which side of the game I'm on."

I raised a brow. "And that is?"

"Truth. Facts. It's what I work for day in and day out. Is she hiding something? Absolutely. No doubt about that." He shrugged.

I was more inclined to agree with him than not, but I couldn't forget that he and Alice had a history. A tawdry one, at that. It could make having him in on this investigation complicated, especially if he didn't come clean about just what that history entailed.

As though he'd read my mind, he took a deep breath. "Look, I'll tell you everything so you can include it in your investigation report. Just not now. We have to find Cheshire and make him talk, not to mention I still have stacks of paperwork to file from yesterday."

He growled the last bit and rolled his eyes.

I almost felt sympathy for him then. "Some days, it feels like it never ends, doesn't it?"

"You could say that. I guess it's time to use your key," he said brusquely, switching subjects so quickly that it almost gave me whiplash.

"Okay. Where to? Or you know what?" I dug the gold key card out of my back pocket. "This should work for you, too, and would likely be a hells of a lot easier. Just think about where you want us to go, and we'll get there."

Nodding his thanks, he took the key from me. With his jaw clenched tight, he swiped the key through the air.

When we stepped out of the tunnel, the land had shifted all over again. Gone were the garbage-lined streets and smog-choked air of the city. We stood in front of a wooden structure that looked held together by a few rusted nails and a few thousand termites holding hands.

There were holes everywhere—in the steps, on the porch, even in the walls themselves. But judging by the volume of chatter and twangy music that flowed from the open windows, there were plenty of people inside.

The sign hanging on the roof read Cat On A Hot Tin Roof. Blue neon lights next to it glowed in the shapes of a martini glass with an olive in it and a pool cue.

"The cat's here?" I asked dubiously before glancing at Hatter, wondering whether he'd only brought me here to get a drink.

"Mmm." He gave a monosyllabic grunt. "Not only is he here, but a word of caution to you, Detective. There's only one way to get that cat to talk, and it's to answer a riddle."

"He didn't require that before."

Hatter shrugged. "He was working off a deal with the Knight. But riddles are the cat's everyday currency."

I sighed. "Fine."

Hatter held up a cautionary finger. "If you don't know the answer, for goddess's sake, don't answer. Say nothing."

I narrowed my eyes. "Isn't that sort of defeating the purpose? How are we to get him to talk if I don't say something?"

"The cat's got a superiority complex. If he believes you stupid, he'll never talk with you again."

I laughed. "Stupid. Because I can't figure out a riddle? I'm the law—"

"Forgetting what I told you back at Potts would do you ill, Detective. Just trust me on this. Answer only if you're sure." He dusted at his sleeves.

The constable was constantly dusting at himself. I'd never seen someone so immaculately groomed, to be honest, so I was beginning to suspect he did it when he was nervous. But why was he nervous now?

Pursing my lips, I gave him an irritated glare. "And why can't you answer, then?"

He shrugged. "Not my case. I'm merely assisting you. The cat has eyes and ears all over Wonderland."

I snorted. "You don't say. I liked him better when I met him previously, and that's not saying much since I pretty much despised him before."

He chuckled. "You weren't on his turf then. You are now. His rules. His way. Always has been. Always will be. Tell me, Detective Elle." Hatter's voice dropped to a deep husky, drawl as he took a step in toward me. "How is a raven like a writing desk?" His electric blue eye practically glowed as his smile teased and taunted me.

My heart slammed against my throat at his nearness. The dregs of Alice's sex magick still pumped through my veins. Hatter played with fire, and a part of me thought maybe he knew it too.

Nibbling the corner of my lip, I was about to answer when a throaty voice rumbled, "Mmm, yes. Do tell."

Gasping, caught off guard by the voice, I turned. My hand automatically went to the hilt of my weapon as I did. But I stayed my hand when I saw who it was.

Cheshire wasn't always a cat. He was a shifter, and his cat form was hardly domestic. It was more like a big, loping, predatory feline with the most amazing black silky fur that practically gleamed like squid ink in the moonlight.

He'd shifted to man form and was just as arresting in that silhouette too, all long and shapely limbs that weren't too muscular, but neither were they spindly little arms and legs. He was well put together, with ebony skin and hypnotic blue eyes. As always, he was wearing his perpetual sickle-shaped grin. He smelled of night and madness, and though I had hated traveling with the beast before, I had to admit to feeling darkly drawn to him too. There was just something irreverent and fascinating about him.

He raised a thick, dark brow. "Well, Detective Arielle," he said with a smirk, knowing the use of that name always set my teeth on edge. "Long time, no see."

Walking like the graceful, sloping predator that he was in every form, he circled me, running his hands through the tips of my bright blue hair as he lifted it to his nose and took a gentle whiff of it before letting it slide back through his fingers.

I flared with siren magick, blasting it at him.

It only caused him to jerk and then chuckle thunderously. "The angelfish has got teeth." He wet his own lips. "And you know just how much I do love my fish, *De-tec-tive*."

He all but purred. Then he glanced over at Hatter, giving him a negligible once-over before resuming his study of me.

"Well, my beauty? How is a raven like a writing desk? Tick. Tock. Tick. Answer quick, or I shall leave."

I'd heard this riddle told before, and there'd been many answers given. Problem was which answer would he want most?

I glanced at Hatter. He was clenching and unclenching his jaw, looking at me with hard intensity, as though mentally chanting that I remain silent and say nothing if I didn't know.

But I knew.

Sometimes it came in handy having a partner like Ichabod.

"Well, I suppose you'd expect me to say because Poe wrote on both, but that answer is too simple. Perhaps, then, it's because there is a "b" in both, and an "n" in neither, but really, that's hardly satisfying."

My lips widened as his did.

Cheshire obviously hadn't expected me to play along. But I was so much more than a pretty face.

"At the end of the day, I suppose the only answer I can give is because they can both produce a few notes, though they are very flat, and they are *never—*"

Cheshire's head whipped up the moment I said it, with a look of mischievous delight sparkling in his glowing eyes, and I knew I'd answered correctly.

"Put with the wrong end in front." A little smug and very satisfied with myself, I crossed my arms and gave Hatter a haughty smile.

His answering nod and expression clearly said, "touché," and it was all I could do not to buff my nails on my chest and gloat. Really, who knew the sexy siren had it in her? Ich would have been so proud.

Cheshire held out his hand, and when I took it, his grip was strong, warm, and very, very inviting. His thumb brushed delicately along the padding of my thumb, making my already-sensitized flesh break out in a heady rush. I knew men of any species, and his meaning was clear enough. Gorgeous as he was, I was still on duty. Also, trusting Cheshire would be to anyone's detriment. He was a lot like the fae—to trust them could very well be the last foolish thing one ever did in life.

Winking, I gave him a no-nonsense handshake, and he shrugged.

"If that's what you wish." He held up his hands. "Then that's what you wish. Come inside, won't you? Share a drink, and we'll talk."

I glanced up at Hatter as I passed. His jaw couldn't have been set any tighter. Clearly, my hidden conversation with Cheshire hadn't gone unnoticed.

Cheshire's tight arse flexed as he bounded up the steps two at a time and disappeared behind the door. He really was pretty, and I knew later tonight I'd regret not taking him up on the offer. I sighed theatrically. Hatter was still at the bottom of the steps.

"What's the matter, Constable?" I couldn't help but tease him over my shoulder. "Uncomfortable working with a siren?"

Licking his front teeth, he caught up as I jogged up the steps.

"Who said anything about being uncomfortable?" His answering grin made my pulse race. My lips curled into a slow grin as I realized he'd been eyeing my arse much the same way I'd been eyeing Cheshire's.

I couldn't help it. I smiled.

The constable was just full of surprises, wasn't he?

CHESHIRE MOVED BEHIND the bar top as he expertly and efficiently withdrew three glass tumblers and filled them full of a glowing, greenish liquid that smoked at the top. Witches brew, no doubt. Very illegal.

I rolled my eyes, knowing what wouldn't end up in my log tonight. Taking a quick study of my surroundings, I was impressed by just how different the inside was than the outside. Seemed to be standard in Wonderland.

The bar itself had a space-opera-meets-steampunk look to it. The brew stand was crank and steam powered, filling the room with a ghostly white fog that seemed to glitter and glow thanks to the golden fairy lights hanging everywhere.

The stools and the bar top were made of a rich hammered-bronze material. Black wrought-iron chandeliers and wall sconces cast prisms of light everywhere. A few yards in front was a stage and a band sweating and powering out some fast-paced music that had everyone in the place ready to dance and drink throughout the night.

The most unusual part of the bar was the floating head that'd been sealed inside a glass jar. The jar was at the end of the bar top, surrounded by patrons who laughed and tapped at it, causing the eyes to open and the mouth to smile.

Hatter leaned in to whisper in my ear. I couldn't help but inhale his cologne as he did it.

"It's the head of an old gypsy woman. She made a trade with the cat a few decades ago."

Turning into him so that my breasts brushed his chest, I asked, "Why?"

Hatter's eyes were hot and hard as he said, "Because it's what he does—trade in deals. He got what he wanted."

"And her? What did she get?"

"She got to play fortune teller for the rest of her life," Cheshire drawled. Clearly, his hearing was remarkable, even in a loud place.

Moving the glasses toward us, Cheshire lifted his, dipped his head, and said, "To murder."

"Macabre, even for you, shifter." Hatter raised a brow as he lifted the brew to his lips and downed it in one deep gulp.

When in Wonderland...

"Bottoms up," I whispered before tipping the glass toward them then swallowing the brew in one go.

The stuff burned like lightning going down my throat, causing my eyes to swim and my lungs to swell like they'd been too quickly shocked from land to water breathing.

Hatter's deep rumble caused my lips to purse with a smirk. It might not have looked pretty, but at least I'd kept it down.

Cheshire made to pour brew into our empty glasses again, but I covered mine.

"I'm good."

Hatter, however, took his and slammed it back. His strong neck muscles rolled as he drank. But the look he turned on me after setting his cup down made my insides scramble.

Cheshire refilled for himself and Maddox one last time, and again, Constable Hatter slammed it back.

I raised a brow once it seemed they'd finally finished.

"Drinking on the job? Seems unlike you, Constable."

"Maddox," he grinned. "And it seems I'm forced to school you again, Detective Elle. When in Wonderland—"

I held up my hands. "Do as the Wonderlandians do. I'm pretty sure I've got it now. But don't expect me to carry your sorry arse out of here if the devil's brew starts biting back."

His devilish grin and laughing dark eyes had my toes curling.

"I'll remember that, Detective. And just so you know"—he leaned in close, whispering hotly into the shell of my ear, causing my skin to break out in a wash of goose pimples—"one should never judge a book by its cover. First impressions are often wrong."

I felt the press of strong fingertips against the small of my back. A dark thrill skated up my spine like black ice, and my heart pounded in my chest.

It'd been so long since I'd fed my siren's needs. I turned, realizing just how close we stood as our lips hovered scant inches apart. The warmth of his burnt-cherry breath washed over me, and I curved my fingernails deep into my palms. The perfume from Alice's sex shoppe had to have been some seriously potent stuff to still be affecting me like this.

"If you'd like to screw," Cheshire drawled, "I've a private room in the back if you've coin enough."

I frowned, whirling on him only to note the arrogant slant of his full mouth.

"Only normal, I suppose," he pressed, "seeing as how you killed your mate and all."

Without thought or even a moment's hesitation, I speared my fingers, now tipped with claws, into the shifter's neck and dug deep into his flesh, enjoying the slide of hot, slippery blood painting my fingernails red. I pulled him toward me and allowed my eyes to shift to that of the demonic creature of the deep.

"If I were you, Cheshire," I hissed, "I'd be very careful with my next words. Very. Careful."

"Release him, Detective." Maddox's sharp words cut through the haze of red, but I only curled my nails in deeper.

Wide-eyed, Cheshire raised his chin, but he didn't utter a sound.

"Detective," Hatter said again, this time placing a hand on my elbow. I trembled even as my mind burned with the hated memories of a time so dark for me that I'd nearly not survived it.

"Elle," he said, his voice a deep and urgent whisper. "Remember why we're here."

Those words were like ice to my flame. Breathing heavy, I glanced around, finally noting all eyes were on us. On me. I heard the quiet hush of whispers as the patrons watched me, an officer of the law, assault one of their own.

I swore and yanked my hand back. No one in here would know why I'd done what I'd done or that Cheshire had set me up to react just as I'd had. I knew it the second I glanced at his face and saw the smug smirk tightening his mouth and eyes. I wrapped my arms around myself, feeling exposed and naked.

A strong arm slid around my waist, holding me close, like an unshakeable foundation in the chaotic storm. I didn't look at Hatter, but I stepped into him just a little, sending him a silent thank you. He nodded once. From his deep inhale, I knew he meant to take over the interrogation, and for once, I was more than happy to let him.

"I'm sure you know why we're here," he said in his eloquent Wonderlandian accent.

Cheshire shrugged one shoulder. The ebony of his skin glowed a deep blue because of the way the light played off his flesh.

"Say I do. What's in it for me, Detective?" His question hadn't been for Hatter.

My nostrils flared. After what the bastard had just done, how dare he think I'd be inclined to help him with anything?

"We can play this game one of two ways, cat. Either you tell us what we want to know go on about your night, or I book you on charges of—"

He snorted and raised a hand. "I see your flare for the dramatic hasn't changed a bit, fish. Fine. We do this your way, then. Show me the claw."

"How do you know about the claw?" I barked.

He snorted. "I know everything, lass. Now, stop wasting my time."

Irritated but also feeling more at ease, I stepped out of Hatter's embrace and dug into my pocket, pulled out the baggie, and slid it across to him.

Cheshire picked it up and looked at it for less than half a second. Then, that infuriating, hypnotizing grin for which he was so well known spread across his face.

"Yeah, I know who this belongs to."

I waited for him to tell us, but as the seconds ticked by, I began to grow impatient. He raised a brow, taunting me, daring me to have another outburst. If I had to take a stab at it, I'd say he wanted me to show my true colors, or at least what most of Grimm thought were my kind's true colors. But he'd already used against me the one thing that would hurt enough to make me forget my training, and I wasn't falling for it again.

"Well?" I asked, nice and slow.

He sniffed, as if disappointed, before licking his front teeth and pushing the baggie back at me. "Like I said, what's in it for me?"

It was against GPD regs to barter. Yes, this was Wonderland, and there was a certain level of wiggle room afforded me. Had it been anyone else, I might have considered it. But he'd pissed me right the hells off tonight, and I wasn't in the mood to play his games.

"You tell us what we need to know, or so help me goddess, I'll book you and put your arse in jail for impeding the progress of an active investigation."

Cheshire chuckled. "Oh, come on, Detective. Is that anyway to treat your old friend?"

And now I was reminded why, regardless of how attractive he was, we'd barely gotten on before and why I'd been in such a rush to leave Wonderland—mostly because of him and his insufferable mind games.

Narrowing my eyes, I gripped the bar top and leaned forward. "I could make you sing like a canary, kitty, if I really wanted to."

I let him feel just a small drop of my magick, that dark power that I kept locked and hidden deep inside of me, that addictive magick that could make any man, woman, or beast yield to my ways. I was forbidden to use the magick while I wore the badge, but I didn't give two hells right now. Cheshire had picked at a pain too completely devastating and too damn fresh for me to take the high road. If Bo caught wind of what I was doing, I could be suspended, but again, I just didn't give two hells right now.

My smile was ruthless as Cheshire's narrowed in dawning awareness of just what he was up against. The air between us sizzled with tension.

But then Hatter was there, stepping between us and gently maneuvering me behind him. "What do you want, shifter?" he asked grimly.

I wasn't sure what Hatter was getting at, until I caught sight of his glowing eye.

"Hmm. Well now, that's the question isn't it? What do I want? You know what I want, don't you, Maddox. You can see me." He pointed to his eye, indicating Hatter's own. "Show me, then."

Rules said I wasn't allowed to promise or bribe anyone in any way to obtain our answers. Those rules didn't apply to someone outside of GPD, though. I didn't like Cheshire. I didn't trust him as far as I could throw him. But he had answers we desperately needed, and right now, I wasn't above making a deal with the devil if that was what it took to finally nail some royal arse with the long arm of justice.

Shrugging out of his jacket, Hatter handed it over to me. I took it without a word, curious about what in the hells was going on. He undid the buttons of his left sleeve and rolled it up slowly.

Even in the dim lighting, I caught sight of the tattoos. My heart hammered in my throat at the exquisite and detailed drawings of demons and monsters on them. Every part of his flesh that he revealed was covered with black and gray artwork.

One drawing stood out the most. It was an image of a sensually beautiful demoness. She had large, bat-like wings outstretched, and they were riddled with holes. Her face held just a hint of a smile, and her long black hair whipped in the breeze. She was nude and reminded me a little of Alice in looks.

But that wasn't what'd caught my attention. No, what I had noticed was the drawing's eyes, the only point of color on his arm. They glowed a vivid, electric blue similar to one of his own.

With a lusty curve of his lips, Cheshire latched on to Hatter's arm, and that tattoo radiated with a soft wash of white light that moved from Maddox into the cat, seeming to lock their hands in place.

Cheshire's eyes closed, and his movements stilled completely.

Hatter, too, had his eyes closed.

I couldn't help wondering what it was the two of them saw. Less than a minute later, Cheshire chuckled and drew his hand back. The light between them died.

Hatter's jaw was held tight, and he drew his sleeve down with hard, jerky movements, as though angry about something.

"I'm not sure you meant to show me that, boyo," Cheshire drawled.

The mystery was almost too much for me. It was on the tip of my tongue to ask them just what they had seen, but Hatter, as though anticipating my question, looked down at me with a glare that brooked no dissidence.

Oh, I was going to ask him about this later. No doubt about it. I had an investigative report to file, and if there was something he was keeping from me, then he'd better believe I was going to suss it out.

"Claw belongs to the bandercoot," Cheshire said with what seemed to be a lack of interest at this point, as though his playthings had suddenly stopped being interesting. Typical cat. "Go. Stay. I don't care. But I have work to do. Oh, and Hatter, just one last thing... friend to friend," he said, but his eyes were for me. "It would be most unwise to trust a fish. They have a tendency to gut you if you do."

I clenched my jaw, but I would not be goaded this time.

Hatter didn't say anything or even look at me, but I saw his reflexive swallow, and I hated it.

With those words, Cheshire was gone, literally there one second and vanished the next. On the other side of the bar and five bodies down, a woman dressed in practically nothing shot up from her seat with a shocked cry as she grabbed hold of her bum and glared at the nothing behind her. After that, it looked like a conga line of sexy women pulled the exact same stunt. I guessed we'd stirred up something dangerous in Cheshire and he was making them pay for it.

But not my circus, not my monkeys.

I figured Hatter would be ready to move on, or at the very least, ask me what Cheshire had meant. But I'd be damned if I told him. The only person still living, besides me, who really knew what had happened that night was Bo, and I knew she wouldn't talk about it. Shockingly, Hatter didn't seem inclined to question me or even leave just yet. Instead, he sat, tapping his finger rhythmically on the bar top, staring off into some time I wasn't a part of.

I flicked a glance at his arm, to the covered tattoos.

"I'm not seeing anything," he drawled after a moment.

"But you did see something. Is it pertinent to our investigation?" My words were tempered. Somehow, I sensed that he'd not appreciate anything more. I hardly knew the man, but I was coming to respect his abilities as my temporary partner and liaison.

"No," was all he said, and then finally, he shook his head as though clearing the cobwebs loose. "Sorry about this." He took back the jacket I still held in my hands and shook out the wrinkles before slipping it back on.

Sliding the baggie back into my pocket, I asked, "You think this is really the bandercoot's?"

"Mmm." He nodded, scrubbing his jaw lightly. "I do."

Something was wrong with him. The vision he'd seen had shaken him. I wasn't sure how, but I knew it had. He was distracted and unfocused. The last thing in the world I wanted was to have to go back for Harry. Hatter had proven himself and then some, so far as investigating went. But I couldn't have him like this either.

"Do you think," he said slowly, "that there's hope for redemption, when the path that saved you is littered with evil?"

His question was so far out of left field that I was momentarily struck dumb. "What?" I blinked, confused by his sudden shift in focus.

His green eye flared once, and then the pall that had lingered over his features since Cheshire shared his vision lifted. A tight but confident smile drew across his lips.

"It's nothing," he said quickly. "Never mind. We should get back."

I was still confused and feeling like I'd missed something obvious, but I couldn't afford distractions. My brain needed to be completely focused on the task at hand. Was I curious about Hatter, more so than ever? Yes. But I was close to having only a one-day supply of water available to me and a key card that would only remain charged for the next few hours.

"To the bandercoot?"

"No." Hatter glanced at a clock hanging on the wall. "At this hour, the zoo will be closed to us."

Zoo? Did the bandercoot live in a zoo? It seemed unlikely, but I knew I'd not misheard. However, he did not seem inclined to elucidate further. After another few seconds of silence I shrugged.

"So then?" I shook my head.

"We wait, Detective. So then, we wait."

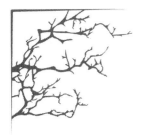

Chapter 7

Detective Elle

WAITING WASN'T SOMETHING I'd ever been good at. The second we arrived back at the constable's station, I knew going there had been a bad idea.

Hatter was switching out work jackets. Apparently, the man was a touch type-A. I inhaled deeply, clapping my hands together and rocking on my heels, which served to draw his attention just like I'd hoped.

"Yes?" he asked, raising one of his devilishly arched brows in question.

"I'm no good at waiting, Constable."

"Maddox," he grumped reflexively. "And I already told you, we wouldn't find the bandercoot at this hour."

I shook my head. "No, I know. But you're going back out. Take me with you."

Harry walked in from the garden just then, popping what looked suspiciously like a bit of mushroom into his mouth as he did so. "Detective," he said in that thick and very hard to understand southern Wonderlandian accent of his. "I wus wonderin' when ye'd be making yer way back to me, then."

I would rather die than beg, but if I was forced to beg, I absolutely would. The fine hairs on my arms were still standing on end and my nerves were shot to hells from the sexual beating I'd taken at Alice's shoppe. No way did I want to be left alone with Harry right now. The goddess only knew what kind of trouble I'd find myself in by night's end.

I nibbled my bottom lip, an action that drew Hatter's eyes instantly. He wet his lips, and it dawned on me that the sensual resonance I usually kept so tightly reined was running rampant through my system right now. And though I'd rarely been one of those sirens who used her charms like a weapon, there were times such as these when the sacrifice must be made. If I wound up in bed with Harry as a partner because Hatter had abandoned me, I'd gouge my eyes out with a rusted spoon.

Fixing a smile on my face, I ignored the huff of excitement that dripped off Harry's tongue as I sidled in closer to Hatter, who was looking at me with two parts wary caution and one part heated anticipation.

"Please, Maddox." I used his given name, taking a gamble that doing so would help my cause. "You wouldn't make me beg, would you?"

At that last bit, I delicately ran my hands up the collar of his tea coat. His face was an implacable wall that gave away none of his emotions.

A muscle in his jaw twitched as he glanced over at Harry, and I knew he was fitting two and two together, not that I cared.

I wasn't completely heartless, though. I didn't wiggle on him or fondle his chest, hands, or arms, even though I was insanely curious about those tattoos and wanted to know more.

I was a good siren.

So far as good sirens went, that was.

"You're a very dangerous creature, Elle," he mumbled with that wickedly dark voice of his that made me think of a fine, aged malt whiskey tapped straight from the barrel.

"Is that a yes?" I asked, voice kittenish and husky as I released more of my charm, wrapping that veil of pleasure around his head like a smokescreen.

I knew what I was doing to him physically, internally. His heart would be racing, blood pumping violently through his veins as it rushed south, shutting off all receptors in his brain save for the most basic and elemental ones—the need to mate, to mark, to screw.

His irises flared, and my smile grew wider.

He latched on to my hands, taking them off his lapels but not releasing his hold on me yet.

"Have I a choice?"

"Not really, no."

His smile was nothing but teeth. Buried deep inside this buttoned-up man was something feral and wicked. I shivered, feeling a little like I could be playing with fire. Not something I was used to feeling around others.

I'd played with fire once before and had been consumed by it. I'd set out to make Hook my slave, but in the end, he'd dominated my siren, and I'd become addicted to the taste of him.

I would never give another male a hold on me like that again, but I'd be lying if I said I hadn't missed the dance.

Hatter lowered his head until his lips were just a few feather wisps' distance from mine, so close I could feel the heated wash of his words brush against my sensitized flesh as he said, "Don't think I don't know what you're about, siren."

His words said one thing, but the fire in his eyes said another. Just like back in the shoppe, I knew Hatter didn't fear my beast. In fact, he rather seemed to revel in her.

I smirked, enjoying our banter much more than I knew I should.

Hard fingers dug into my wrists unmercifully. He, in turn, was testing me, seeing just how far I planned to take our little tête-à-tête. Well, fair was fair, after all. I'd started this game.

Spreading my legs until every inch of my lower anatomy brushed against every inch of his lower anatomy, I moved into him until hardly any space was left between us. Something hard and long poked into my thigh, and I almost purred.

That damn sex magick had stirred the waters, and come hells or high water, I was going to have to find some way to still the ripple before it became a full-blown tsunami of lust.

Leaning up on tiptoe, I whispered, "Then you know a siren always means what she says. Or doesn't say."

With the lightest of touches, I pressed my hand to his flat belly, delighted by the corded feel of his abdominals. Hatter was a walking, talking contradiction. A scholar with the body of an incubus. The appearance of a saint with the heart of a sinner.

Oh yes, I very much liked what I saw.

Lips pursing as though digesting my words, he chuckled from deep in his gut. "Then come, Detective, though I rather think you'll find slogging through mud and weeds not at all to your liking."

"You have no idea what I like, boy." Then, with a flick of my fingertip to his nose, I stepped well outside his personal space and spread my arms. "After you, Constable."

Clearing his throat, he suddenly looked discombobulated, and I felt a teeny bit predatory because of it. Sirens liked nothing so much as the scent of blood in the water, no matter how insignificant an amount.

When I looked up at Harry, his jaw was gaping open and he was breathing raggedly.

"Wipe your chin, hare. You're drooling."

Hatter smirked. He looked as unflappable as usual when he brushed past me. But his brush was a deliberate press of chest to chest, and I heard his smoldering chuckle when I gasped from the contact.

As we traveled through the portal again, I thought maybe I'd been away from the siren game too long. That incidental bit of contact should not have been enough to make me feel as though I'd just taken a shot of liquid lightning straight to my veins. It should not have roused the beast as it had.

Even now, I was still sparking. I kept telling myself this was nothing but sex magick at play, but deep down, I worried that maybe I'd poked at a sleeping dragon. I nibbled the corner of my lips, stomach twisting and diving toward my knees.

"Penny for your thoughts," Hatter said in a voice that told me he knew damn well where my muddled thoughts were at.

"Wouldn't you like to know?"

His look was intense as he quietly said, "Maybe I would."

I frowned as we stepped through the portal, wondering if he was still playing as we had been. But my thoughts were quickly diverted when I took my next breath.

The scent that lingered in the air was one I'd smelled before—at the Charming estate.

Blinking, I went absolutely still as we studied the layout of... wherever we were.

Hatter had led us here, and by the looks of the dirt path ahead of me, littered with halo-shrooms on either side, I could only assume we'd arrived at the crime scene Hatter and Harry had been at the day I'd arrived in Wonderland.

Several lit wall torches set within the stone siding of the pub behind us cast a soft, golden glow across the gathering veil of night. The cacophony of drunken patrons and plinking piano keys behind us was a hum of soothing white noise. I looked at Hatter, wondering which way we might go—down the path and into the forest, or into the bar. My money was on the bar. Potential eyewitnesses could still be in there, and it was a well-known fact that if you got a man deep enough into his cups, any number of surprising things could come out of him.

But Hatter surprised me by turning onto the path and heading down the winding dirt trail instead. He paused and looked back at me.

"You coming, Detective?" he asked with a sly grin.

I glanced at the pub one last time before turning and jogging to catch up with him. "Of course I am."

The forest was thick with night. The chirping of insects was a low hum. Ancient, gnarled trees with massive limbs and exposed roots twisted through the forest to form a giant green labyrinth. I stepped up and around them as best I could, but my boots continually sank deep into the surprisingly swampy marsh beneath. I had to jiggle my heels each time I stepped out of it. Soon, all I heard was the sucking squish of our walking and our steady breaths.

"Rained the past few nights. Wasn't this bad when we were here last. But the path up ahead should be dry. Tree boughs are tight enough that it should have kept out most of the rain."

I wasn't sure if his words were prophetic or whether he'd had a vision, but he was right. Soon enough, we were out of the swamp and on terra firma once more. I jiggled my foot.

"Thank the goddess," I muttered beneath my breath. I might be a water elemental, but even I had my limits when it came to tramping through muck. I wrinkled my nose as I thought about how badly I'd need a bath when I got back home for the night.

I was rather surprised, though, that as meticulously groomed as Constable Hatter was, he seemed far less bothered by the mud than I.

I was dragging my muddy boot along an upraised root to clean it when I caught the scent of something very familiar. I went immediately still and sniffed, dragging air deeper into my lungs, forgetting all about the muddy boots.

Hatter, keenly aware of his surroundings, paused just a moment later and looked back at me with a curious frown on his face.

"What?" he asked, as though aware of my unnatural stillness.

Holding up my hand, I frowned hard as I tiptoed softly by him, keeping to the path laid out by MICE—a glowing trail of luminescent orange mushroom caps that marked a clean trail for crime scene investigators to walk through. I ignored many of the tiny orange flags that'd been shoved through the muddy soil to mark spots of interest for further investigation and continued to let my nose lead me.

"Detective Elle?" Hatter whispered more sharply this time, but again, I held up my hand and shook my head.

"Something. Something," I mumbled, following the scent trail like a bloodhound would.

I walked outside of the obvious area where the body cast had been sprayed in white, moving several yards deeper into the woods, following my nose toward the source of the water I smelled.

Hatter stayed by my side, saying nothing, for which I was grateful.

"This could be nothing," I mumbled beneath my breath as I started trotting to my left, where the sulfuric stench became more overwhelming.

"What could?"

I glanced over at him, noting that his blue eye was lit up like a firecracker and burning like flame in the night. I vaguely wondered if he was seeing a vision, but I was like a dogfish with a bone.

"Where's the water?" I muttered. "Where's the water?"

"Water?" he repeated. "I—we did not see any."

The smell was punching me in the olfactory senses. I knew it was here somewhere. I jumped through a screen of heavy shrubbery, wincing at the twigs that cut into my arms.

"Detective," he said with a surprised grunt.

I looked ahead and then stopped moving. Shimmering like black ink in the moonlight was a deep pool of natural spring water bubbling up from the earth. The surface of the water was a scummy green, which I ignored. I sniffed again and then grinned, yanking off my shirt with a hard jerk.

"Detective?" Hatter asked questioningly.

"Tell me, Maddox." I smirked. "Did anyone bother to dredge the pools around here?"

This wasn't the only body of water around, but it was the only one of interest to me. I smelled sulfides. Sulfides that, once again, didn't belong to the flora and fauna in this part of the Grimm universe. It was a type of sulfide that belonged to mountainous sulfur springs only. So what the hells was it doing here? Two separate realms, but the same sulfides? That wasn't a coincidence, surely.

As I undid the button of my pants and slid the leather down my athletic legs, I was shivering, not from fright but from near orgasmic excitement. There were few things in life better than a swim into the unknown.

Hatter's eyes were hot brands as they traveled the length of my near-naked form unashamedly. The last thing I had to take off was my shirt. I didn't want to. The magick of my waters was imbued within the fabric itself. But I also couldn't afford to walk around Grimm nude until my shirt air-dried. Mixing my water with any other would dampen its effect and make it difficult to breathe. I couldn't contaminate my waters and survive. Father had thought of almost everything when he'd exiled me.

With a grunt of determination, I undid the buttons one by one. I could feel the weakening of my waters already. The shirt had a day of magick left to it. I'd need to return to my waters before day's end tomorrow. I dreaded the thought of depending solely on the trapped water inside my shell.

The teal shirt fluttered to the ground like feathers at my feet. Already, I felt weaker. My breaths turned shallow, and I had to stave off the panic that came anytime I felt myself bereft of my waters. But I still had my shell, and though its magick wasn't nearly as strong as that of the sprite's work, it would do well enough.

"I take it by your state of undress that you plan to swim, siren." Hatter's words rippled like hot velvet.

I laughed. "Does that bother you, Constable?"

"Oh, so now I'm Constable again, am I? I thought we moved beyond that back at my quarters. Or were you simply teasing me as a siren is often wont to do?" he asked not with anger, but with a teasing lilt.

Hatter knew far too much about my species. I should hate him for it. And yet, I completely didn't. Choosing to ignore his not-so-subtle dig at me, I took a running leap and dove square into the center of the deep but narrow pool.

The moment my flesh touched water, the sizzle of my transformation took over, and I sighed with relief. This might not be my water, but the feel of its liquid coolness was like a drug to my overheated senses.

Focused on the task at hand, I swished my tail, swimming powerfully toward the source of the scent buried deep below the earth. Again, I was overcome by the familiarity of the slightly sulfurous yet peaty smell.

The pool was deeper than I'd first imagined, taking me many leagues down as I continued to inhale and taste the waters on my gills and tongue. Again, just as before, the sulfides were naught but a trace element, so minor that they could only have been detected by a water elemental.

Then another odor caught my attention. Something sharp, and metallic. Not blood necessarily, but it could be.

It was dark as pitch down here and nearly impossible for me to see anything despite my ability to see in near dark. But that did not deter me. Most of the universes' waters were so black that we often swam blind.

Frowning, I pushed my muscles harder as I allowed my instinctive nature to guide me. The pool had no life in it, no plants or animals. It was as dead as the Sea of Balam in the eastern realms of Grimm. Completely lifeless. The natural essence of this water should have been pristine and unsoiled, but there was definitely a contamination about.

No longer within the range of sunlight, I was completely immersed in the deepest darkness of my world, relying more on my sharp awareness of water purity and disturbances than sight.

When I hit two-hundred meters deep, I knew I'd arrived.

I ran my fingers along the roughened mud walls of the pool and paused when my fingers tapped along a portion much rougher and less packed than the rest.

Using just a touch of my magick, I began sifting through the granules of mud, forming a hole deep enough for me to put my fist through, and then my forearm, and finally my entire arm's length, but still I found nothing when I wiggled my fingers.

There was definitely something there, though. I felt the rippling distur-
bance of a foreign body, but I could no more see it than the air I was forced
to breathe when upon dry land.

Glowering, I tried to work out just what I could do. If I excavated away
too much of the mud wall, I could cause the entire structure to weaken and
collapse down on itself, potentially fracturing whatever clue lay hidden inside.

But if I didn't dig deeper, all I'd have was my gut feeling that something
important rested behind this location, however many feet deep, with nothing
to show for my efforts.

Water bubbles burbled from my lips in exasperation as an insidious little
thought began to take root in my mind. Very few creatures in Grimm were capable of going to such lengths to hide their treasures within the waves. Sirens
could, of course. But sirens enjoyed looking at what they'd taken. It wasn't in
our nature to bury our possessions.

I had no choice. I had to risk it. Closing my eyes, I focused my mind solely
on the very delicate, very intricate task of pushing aside the mud while keeping the integrity of the walls intact.

It took several long, painstaking minutes of intense mental manipulation
before my fingers finally felt the press of something hard. With a cry of jubi-
lation, I swiped the object out, packing mud back into the hole just as quickly
as I could. The earth shuddered, but it did not fall.

Breathing a deep sigh of relief, I wilted against the wall, hugging the foreign object to my breast for half a second as I waited for my excited pulse to
return to normal. If that wall had collapsed, the item wouldn't have been the
only thing to have been buried.

Fingers shaking just a little, I brought the object up to my face. It was too
dark to see anything still, but I had other ways of figuring out just what in the
hells I'd put my life on the line for. Pressing down on it with my fingers, I discovered it was long, hard, and flat with roughened outer edges.

Bringing it up to my mouth, I delicately touched the tip of my tongue to
it.

Definitely metal.

What in the hells was this thing, and why had someone worked so hard
to hide it? I hoped with the last dregs of my soul that this might crack the
case wide open, but I doubted I'd be so lucky.

Just then, a piercing wail snatched me from my thoughts, causing me to wince and twitch. I looked up just in time to feel the water move with yet another sonic frequency wave across my flesh.

The sound came from above. Hatter was up there.

In a flash, I shoved at the water with my tail, speeding up from the deep, breaking through the surface less than three minutes later, to discover that the shrill, piercing wail had come from Hatter himself. He whistled again just as my head popped above the water.

Dropping the fingers from his mouth, he jerked his chin to indicate the space behind him. "We've company, Detective."

His words were rough and hurried. I fixed a stern frown on my face.

"So? This is your investigation and—"

"No longer," an uptight male voice snapped as I came forward, and my heart sank.

Even blind, I'd have known who it was. The bastard, the prick of a schoolyard bully, Special Agent Crowley, aka... Big Bad himself.

He wore his perpetual ensemble of black leather jacket, scuffed-up jeans, dark boots, and reflective sunglasses. With his head of dark, shaggy hair and week-old scruff along his jawline, he always looked a little wild, courtesy of his shifter heritage.

"What the hells are you doing at my crime scene?" I snarled, using a nifty parlor trick Ich had taught me years ago to hide my find in my curved palm. Then I slammed my hands down on the ground as I smoothly exited the water, transforming my tail into legs instantly. Water puddled around my feet. I made no effort to snatch up my clothing, but instead, scowled fiercely at him with my hands on my hips.

His gaze was insolent as it traveled the length of my body. Leaning against his chrome motorcycle, Crowley crossed his feet at the ankles and smirked. Behind him was a posse of black suits littering the crime scene like ants at a picnic. Whatever evidence there might have been was now surely gone. I pursed my lips in disapproval.

"You're no match for me, *little mermaid*. I'd eat you up."

I grinned, but it dripped with condescension. "Funny, because I don't think I was offering, dog."

Crowley might be a special agent, but he was a class-A pig who thought his looks and his badge were enough to get him by in life. He was known to use both to a punishing degree.

Hatter, about whom I'd almost completely forgotten in my seething hatred, came over to me with my clothing draped over his arm. Nodding my thanks, I snatched my shirt up and put it on first, able to breathe just a tad easier when its comforting presence pressed down on me.

"Shut this little shindig down, detectives," Crowley snapped, voice all business and with a hint of a growl to it.

"Says who?" I snapped right back, knowing damned well I wasn't going to like the answer.

"Says the Bureau of Special Investigations." He flashed an official looking document at me that no doubt stated we were now trespassing on the absolute directive of the Grimm upper echelon.

The Bureau of Special Investigations, or as we in the business liked to call it, the Bureau of Silence—BS for short—only dealt with cases that involved a person or persons of such a high level of notoriety that, at all costs, knowledge of it must be suppressed.

My nostrils flared. As much as I wanted to rail and scream at the injustice of having this scene yanked out from under our noses, at least I had something to show for our efforts. I curled my fingers tight around the piece of metal firmly tucked in my palm. Licking my front teeth, I snapped up my pants.

"Whatever you say, Crowley."

He snorted. "C'mon, fish. I figured you'd give me more fight than that. And I don't think I need to tell you that if you've found anything while trekking down there, it now belongs to the BSI."

I growled and took a step toward him with my hands balled tight by my sides, feeling the heavy presence of that metal. It was just the reminder I needed to keep me calm. No one knew about the metal shard but me. I grinned. "Thanks for the warning, Special Agent. Trust me, I know my job. If there was something down there, you'd have been the first to know."

He snorted and rolled his eyes. "I don't trust you as far as I can throw you, Elle. And I think we both know why."

My nostrils flared at the reminder of our one-time only and very unfortunate past. Balls. I'd been desperate, and he'd been there. Spreading my arms wide, I turned slowly for him, letting him inspect me from every angle. Once I was facing him again, I executed another smooth little parlor trick, tucking the metal between my fingers and hiding it in plain sight, showing him empty palms and praying to the goddess that none of his cronies happened to walk behind me.

"I'm pretty sure I'm not hiding anything."

From the corner of my eye, I caught Hatter tense. No doubt he'd caught the flash of silver. He moved just an inch closer to me.

Crowley's eyes were hot, hard, and full of lusty anger. "Get dressed and get the hells away from here, Elle. I won't be so nice again."

Glancing at Hatter, Crowley smirked. "We good, Constable? Or would you care to read the document yourself? It's sealed with the king's signet. I would think that should be good enough, no?"

Hatter's arm twitched, reminding me that he still held my pants. Without saying a word, I took them and began tugging them on, carefully slipping the metal sliver into my pocket.

"For now," Hatter said. "But mark my words, demon dog. You've not heard the end of this."

Crowley smirked, and I could practically read the seething hatred behind his sunglasses as he said, "You're nothing but a lowly constable. How's about you just stay in your lane there, arse for brains, while the big guns talk this one out."

"You've still got such a way with words, Crowley," I snapped, then marched off without looking back. I wasn't even wearing my boots, but I didn't care. Grabbing them off the ground, I hugged them to my chest and took several deep breaths to ease the tightness of fury in my stomach.

Seconds later, I heard Hatter's footfalls keeping pace with my own. The crime scene was now littered with MICE and yet more special agents. Whatever the two hells had happened here, it was now serious enough to involve them. I had a bad feeling about this.

A very bad feeling.

Taking the key card out of his inner pocket, Hatter swiped the air, and neither of us said a word until we were ensconced in the safety of the between.

He whirled on me just as I whirled on him.

"You found something," he said.

"I found something," I said at the same time.

His lips curved into a seductive grin of satisfaction that made my already-frazzled nerves feel tingly.

I reached into my pocket, withdrew the piece of metal, and handed it to him. I'd not been able to get a good look at it at the scene, but examining it, I saw there was something oddly familiar about its shape and size. The flat piece of metal looked like it might have been overlaid in gold at one point. There were filigree patterns etched in acid on each of the four corners and words at the center that had been scratched off as though by a metal file.

"What is this?" Hatter asked with a frown as he glanced at me.

"Maddox, give me the key card." I held my hand out to him impatiently.

He reached into his pocket and, without question, handed it back to me. I took it one with one hand, picked up the distressed metal with the other, and pressed them together. They were the exact same size, a perfect match.

I looked at him just as he looked at me.

"Is it a key?" he asked.

It was hard to tell. So much of what would prove definitively whether it was a key had been scrubbed off, but... "My gut says maybe."

He frowned. "Looks like it's been there for ages. This murder just recently took place."

I pointed to the roughened edges and the smoothed-down center of the metal. "Look here and here."

He did, peering closely, a frown tightly marring his brows. A second later, he stood and glanced at me. "I see what you're saying. It looks jagged in spots. Too rough."

"Exactly. Someone tried to make it appear water worn, but it was poorly executed. Over time, water will cut through even the most jagged of canyons, turning its pathways so smooth they're nearly silk. This isn't water-smoothed, though it was an attempt to make it look that way."

He nodded. "It's not weathered so much as distressed."

"Exactly."

His look was open and frank. "But how can you be sure it's tied to my case?"

I twisted my lips and handed him the metal. It was part of his investigation, after all. We were marking the evidence with our fingerprints, which was not smart, but the thing had been buried in tons of sediment and had likely been rubbed clean of all markings, anyhow. We were knee deep in it, now. We'd broken the very laws we'd sworn to uphold.

"I can't." I shrugged.

"By rights, we ought to hand this over to the Bureau," he said, before curling his fingers over the evidence, silently asking me my opinion on the matter.

I knew that, for all his eccentricities, behind that quirky façade was a brilliant mind. The constable knew as well as I that it stunk like ten-day-old fish entrails anytime the BS went meddling.

I bit my bottom lip, and his eyes tracked the movement.

"They don't even know it exists. And tell me, Maddox, why now? This scene is how many days old?"

"Not even twenty-four," he said, stroking his immaculately groomed goatee.

I pursed my lips and shook my head.

He grinned, putting the evidence in my palm and closing my hand over the metal. "Methinks something's afoot, dear Watson."

I snorted. "You're mad."

"That's what they say, Detective, but I say we're all just a little bit mad here. Perhaps we should go have a chat with Pillar and see what she has to say."

"Can we trust her?"

"I don't know." He took a step into me, invading my space with his heat and wicked, smirking lips. "I'd say we'd be fools to trust anyone right now."

I was working a separate case. This case and that one had nothing to do with each other. But the sudden appearance of Crowley made me think that was wrong. Maybe there was much more here than met the eye and maybe, just maybe I'd found myself smack dab in the center of a conspiracy with only a madman by my side.

"Can I trust you?" I asked him.

His fingers brushed petal-soft skin beneath my jaw, tipping my face up until our breaths mingled.

"I rather think the real question is can I trust you, Detective Elle? You show up, and suddenly, everything's flipped on its head. Why is that?"

Fire and heat laced his words, the obvious and the subtle wrapped up in one. My heart beat like a racing stallion in my chest. I grabbed his wrist.

"You play with fire, Maddox," I whispered.

His dual-colored eyes flared and his pupils widened, nearly obliterating the irises, as he growled low. "You think you have my number, Detective, yet I can assure you, you do not." Then he released me and stepped back as he casually dusted off the edges of his shirt.

I trembled from head to toe, staring at the tunnel of starlight ahead of me as I struggled to breathe. My claws were unsheathed, and my teeth ached, feeling sharp and pointed at their tips.

This had to stop.

This had to.

Tonight, I would go back to Alice's shoppe and feed my need. The siren in me was awakening, and if I didn't feed the beast soon, I would arouse a bottomless hunger that could only be assuaged by blood.

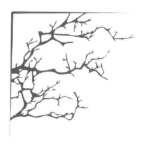

Chapter 8

Detective Elle

WE STOOD OUTSIDE OF a derelict-looking home that sat high on a hill, all by itself. It was a Victorian gingerbread, a dilapidated structure that had clearly seen better days. The wooden siding was mostly gray, with peeling bits of chipped paint. There were no glass windows, just holes where they should have been, and boards nailed over them to keep the unwanted pests out.

Rocks—more like massive boulders, really, smoothed down from years of hands brushing against them—lined the pathway and were painted with phosphorescent green runes that rolled with powerful waves of magick.

The house itself was divided up into three separate but joined sections that created a sort of trident shape. Ghostly, skeletal horses, their eyes blazing red, and their skeletal riders rode on swirling air currents. The night was full of spine-tingling sounds—the cackling of laughter, the hoot of owls, and the symphonic wail of the wind.

To say the place was haunted would be an understatement.

I glanced at Hatter, who looked unflappable as ever, and he at me, his face clearly saying he'd thought I'd lost my nerve.

I snorted. "You clearly have never visited my father. This place looks like fairy garden compared to that hells."

Then, shoving my hands into my pockets, I started down the pathway. But Hatter grabbed hold of my elbow and guided me down a hidden trail I'd not seen.

"Enter through the front door, and you'll become as one of them, your soul instantly sucked out of you, doomed to haunt this place forever."

"Cheery thought," I said back and smirked.

The trail he took us on was less dead-looking than the rest of the grounds, though it shimmered with a thick weaving of magick.

"How do you know of this pathway?"

He pointed to his eyes. "I can see magick in all forms."

I raised my brows. "You do know you'd make an excellent addition to the Grimm PD. I'm just saying. I think Bo would shart herself to get her hands on the likes of you. Not sure there are many of your kind in all the realms."

"What if I told you, Detective Elle, that I'm the only one?"

The way the moonlight framed the black velvet hat on his head and cast shadows onto the hollows of his throat and cheeks made him look more sinister and devilish to me than he ever had.

I wet my lips, and he snorted, as if the bastard knew exactly how much I liked it.

"Then I'd say I'm lucky indeed to have had you assigned to me. We work well together, Constable." I shrugged at his raised brows. I wasn't very good at mincing my words. I'd never been that kind of girl.

"A compliment from the siren? Maybe I am dead."

It was my turn to snort. "Keep teasing me, and I might just decide to shove my claws through your soft belly meat. I've not eaten in days, you know."

He went still, completely serious, and I instantly regretted my words. I knew my history and what everyone thought of me, mostly because the stories of my kind weren't exaggerated. We were man-eaters in the most literal sense. A muscle in my jaw twitched.

"I am—"

"You're not what they say, Elle. I know that well enough. Don't apologize. Don't ever apologize for being what you are."

I might have said more to him then, but he was slowing down, and when I glanced over, I saw why.

We'd walked a very long way around the house to the back where, at the heart of its structure, looked to be an opening the size of a man's body that led straight into the earth itself.

He gestured for me to follow, and without hesitation, he marched straight into the opening and was swallowed up by the unyielding shadows within.

More nervous now that I was alone, I knew I had no choice but to follow. Squeezing my eyes shut, I took the last step and was instantly sucked into a vacuum of complete and utter darkness. There were no noises. No smells. Not even a source of light to guide me by.

Pulse beating on the back of my tongue, I took a cautious step forward, and then another, and another still. With each step, I felt a lessening of that vacuum, a slow release of pressure against my form until, with one last step, I'd gone from complete black into a swirling miasma of radiant fog the colors of the rainbow.

The world smelled of flowers, a clashing mix of hundreds of thousands of flowers that offended my nostrils and made me cough into my fist.

Hatter was there a second later. "It does reek in here, but at least it doesn't smell like dog waste."

I chuckled, waving a hand underneath my nose as my eyes continued to leak water. "There is that, I suppose."

"Shallow breaths. You'll adjust soon," he said. "Follow me."

Not releasing my hand, he led us down a long narrow corridor that still swirled with colorful fog at our ankles.

"You can release me now. I'm pretty sure I can find my—"

He shook his head. "No. If we are separated in this place, we might never find our way back out again. What comes in together must remain together. It's the law in this twisted sepulcher the caterpillar calls home."

So why hadn't we walked in holding hands? I wasn't certain Constable Hatter was telling me the full truth, but then again, this place made my skin crawl, and I wasn't exactly keen on getting lost here either.

"Fine," I rolled my eyes and kept pace so that we walked side by side.

He glanced down at me. "You don't sound fine."

Thrusting out my chin mulishly, I whispered, "I don't much care for dark magick, if you must know."

Soon enough, the dark hallway, lit dimly by far-spaced candlelit wall sconces, began to fill with creeping, slithering, twisted, wrist-thick vines. Flowers of every variety bloomed from them, some snapping their sharp, nasty little fangs, others weeping their venomous toxins. I hissed as one in particular—a blood-red bloom that looked like a lipstick tube—reached for me, dripping a viscous, clear fluid.

I squeezed in closer to Hatter, pressing my side to his as much as possible.

"We're here on official Grimm business. The blossoms will not attack us, Elle. No cause for concern."

I clenched my jaw and nodded, steeling what vestiges of pride I still had left to me so that I wouldn't do something stupid, such as scream like a banshee and draw my pistol to shoot wildly at the flowers.

Scrubbing at my mouth with my free hand, I whispered, "Just walk faster, Constable, if you please."

Neither of us spoke again until we'd cleared the hall of horrors and found ourselves in a spiraling chamber of rocks that echoed hollowly with the steady dripping of cave water.

I frowned. "How the hells did we get so far below ground?"

"This is Wonderland," he said with a shrug.

I spotted a hunched figure sitting at the center of the stone chamber, looking as wizened as Thantor. Her ears were as long as his, her skin as wrinkled and liver spotted as well. She was writing on a rolled sheaf of parchment. The gentle scratches of her quill were oddly soothing.

Resting beside her was a vase full to overflowing with hundreds of sticks of incense, the cause of all the colorful smoke that'd guided us to her.

She wore a thick overcoat with odd striations that made her appear as though she were divided into three parts, much like a caterpillar. She had no hair on her bald head, but she did boast two impressive-looking black antennae that swiveled toward us.

"Thantor warned me ye two might come," she said in a voice as ancient sounding as dried parchment.

I winced, her voice grating sharply on my ears. Hatter was as calm as ever as he dipped his head. She glanced up, and I was shocked to see that her eyes were milky white. She was blind.

My heart sank. There was no way she'd be able to help us identify the key card, if that was indeed what it was.

But Hatter didn't seem to share my misgivings. Reaching into his pocket with his free hand, he pulled out the distressed bit of metal.

"What is that?" she asked as she gently set her quill down and held her hand out, palm up.

We walked forward. Hatter dropped the metal into her palm.

"It's why I've come. We believe it could be—"

"A key card. Yes, it is," she said as she traced her fingers over the roughened edges and frowned hard. "Useless now. Why have you brought me this?" She looked up, voice tight with impatience.

I licked my lips. So it had been a key card. We'd been right, then, and my gut was telling me we were right about the rest too.

Hatter looked at me, and I knew he wasn't sure how to proceed. I stepped in front of him.

"You're a mystic. Surely it isn't above your pay grade to tell us who this belonged to and why it was found where it was."

She snorted. "Mystic? Hardly. Ye ken that I only channel a little of me master's power. What ye ask for is more magick than I possess."

My shoulders slumped. We'd tried. But I shouldn't be working on Hatter's case, anyway. "Maybe we should just—"

Hatter jerked his head and growled. "Give us something, Pillar. Anything. I know you know more than you're letting on."

Her lips curved into a sickle-shaped smile that looked grotesque on her ancient features.

Confused as to why Hatter seemed to be taking this so personally, I stared at him. Sure, getting cut off at the knees by BS wasn't fun, but anyone with any time on the force had experienced it before. It sucked, but what was there other than to let go and move on?

"It'll cost ye, madness. Are ye sure ye wish to pay up? We both ken what the giving does to ye." She laughed, and the sound was cruel, edged with flinty darkness that made my skin crawl and my insides squirm.

I looked back at him, noting the hard tick in his cheek, the way his molars ground together, and the sheen of sweat that had suddenly covered his brows and upper lip. It seemed Pillar meant more than just what he'd given Cheshire. Whatever it was, Hatter didn't like it and didn't want any part of it.

"Excuse us, ancient. I just need to speak with my partner for a minute," I said smoothly, then jerked on Hatter's hand, dragging him behind me.

He looked shocked but came without complaint.

I walked until we were well outside the range of the gnome's super hearing and then hissed beneath my breath.

"What does that bat want? More sight?" I gestured to his eyes and noted his nostrils flaring. "Or... that?" I pointed to his arm, still not really sure how or what he'd done back at the bar with the cat.

He licked his front teeth, looking like he wouldn't tell me, and I cocked my head.

"We're partners in this, Constable. You're—"

Hatter glowered. "Partners," he scoffed, looking hard and angry. "Disabuse yourself of that notion right now, Detective. I'm but a lowly constable in this realm, as you continually like to remind me."

Shocked by the weight of his vehemence, I nearly dropped his hand, but he clung tight to my fingers, refusing to let me go.

"What the two hells is the matter with you? And you bloody well better tell me the truth. I understand the willingness to do whatever it takes to solve a case," I said. "Believe, me I get that. But this feels wrong, and I want to know what is really going on here. You're off this case, so why pay a price you don't want to? We tried, we failed. It's time to move on. Or is there something you haven't told me yet?"

With a growl, he dropped his head into his hands and took several deep breaths. I didn't know what had happened back there, but something had been stirred up in him. I wasn't exactly the nurturing type. It wasn't part of my chemical make-up. Sirens took; we didn't give. But he'd been good to me in this twisted place, and I felt compelled to help in whatever small way I could.

"Listen to me, Maddox," I said slowly, and I saw him shudder. Looking back on it, it was clear to me he'd never much cared for my calling him either Hatter or Constable. If he wanted me to call him Maddox, then so be it. "Are you listening?" I whispered.

He glanced at me, and his eyes were blazing, the blue one burning like flame. He was having a vision, and I couldn't remember if it was the past or the present that the blue eye could see. All I knew was that something wasn't right with him.

"For however long I'm here, we are partners. And you should know I have no partner at home. I don't much care to share the spotlight."

At that, he grinned. It was slight, barely more than a stretch of his lips, but it was something. "How very unsurprising of you, Detective."

I sniffed and grinned. "Well, be that as it may. You are my partner here. And having partners means that when one of us can't, the other must. I don't know the history between you and that antediluvian demoness back there, but I do know that I want to help. So let me help. Tell me what to do."

"She wants part of my soul, Detective. Gnomes aren't immortal like their masters, and Pillar is coming to the end of her string. She wants what we all do."

"More time," I guessed and then sighed. "How very unoriginal of her. Have you given her soul before?"

Immediately, his shoulders tensed up and his jaw clenched tight. His hand in mine squeezed so hard that it was almost painful. Though I desperately wanted to ask him what in the two hells had happened to him before, I knew I couldn't pry. It wasn't my place.

"I did," he bit out, "and in the end, it cost me everything."

The bitterness dripping off his tongue scorched my flesh and made me wince. His blue eye blazed, casting a brilliant glow on our surroundings as his gaze turned inward.

I had very little soul of my own left, not enough that I could give any away. But I wasn't without my own charms.

"Can I just ask you one thing?"

He looked at me and nodded, but his face was a rigid mask hiding so much pain that I felt it like a punch to my chest. And because I knew that kind of pain, because I had my own, I knew I couldn't let him do this.

"What?"

"BS stole your scene from you. Whatever was there is there no more, I can assure you. This key card is inadmissible as evidence."

His eyes closed because he already knew all that.

I pulled his hand to my chest and closed my other hand over it, squeezing hard. "Why does this one matter? We can walk away now, forget it, move on to solving my case or whatever else you have waiting for you. Whatever you tell me now, I'll believe you."

He opened his mouth, and I interjected one final thought.

"But don't lie to me, Maddox. What do you know that you're not telling me?"

A heavy breath trembled out of him, and his nostrils flared as he glanced to his left, staring at the wall sconces like a man possessed. His voice was flat when he said, "I... I *saw* something."

His eyes closed, and he started to tremble.

Worried, shockingly more for him than anything else, I stepped forward, forcing him to back up on his heels until he was pressed against the wall, staring down at me with miserable, haunted eyes.

"When? What?"

"Three days ago."

I cocked my head. That was before I'd gotten here. Suddenly feeling cold all over, I shook my head. "I don't understand. What did you see?"

He was gritting his teeth, and I knew whatever he'd seen, he didn't want to tell me. Suddenly, he reached up and snatched his hat from his head then leaned his head against the wall with a harsh thud and groaned. "You aren't what I expected, Detective. I thought I knew what it was I'd seen, but this makes no sense to me, and..."

"You're speaking nonsense, Maddox. Just spit it out," I said sharply.

His eyes were no longer blazing as he looked at me. "I knew you'd be coming before I even got the call. There is only one siren in the GPD. That was easy enough to decipher. But I saw a badge, Elle."

I narrowed my eyes. "So? And what? All law enforcement personnel have badges." I pulled his jacket back a bit to expose his own.

His hand clamped over mine, holding my hand to his chest. The beating of his heart was a steady drum against my palm.

"Aye. But not all badges bear the GPD stenciling, and more than that, I saw the proverbial smoking gun. I saw a figure in blue standing over three dead bodies—mine and yours."

I stepped back, my grip growing lax. But he clung to me tightly.

"What are you saying, exactly? We die?"

"No," he growled, "not our bodies, but those of our DOAs. I didn't know you then, Elle. I didn't know about your dead bodies, so why did I see them? Only once I was given your case file and I read through it did I realize our cases were connected. It's why I agreed to guide you, why I didn't just hand this off to Harry. I'm saying this smells. I'm saying there's a conspiracy. And I'm telling you the GPD is in it up to their eyeballs."

If he wasn't who he was, if I hadn't witnessed his power for myself, I'd have doubted him. I still doubted him, truth be told. It wasn't that law enforcement didn't come with its own dark stain and history, because it did. But I knew everyone in GPD, from the lowliest filing clerk all the way up to the chief, and there wasn't a doubt in my mind that they were all clean, all good guys just fighting like the two hells to get by.

"You're wrong. And if you're saying that it's me, then you can just disabuse yourself of that no—"

"No." He lowered his head, shoving his face toward mine. "No, it's not you. I know that now."

I started to think about the things he'd done since I'd arrived, how he would look at me, stare at me. I'd thought it was curiosity or even attraction, but what if I'd been wrong? What if it wasn't lust that made him study me, but rather distrust?

"Why are you telling me this? How can you trust me? You say one of my own is corrupt, but yet you tell me everything?" I didn't try to mask my sarcasm. "What is this? Some sick joke?" I tried to snatch my hand away, but he wouldn't let me, growling beneath his breath as he held on like a clamp.

He scrubbed a hand down his face. "This is not a joke. I'm only telling you this because if you hadn't brought that key up from the pool, we wouldn't be here now. I trust you, Elle. And I'm worried that we've got a noose around our necks and you don't even feel it yet."

I reached for my neck, rubbing at its hollow. "What are you saying exactly?"

"I'm saying the timing of all of this is suspect."

I'd thought the exact same thing, about how my murders and his had seemed so similar on the surface. The sudden appearance of BS only further strengthened Maddox's case. But I wasn't ready to believe in a conspiracy, either. I just wasn't ready.

"I know those guys," I hissed, leaning up on tiptoe. "I know them all. We're the good guys."

He frowned and glanced over my shoulder.

But it was his lack of words and the fact that he refused to fight with me that filled my body with cold dread. Was I wrong?

Why had my case not been solved ages ago? It was a stain on the royal family to have an unsolved murder on their grounds. Sure, they'd been helpful, to a point. But Crowley showing up and locking down Hatter's scene wasn't a coincidence. It never was where BS was concerned.

I squeezed my eyes shut. "Say I believe you."

"I'm not lying."

I glared at him. "Say I believe you; then you have to trust me. With everything."

He was silent, staring at my mouth, nostrils flared, reminding me of a predatory wolf, not sure whether to leave be or take the kill.

Finally, he looked into my eyes. "Fine."

I nodded. "Good enough for me. C'mon."

I turned, yanking him back with me toward Pillar's chamber.

"What are you doing?" he hissed. "It's my soul she wants."

Back in her chambers, Pillar's antennae were turned toward us. She was listening.

I leaned in to whisper heatedly in his ear. "I'll be damned if she steals more from you. Just take my lead."

His fingers clenched mine tight, but it felt more like solidarity than simply needing to stay connected, like he was taking strength from me just as surely as I was taking mine from him.

My stomach fluttered at the thought, and I glowered, marching back up to Pillar with hurried steps.

I wanted so badly to threaten and act like a raging, tempestuous elemental. But I'd already screwed up once, and I couldn't afford to lose my composure again. If it was true what he'd told me, then I had to tread carefully.

I forced a smile. "I will pay your fee, gnome, so long as your information is good."

Hatter jerked, and I elbowed him, telling him silently to shut up and do nothing. I felt him seething behind me, but he remained blessedly still after that.

She snickered but didn't stop her scratching on the parchment. "Oh, my information is always good. But it seems we have a problem, princess."

My shoulders stiffened, and I clamped down on my tongue. It wasn't that I thought Maddox didn't already know who I was—it wasn't much of a secret anymore—but I hated that title with the strength of ten thousand suns.

Finally, the she-devil set down her quill and stared at me with her milky white eyes. Her smile was pure venom.

"You have no soul left."

I jerked. That wasn't true. I had some. I had enough.

Maddox stiffened, and I was forced to dig my fingers into the top of his hand. There was little in all the realms more dangerous than a siren, except for a siren without a soul.

I grinned, never letting on how much I was hurt by the emotional wall he'd just demonstrably put up. No one knew the truth. The only one who had known died that night. I was only a tenth of the person I'd once been. But bloody hells, I would cling to that last shred of humanity if it was the last thing I did. It was what he would have wanted from me because he'd been the only thing in all the worlds that could ever love a monster like me. He'd shown me another way, and I would honor his memory in the only way I knew how.

"I may not have a soul, Pillar, but I have other things, as you well know. Things a gnome like you would kill to get her claws on. Am I wrong?"

She said nothing, only sat upon her little stool trembling like a sapling in the breeze, as her tiny, liver-spotted hand furled and unfurled.

"On my oath as Princess of the Deep, I will give what you desire, but first, show me your hand. If the information is of worth, you will get what you wish."

She hissed, exposing long, pointed silver fangs. Ancient or no, Pillar was still a worthy foe.

"And how can I trust ye? A filthy siren? Nasty liars, ye all are."

I laughed, and the sound was chilling, echoing around the chambers like the haunted cries of the damned.

"Because I've given my oath. If it's worth it, I will give you what you want."

Pillar wet her desiccated lips as avarice filled her gaze, and I knew the temptation was far too great for her. Sirens were killers, but there was more to us than that. It was what made us so alluring and why so many treasure hunters had betrayed, lied, stolen, and killed to get their hands on us, tempting fate over and over again in the hopes that we just might show them mercy.

She inhaled deeply and then said, "The Goose. Speak to the Goose. Now, give it."

Reaching forward, she fisted my shirt in her hand and, using far more strength than I thought possible, yanked me to her, slamming her shriveled lips over mine.

My powers flowed like living waters through me and into her, ramming down her throat, making her squirm and cry out, making me sing and filling the chamber with the tenor of the most mystic of songs.

Powerful hands pulled me back, and I gasped, heaving for breath as my powers swelled like a surge inside me. Tears rolled down my cheeks, and Pillar sat in a trance, laughing maniacally as her features transformed, twisting her ancient, withered frame—even if only temporarily—into something more beautiful than it had ever been before.

Massive wings an electric shade of neon-blue burst from what I'd thought had been a coat and now realized had actually been her flesh. Her limbs grew long, strong, and sure. Hair the shade of deepest chestnut sprouted from her head, and her cheeks pinked with verve.

Fire raged through my bones and my body. The siren had come alive, and now she needed to feed.

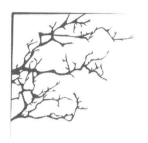

Chapter 9

Constable Maddox

TAKING OUT THE KEY card, Maddox swiped at the air, desperate to get Elle out of there. Instinctively, he knew where to take her.

She was a siren.

She'd unleashed the full strength of her charms upon that wee demon, and now she needed to be fed. The lights of the between rolled by so fast that they made him dizzy, but he held her writhing body tight to him as her back arched and snapped, the bones shifting furiously beneath his hands. Her skin was on fire, and she was screaming. She was too wild, too full of the dark power for any but one to handle her safely.

Squeezing his eyes shut, he whispered to her, though he knew she could not hear him over her screaming. "I've got you, siren. I've got you."

He was clawed for his efforts, but he never loosened his grip on her. By the time they arrived at the Crypt, Elle had nearly gone through her entire metamorphosis. She had long curved black claws, sharp fangs, and lavender glowing eyes. Even so, he found her to be the most alluring creature he'd ever seen in his life.

He raced from the tunnel toward Alice's shoppe, banging wildly on her door with his foot. She yanked it open just a moment later.

Alice stood in shock, staring down at the screaming banshee in his arms, then up at him. A second was all she needed before instinct kicked in.

All around, the sounds of lustful moans had ceased as dozens of eyes turned on them.

"Help her," he pleaded, and she nodded.

"Bring her to the back. Celestria is on call tonight."

He marched behind her, all the while fighting to keep Elle from shoving frenzied claws into the soft meat of his face and belly.

Her cries weren't human any longer. They echoed with the haunting tonal quality of a siren's desperate need. Her skin rippled, glowing with streaks of jagged blue beneath her flesh. Whatever Pillar had taken from her had left Elle in a desperate state.

"Hurry, Alice, dammit!" he snapped when she turned down yet another hall.

Her tall heels clicked on the polished white tile, and her sheer nude gown twinkled as the light reflected off the inset gems.

Finally, Alice reached the very back of all the rooms, the ones reserved for the darkest, most desperate of cases. The ones reserved for Celestria alone.

She opened the door and stepped aside. The room was dark, save for a pool of reflective navy-blue water at its center. Inside of that was a monster, a beast, a thing of nightmares and unimaginable beauty.

As if on cue, Celestria's head cut through the water. Her lips were coral, her eyes black as sin. Her skin looked as though it was formed of pearls, and her hair gleamed like molten gold inside a heated crucible. She licked her lips and reached out, not with hands, but with eight long tentacles.

Elle screamed louder, higher, clawing at her own face as she bloodied herself, jerking with spasms that ripped his soul in two. What had she done? Why had she done it? What the hells had she been thinking?

But he didn't stop to ask her any of those things. Instead, he shifted her heavy weight into Celestria's waiting reach and shuddered when the tentacles grabbed her tight.

"Elle," he croaked, just as the monster snatched her away and took her into the abyss beyond, out of sight.

The sudden silence was unnerving.

He looked at Alice, feeling her weighted look on him.

Her silvery white brows had risen high, a question for which he had no answer.

"Follow me," she said with a crook of her finger. With one last hungry look at the pool, he turned and followed her out the door.

Alice took him to her office, what had once been their office, ages ago.

"Sit." She pointed to a tufted leather chair.

He dropped his weary carcass into it, dropping his elbows to his knees and his head into his hands as he let out an exhausted groan.

Behind him, he heard Alice pouring drinks into crystal. A second later, a tumbler was thrust at him.

"Take it. Drink it slowly."

Taking the drink, he nodded his appreciation. His head throbbed like the devil, and he knew that she wanted answers. Not about the case. Alice didn't give two hells about that. She never had.

After sniffing the rich sweetness of the brandy, he took a long, satisfying pull from it. The liquor began to work its magick in seconds, easing his rattled nerves. He scrubbed at his bruised cheeks, pulling his hand away to note the dark stain of blood on his wrist. It was a miracle she'd not hurt him worse. In her delirious state, she should have shredded his flesh to bloody ribbons. That she hadn't showed him she'd held herself back. She'd had just enough mental awareness to keep her powers in check.

He blinked, awed by the knowledge that, even in her pain, she'd not fully given in to the monster's need.

Why the hells had she done that? What was she going through right now? He squeezed his eyes shut.

"She's got you all twisted up, hasn't she?" Alice's words were low, innocent even, but he wasn't fooled.

"Alice," he snapped. "If you're going to start this now—"

"What?" she retorted. "You'll what? Leave?" She laughed, and the sound was grating to his ears. "I hardly think so. Not with your new toy here. Does she know, Maddox, huh? Does she know the bastard you really are? Business and pleasure don't mix. Or have you forgotten that so soon?"

He pounded a fist on her desk, rattling the heavy metal paperweight in the shape of a key on her desk.

"Enough! She's an officer of the law, nothing more."

She rolled her eyes, taking a small sip from her tumbler. "Did I ever strike you as a fool?"

He clamped his jaw shut, remembering that once, there'd been better days between them. But those days were gone, and all that was left was the ghost of things that had once been.

Setting down her half-finished glass, she shook her head. But her eyes said what her lips did not—she hated him then, and she hated him still. Forgiveness wasn't in Alice's nature. It never had been.

"I hope she breaks you. Just like you broke me. The second Celestria is done with her, you take your bitch and leave." Then she scooted her chair back and left.

Anger, fury, but also a deep-seated self-hatred filled his bones. He stayed in his seat, slamming back the drink she'd given him along with the rest of hers. Then he reached behind him, took the bottle she'd left, and finished that off too. By the time he was done, he was numb.

The pain didn't hurt so much anymore. The memories weren't like knives, but more like a jagged piece of flinty rock trying to pierce his emotional wall, but it only hurt a little.

And he was able to forget about her again. About his little butterfly, the only thing he'd ever loved in all the world. Full of innocence and purity, she was the ghost that would forever haunt him and never leave him, and the truth was that he never wanted her to.

He wanted to remember. He wanted the pain because if it still hurt, than she still lived.

Detective Elle

I WOKE UP LYING IN cool water, but not my own. I had been floating in a world of nothingness, feeling as though I'd lost my way, but suddenly, I was back.

Back to being me again.

I frowned, not sure what had happened or why. But I felt good in a way I'd not felt in a long, long time.

I sat up, flipping my tail, and noted what had to be thousands of tiny bruises all over me. Holding out my arms, I saw suction marks there, too, and stared into the abyss, sensing a darkness lingering down, down, down.

I shivered. What the two hells had been done to me, I'd probably never know, but I knew it was time to get out of there.

Swimming to the edge of the pool, I gracefully pulled myself out.

My clothes had been neatly folded, and I frowned, reaching for them. But when I pulled on my shirt, I did not feel the magick of my waters encase me.

Grimacing, I rubbed at my chest, feeling the slight burn of water still left in my shell. The sprite's magick had run out for me. I had to make it back to my waters soon.

Feeling jittery and dizzy, I dressed as quickly as I could. But even so, when I walked out of the room, I had to cling to the wall for support.

A second later, I felt hands on me and knew without looking up that they belonged to him.

"I thought I'd lost you for a second there, Detective."

I glanced up at his handsome profile. He was covered in faint, fresh scratches, and for the first time, I didn't feel the sizzle and burn of the siren magick like I had before. Even so, I was very aware of the power of his body—the graceful predatory sloping walk of his, the way he moved, how he breathed, even how he swallowed.

I liked his looks. I liked them a lot.

I rubbed at my forehead. "Do I even want to know what happened to me down there?"

"I expect not, Detective."

I frowned. "Well, if you're going to force me to call you Maddox, then surely you can call me Elle."

His lips twitched. "As you wish."

I cleared my throat.

"Elle," he finished, and I grinned back.

"Yeah, whatever. Look, I feel as weak as a newborn colt. I need my waters."

He frowned, staring down at me even as he pushed open the exit door. I didn't have to ask where he'd taken me. Judging by the continued stream of lusty moans and groans, I knew we were at the Crypt. I really, really wanted to know what in the two hells had pulled me back from the siren's need, but I was also just as sure that sometimes, ignorance really was bliss.

"But you've been swimming for the past two hours. Surely, that helped."

I nodded, gasping a little as I took my first drag of smog-filled Wonderlandian air. Clutching at my shell, I squeezed it tight. Its tiny bit of warmth helped, but not by much.

"I'm... I'm not like other sirens. There are things about me that—"

He turned me toward him and put a finger over my mouth, and for just a second, I tasted the salt of his skin on my tongue. He shivered as he pulled away.

"Then we go."

"We?" I raised a brow. "I don't take just anyone to my waters. In fact, I don't take anyone at all."

He raised a brow right back. "I can't go back to my office. I can't deal with Harry right now. Or anyone, for that matter. And our investigation is at a standstill until sunup. You asked me not to leave you alone earlier. I'm asking you now to return the favor."

I almost smiled until I realized just how serious he was. His eyes looked haunted, and there were dark circles beneath them, as though he didn't often sleep. So I took his callused hand in mine and squeezed gently.

"Then give me the key."

He handed it over without question, and I felt a moment's awkward pride that his eyes no longer looked quite so grave.

Swiping the card through the air, I thought of home and heaved a world-weary sigh when we were once again caught up in the between.

His arms circled me, and though I knew none of this was professional, I felt weak, and I rather suspected he did too.

Whatever had happened to me must have been brutal. I'd noted no less than three deep slash marks on his cheeks and neck. I recognized a siren's furious markings.

Wrapping my arms around him, we held each other as we sailed far to another realm.

Long before I was ready for it, the pathway disappeared, and we stood not upon stars, but sand.

My sand.

A sound full of desperate yearning and longing spilled off my tongue as I shuddered. The rolling waves of home called to me like a lover's lament.

There was nothing in this place. No grass, trees, birds, game, or any other life. The waters were empty of all of it, but there was still no other place in all the realms I'd rather be. There was peace in this nothingness. It was a place of perpetual night, with silvery clouds and a fat, buttery moon resting high above me.

The breeze smelled of salt.

Maddox smiled. "It's pretty here. Quiet." He looked at me.

I shrugged. "Suits me."

"The cities must be madness for you," he said, finally pulling back from me.

I frowned, loathe to admit that I actually missed his touch and feeling a prickling of guilt that I should. But I'd not been touched like that in so long. So damn bloody long.

I shrugged. "It is what it is. My penance, or so he says." I wrinkled my nose when I heard the note of bitterness and turned on my heels.

With angry, jerky movements I stripped, tossing the shirt over my head. Within hours, it would shift back into the water it'd been fashioned from.

Kicking the pants off, I didn't look back as I turned and walked to my waters. The moment the water touched me, I sang. The song was a loud, wailing lament full of sorrow, desperate fear, and longing. I could no more hold back my song than I could stop coming to these damned waters.

I felt Maddox's eyes bore into me, but I couldn't look back at him. With a powerful kick of my tail, I sank into the dark waters, and only then did I unleash it all.

The pain. The fury. The injustice of what had been done to me. To us.

The feelings churning up in me could not be allowed. I'd sworn I would never feel them again. I'd never want them again.

But I'd been lonelier than even I'd known, and I was forgetting, losing myself, seeing things that couldn't possibly be.

Like maybe Maddox was a man who also knew the depths of true, soul-stripping pain.

And so I screamed, even as my waters healed me, as they reshaped and formed me into a powerful being that could easily lure a ship and all its booty to the depths of Davy Jones's locker.

And for just a second, as my tears mingled with the waves, I felt the old hunger and wished I could give in just once more. Just this once. Just so that I could stop the hurting. Stop the feeling. And stop the damned bloody memories that would haunt me until the day I died and returned back to the waters I called home.

But as I drifted alone in that darkness, I knew I never could.

I *never* could.

And so, with a cold fury sunk deep into my bones, I snatched another golden pearl from the sandy bottom and raced for the above, screaming out to the sprite the moment my head cut water.

"Caytla, come, you damn bloody wench!"

And come she did to watch me sell the last dregs of my soul to her over and over again.

Chapter 10

Constable Maddox

He sensed the difference in her immediately. Gone was the weakness. Her steps were sure and confident, just as they'd been the first night she'd come to him.

Her shift from siren to human was seamless, and he feasted upon her luscious curves as she dressed. It'd been ages since he'd lain with another, not for many months. But not since he and Alice had he actually felt anything other than carnal lust.

Her shirt was a deep, shimmering coral this time, and it contrasted prettily with her unusually electric-blue hair. Her eyes gleamed, and her skin sparkled with a pearlescent sheen.

She wasn't just beautiful. She was breathtaking.

She wore no boots or pants, only the shirt. Her long legs were naked and on full display. Sirens weren't a modest bunch, but then, their sole reason for being was to lure in the unsuspecting.

And yet he didn't fear her. Not that she wasn't terrifying. He'd seen her at her lowest and in her most terrifying form. But even then, he'd sensed a great effort from her not to give in completely. If she'd wanted, she could have eviscerated him on the spot.

The wind brushed through the long strands of her hair, but she stared out at her waters with her long legs crossed at the ankles and her chin resting on her knees.

She looked lost. Alone.

He blinked. "I'm a father," he said, not sure why he'd admitted that to her. He never talked of his past, and especially not of his butterfly. But Alice had poked at the memories, dredging them up from the dark pit, and now the ghosts were haunting him.

He felt her look at him, soft and nonjudgmental. He turned to her. She swallowed and reached up with a hand that had, just hours earlier, sliced deep grooves into his flesh. This time, she brushed her knuckles down his jaw tenderly. He trembled and squeezed his eyes shut.

"I thought that maybe you were," she whispered.

He looked at her, really looked at her, seeing beyond the obvious beauty of her exotic but deadly appeal to the complicated woman beneath. To the only one of her kind who wore a badge. To a woman who had so completely altered her life that it was nearly unrecognizable from what it had once been.

He'd heard the rumors of the mad siren. Everyone had. The mystery of her banishment, and how she'd wound up in Grimm PD, intrigued him. But more than all that, he felt almost like she wasn't just his responsibility while she handled her investigation through Wonderland, but like she was more. Like she'd always been more. He just hadn't known it then, or maybe he had.

For so long, he'd dreamt of these waters exactly—barren, stripped of life, but even so, teeming with it. He'd always known, deep down in the very secret part of him, that those waters would one day be his too. He hadn't known the waters would come with Elle. No one in the lands knew where the mad princess had been banished to. But here she was, and suddenly, he felt like he could breathe again.

For so long, he'd been dead inside, but he felt the life flowing through his veins again, coming to desperate, raging awareness. And that thought scared the ever-loving hells out of him.

But he wouldn't tell her any of that. It was his secret alone, and would always remain so.

"How could you know I had a child?" he asked, voice thick with so many unnamed emotions.

She dropped her hand, and he scowled at the sand by his feet while drawing lines and circles in the sand.

"Because of your reaction with Pillar. And what you told me about how you'd shared your soul, but it hadn't helped. Only the loss of something truly cherished could have imprinted such a terrible mark on one's soul. I could kill that gnome."

A ghost of a grin feathered over his lips at her impassioned words.

"What's your child's name?" she asked softly, but still, he heard her words like a cannon, even over the roar of the waves crashing upon shore.

His soul felt as though it had shattered in his chest. "Her... her name was Mariposa. She was two."

He swallowed, trying not to let the memories draw too close. Trying not to remember too clearly her snow-white hair, so much like her mother's, and the dual-colored eyes, just like his own.

"Was?" she whispered, and he should have known she'd latch on to the truth quicker than most. "I'm sorry."

Tears swam in his eyes, and he swiped at them with his wrist as he thought about that terrible night, the night that had changed the trajectory of his and Alice's life forever.

He shook his head, clamping down on his tongue. Talking about her had been a mistake. He stared at the waves in silence, feeling raw and exposed, wishing like the two hells he'd not started this conversation.

After a long minute of heavy silence, she sighed. "I killed my lover. At least, that's what they say."

The words sounded strained, like she hadn't wanted to say them, and he looked at her, noting the slide of tears down her cheeks. She was completely still and white as a sheet. Sadness blanketed her small frame.

He wasn't sure when he'd moved, but suddenly, they were pressed close to one another, not an inch of space between them.

He reached for her hand. Her fingers were cold, but she didn't let him go. Instead, she clung tightly to him, even as she continued to stare out at the expansive, dark waves of the eternal pools.

"Did you?" he asked softly, grateful to her for changing the subject, but equally worried about her because he knew it wasn't an easy topic.

She shivered violently, her teeth clacking so hard that he worried she might bite her tongue.

Her gaze cut to his, hypnotic blue eyes swirling with endless depths of desperate pain—pain he, too, experienced. "What does it matter? Perception is reality, no?"

He shrugged. "It's what they say, but I've always thought *they* were a pack of arrogant pricks that could go hang."

Through her tears, she laughed. The sound was soft, ethereal, and real. In that moment, he didn't stop to think about right or wrong, or even care. He placed his finger beneath her chin and tipped her head upward. She gasped but didn't look away as he leaned down and kissed her.

The touch of her on him lit a fire in his blood, made his body both languid and heavy, desperate for more. But it wasn't lust that drove him. It was the knowledge that, in her, he'd found someone who understood intimately the demons he lived with day in and day out.

When he pulled back, they were both panting and clutching at each other with desperate hands. Her hands were on his cheeks, and his were on her wrists, as though holding her to him, afraid to let her go, afraid that if she left him, he'd crack again, and all the demons would come flooding back out.

"You asked me earlier about Alice," he said softly, regretting the necessity of revealing such a personal part of his past.

She shook her head. "You don't have to. I don't need to know."

He frowned, not wanting to share, but also kind of wanting to, too. "The case," he tried again, words slow and reluctant.

Her brilliant eyes searched his face, studying, imprinting, memorizing him. He held still beneath her look. Elle wasn't a seer, not like him. She couldn't see who he'd been, the terrible thing he'd done. But when she looked at him like that, probing, searching, he thought that maybe she saw a lot more than she let on to the rest of the world. It was what made her such a damned bloody good detective.

Her small nostrils flared. "Your life. Your business. Don't tell me anything because I don't want to write that report. There are certain pains, Constable, that are our own and belong to no one else."

Closing his eyes, he hung his chin to his chest and took three deep breaths before trusting himself to speak again. She had to know at least some part of the truth, and she was protecting him from that truth now. His throat felt tight and hot when he cleared the gravel from it.

"We should go back now," he said, the words so low he hoped she might not hear, wishing in some small part of his mind that they could just stay here forever, locked away on this isolated, lonely island together and never again have to face the pain of a world gone mad.

She nodded. "Yes, Maddox, we should."

He heard the tightness of her words and understood what she was really saying. They couldn't be together. Not now. Not ever. They'd flirted earlier, but it had been easy then. They'd not shared anything of true worth between them. But now, they understood there were dark, terrible moments in their pasts and things had to remain professional.

He dropped her hands, standing and dusting himself off. She was right, of course. On the day he'd seen his beloved butterfly crumpled in a heap on the floor, he'd decided that never again would he allow himself to love anything else.

There would be work, and only work, to keep him company.

He didn't love Elle, but he sensed that she was a woman who could break down all the defenses he'd taken years to build, and that made her more dangerous than just about anything else in all the realms.

"You're right, Detective. We definitely should." His words were cold, but courteous.

For just a moment, he saw her eyes fill with something that looked suspiciously like regret. But then she was smirking, and her mask was on just as surely as his was.

Reaching for her pants, she yanked them on. "Tell me, did Pillar give me anything good?"

He nodded, keeping his eyes on the waters and not on her body. "Yes. She said we should speak to the Goose."

"And who the hells is that?"

"Mother Goose."

"Oh goddess. The woman with all the brats?"

He chuckled. "Aye. But first, the bandercoot. Are you ready?"

"Yes. As I'll ever be."

Detective Elle

I FELT LIGHTER, FREER. I didn't know whether it was the talk I'd had with Maddox or that kiss. But the bottomless pit of self-loathing and pain didn't feel quite so bottomless tonight.

I stopped myself, thinking that maybe I should revert to calling him Constable, or even Hatter again—anything to create some distance and remind myself that, at the end of the day, we were colleagues and nothing more.

We were travelling the between again, moving back from my realm to his. But in the back of my mind, I knew time wasn't on our side. I had less than a day's charge on the key card and a boss to whom I needed to report, who I wasn't sure I could trust anymore.

I glanced at Hatter from the corner of my eye. His face was a stony mask. His full lips were set into a thin line, and for a second, I suffered a moment of dizzying regret at what might have been.

Why had we shared so much? Why couldn't we just have kept things between us superficial? I'd not even thanked him for saving me after Pillar's, and I didn't know whether I even should. He didn't exactly seem like he wanted to talk.

And why should I care anyway? It wasn't like I'd see him after I was done here. I had one more day. Who the hells cared about any of this?

"Balls," I muttered.

"Pardon?" he asked in his urbane Wonderlandian accent.

I grimaced. "Nothing. Just... you know, thank you for taking me to Alice's. I'm not sure what you did to me there, but it could have been worse."

His lips twitched.

And mine did too. My stomach fluttered remembering the press of his cherry-wine-tinted lips on mine. I flattened my hand to my stomach and pressed.

"I know. I'm goddess awful at thank-yous. Least that's what Ich always tells me."

He glanced over at me. "Ich?"

I rolled my wrist. "Ichabod Crane, my sometimes partner."

If I'd hoped to see even a hint of jealousy in his eyes, I was quickly relieved of the notion. His face was an implacable and unreadable mask.

I squeezed my fingers. The case. The case, and then I'd go home.

Locking the strange thoughts and feelings in a box that I would never again open, I shoved it down deep and took one last breath. The kiss had happened, truths had been shared, and it was over.

It had to be. I wasn't the type that could afford to get my feelings entangled. Seemed like anytime I did, things never ended well for my lovers. There was always a price to be paid when a siren thought she could have her own happily ever after.

Squaring my shoulders, I nodded, silently communicating my resolve. He dipped his chin, letting me know he understood and agreed as well. Nothing but the case. That was all that mattered.

By the time we cleared the pathway, my head was back in the game. We stepped out into a chaotic, busy city square, this one less filth-ridden than central Wonderland, but still with the fast, dizzying pace of city dwellers.

The buildings towered high into the heavens, twisting and turning into fantastical and strange designs. They appeared held together not by bricks and mortar or even thatch, but by fat, thick vines full of wicked thorns that actually seemed to inhale and exhale at measured intervals. I grimaced. I really hated vines.

Hatter began a brisk march down the cobbled street, turning toward our left and heading deep into the city center.

A vendor selling oysters on the half shell was hawking his wares with that fast-paced patois all vendors seemed to share. "Oysters, get yer oysters, 'ere," he said in a high-pitched squeak.

My stomach chose that moment to growl. Loudly. I frowned, realizing I'd not eaten much in days. That wasn't uncommon for me when I was on a case.

Without missing a beat, Hatter turned toward the vendor and held up two hands. In seconds, the vendor, with a gray Fu Manchu mustache and thick, walrus-like chin rolls, was shoveling fat oysters on the half shell into a broadleaf sack. I reached into my pocket to pay, but Hatter was quicker. He handed me the sack.

"You didn't have to pay for my lunch," I said as I turned to follow him down a smoothly paved sidewalk.

"It's customary to say thank you in times like these, Detective," he said smoothly, with that hint of mocking laughter he always seemed to have.

I rolled my eyes and snatched the sack out of his hands, far too hungry for niceties or false modesty. I was starving. Reaching into the sack, I scooped out a handful of oysters and tossed them into my mouth, shells and all.

I felt his stare on me, and when I turned, it was to note a hint of revulsion in it. I grinned. "What? Good for calcium."

"If you say so, Detective."

Snorting but not bothering with words because these were the sweetest, most succulent oysters I'd tasted in quite some time, I demolished them in seconds flat. Hatter had barely gone through half his sack, when he shoved his bag into my chest.

"Here. I'm done anyway."

I tipped my head in a nod and, in another few minutes, had his sack cleaned out too. Stomach pleasantly bulging, I burped once—a sign of a good meal where I came from—and grinned.

"That did it."

"Goddess, you've the manners of a feral dog," he said, lips curled, but eyes glittering with humor.

Shrugging a shoulder, I wadded up the empty sacks and tossed them into a trash receptacle made of twisted vines and thorns.

"Yes, well, if you'd fed me better..."

"Ha. Ha. I laugh." He snorted, and I grinned back. The constable was fun to tease.

I rolled my wrist. "Sirens burn an ungodly amount of calories in or out of water. It's part of our chemical make-up. And unfortunately, when I'm on a case, I tend to forget that I should eat at least a thousand calories every four hours or so."

His peaked brows rose high, as if surprised. "I did not know that."

Again, I shrugged. "Think about it, Constable. Have you ever seen a siren with an abundance of curves?"

Scrubbing at his jaw, he murmured, "Come to think of it, I've not."

I was curious about just how many sirens he'd come across in his life, but decided against asking since that seemed slightly more personal than not.

"My point, exactly."

Suddenly, Hatter grabbed at my sleeve, tugging on it. I looked up and saw that, instead of continuing down the street, he was now walking toward a massive black wrought-iron trellis covered in—who would have guessed it?—breathing vines and thorns. A sign on the trellis, which was actually more of an arched entryway, read The Looking Glass.

Above us, the sky reverberated with the bass rumble of thunder. Forks of jagged lightning cut through the darkening canopy above us. The storm had come on quick. I frowned, smelling the water that saturated the air. There was going to be the mother of all storms in just a few seconds.

"Hatter, rain and I do not mix." I hugged my arms to my chest.

"C'mon, siren. Let us get you to dry land."

As we stepped under the archway, the vines grew and grew, twining and twisting as they often did, to create a waterproof screen above us. The second we had a mostly solid covering, the sky opened up, and it sounded like a geyser of water had just ripped open the heavens, spilling like a silver blade into what now looked like deep night.

Pedestrians were running, seeking shelter wherever they could find it, and the Looking Glass, which had been all but empty just seconds ago, was now jam-packed with bodies waiting out the storm.

But Hatter wasn't waiting around with them. He was still tugging on my shirt, winding a slithering path through the crush of Wonderlandians as we made our way deep into the heart of the place.

We continued to walk down a long, dimly-lit pathway until I felt the cool wash of cavernous air pressing against me. When we stepped off the pathway and into the darkness of a room, our heels clacked jarringly in the absolute stillness. Not even the sound of the tsunami-like rain reached us back here. It was dark and blessedly quiet.

"Take my hand, Detective," he said, and I did without question.

Instantly, I was more at ease when I felt the rough smoothness of his palm press against mine. Just after our hands joined, though, I felt the ground beneath our feet give, and I cried out in surprise.

"It's fine, just the automated pathway that guides us through the zoo."

"This is a zoo?" I asked, frowning at the absolute pitch black of the place. Only the coolness of the air gave me any kind of sensory information about direction.

"Of a sort."

"I don't like it. I don't enjoy being without my senses. What the hells kind of zoo is this, anyway?"

His chuckle was deep and throaty, alleviating my restless anxiety as I moved just a little bit closer to him, needing the tactile sensation of touch so as to not completely lose my nerve. I lived in the deep, and I was used to darkness, but there was always something around—lights, colors, the movement of currents. Here, there was absolutely nothing at all. I tried to look over my shoulder, but Hatter's deep voice stopped me cold.

"Do not look back, Detective. This place was built by a creative madman, a genius to be sure, but one with a terrible sense of humor."

"Let me guess, the ground drops out from beneath my feet and we go tumbling into the never?"

"Something like that," he said, sounding amused.

I huffed, digging my nails into his palm as my own were now starting to perspire.

This was why anyone not of Wonderland needed a guide. If he'd not been here, I'd have tried to walk out.

"Why are we here?"

"Because here is where the bandercoot lives," he said succinctly.

I jerked and looked at him, or at least where I suspected he might be. "What, here? In a zoo?"

"Of sorts," he repeated and patted my hand like one would a little child asking too many bothersome questions.

I thinned my lips but said nothing else.

We sped by in the darkness for what felt like an eternity before I finally saw my first wisp of color. Just a vague blink of it really, silvery blue and brilliant, like a blaze in the absolute pitch black of the place. Then there was another blink and another until the blinks began to coalesce and take on form.

The pathway we were on suddenly gleamed like cut diamonds beneath my feet, like a trail of glittering stars, and above us was a glass-like dome with strange and wondrous creatures that glowed in every shade of phosphorescence, odd and unusual things of no form, but they danced and swayed like silk in water.

I *ahh'd;* enchanted, despite myself.

"What in the bloody hells are those things?" I asked as one particularly pretty one, the color of reddest plum and with a trail of what looked like aquatic feathers, disappeared back into the void of darkness beyond.

"No one's certain." He shrugged. "All we know is that they're terribly lethal. One touch of those pretty feathers to skin will eat away one's flesh like acid. We lost many lives before we figured that one out. So they are kept behind the dome where we can admire them and not die."

I chuckled. "They look aquatic, but I've never seen anything like them."

"I'm sure you haven't, Detective. Wonderland is unlike any other realms out there."

I nodded. "I'm figuring that out."

"Do you like it here?" he asked thoughtfully, quietly, as though he wasn't sure whether he should.

"What, the zoo? Or Wonderland itself?"

His grin was crooked as he spread his arm to encompass the strange but alluring place. "Either. Both. Doesn't matter."

I narrowed my eyes.

The smile slipped from his face. "I'm sorry. I shouldn't have asked something so personal."

"Hardly personal," I corrected, "just curious that you'd care, is all. Yes and no is the simple answer."

He looked at me with raised brow, saying nothing, but I knew what he was thinking.

I turned to look back at the tunnel of never-ending glass and the odd little floating creatures that danced above it.

"I don't hate Wonderland. But I've a healthy respect for it. Though, some of the people are..."

"Odd?" he supplied.

"Well, I was going to say interesting. But odd definitely applies."

That crooked grin of his tipped his mouth again, and I'd have been a liar if I'd said I didn't want to kiss him right then—not with the same hunger and carnality I'd felt after leaving the Crypt yesterday. But I could still imagine the phantom press of his lips on mine and the buried strength within that he kept so tightly checked.

Bothered by these thoughts, I turned back around and said nothing, holding on to his hand with only the lightest of touches, wishing I could just wrap up this investigation and leave already.

"Do you think I'd like Grimm?" he asked into the thick silence between us.

I huffed and shook my head, trying in vain to clear the intimate thoughts from my brain. "If you can handle Wonderland, I'd hazard a guess that you could handle Grimm, Constable."

Neither of us said anything more for a while after that.

Soon, though, the surroundings shifted yet again. This time, the automated pathway took us into another cavernous room, just as dark as the one before. In this one, there were long, vertical mirrors that seemed to stretch toward infinity in both directions. Within them were creatures, strange and unusual beasts I'd never seen before in my life.

I breathed, leaning forward on my tiptoes. But Hatter placed his hand against my chest and pushed me back. "Careful," he warned, and I nodded, but turned quickly to look at the mirrors. Each reflective surface shimmered with a different landscape inside, all of it of Wonderlandian nature. There was a fascinating oddness to everything.

One showed us a green sky and blue grass, with prancing, hopping bunny-like creatures sporting fangs as thick as my wrist as they tore into the carcass of one of their fellows.

Another glass showed us a seascape, and within it were fish that looked like flowers, their tails hooked one to the other, creating unbelievable works of living, moving art.

In another, there was a forest of those writhing, breathing vines, with strange, furry, bipedal man-like animals. They looked like black-furred monkeys with long white tails but with smooth green heads and reptilian-slitted eyes. What must have been a male and female stood side by side on that stretching, breathing vine, staring right back at me just as surely as I stared at them.

And on and on the house of mirrors went. I saw things I'd never imagined possible, like rocks that writhed and wriggled like worms on a hook, and an enormous field of flowers with melted-looking faces inside their blossoms that coughed and hacked out plumes of colorful and noxious gases.

I swallowed hard, glancing to my left and right, dizzied by the endless scope of the place. Hatter reached out his hand and touched his finger to one particular looking glass.

The constantly revolving swing of mirrors stopped instantly, and the pathway stopped moving. In what seemed like a very mundane image of a forest was a thatched-roofed cottage with a cheery plume of smoke coming out of its chimney stack.

But the sounds coming out of the cottage—obnoxiously loud caterwauling and the screams of babies and children—made me wonder if there wasn't a murder taking place right now.

I glanced at Hatter in question, but he merely pointed at the mirror without looking at me. When I turned back, I was shocked to see an animal standing on its hind legs, with beautiful, silky fur marked with leopard's spots, walking forward.

This beast didn't act like a beast or even look much like one. Its face was a mix of rabbit and rat, with its long pointed snout and bright pink nose. But on its face, it wore a small pair of golden-framed spectacles, and it was dressed in its Sunday-best pea-green suit and paisley tie. He, and it was surely a he, even wore a pair of patent-leather shoes.

But the shoes were scuffed at the toes and had seen better days. The suit was holey in places, especially around the collar, and the tie was askew. This was a harried looking fellow if ever there was one.

He plopped his hands onto his rather substantial paunch and eyed us speculatively. I immediately noticed the length of his claws. They were enormous in proportion to the rest of him and were a perfect match to the one I still carried. I idly ran my fingers over the bulge in my pocket.

"Constable Hatter," he said with a squeaky-pitched Wonderlandian drawl. "Well, this is a surprise."

I blinked. Not that I should have been surprised, but I was. I'd never seen a talking rodent before, though I'd heard rumors of their existence in Wonderland. I'd always thought the rumors nonsense, until now.

The bandercoot twitched his nose thoughtfully, causing his meticulously groomed and evenly trimmed whiskers to twitch too. He turned tiny black eyes upon me. "And I see ye've brought company, ye have. 'Ew is she?"

Hatter grinned pleasantly. "Boris, this is Detective Elle from Grimm PD."

"Oh my, oh my," he said, rubbing his little bright-pink paws down his front repetitively. "I knew I'd get caught. Told him so, I did. But he promised me it weren't nothing. I needed coin, ye see, to feed the missus. We just had a new bairn, ye ken. Times been rough, not many comin' to see me no more. Ye understand, don't'cha?"

He rambled, causing his whiskers to twitch spasmodically as he swallowed with obvious nerves, looking at Hatter then at me and then back at Hatter again.

I cleared my throat, remembering at the last second not to take a step. "Boris, was it?"

He clamped his mouth shut and nodded miserably, his tiny eyes looking frighteningly large behind his spectacles.

"I'm guessing, then, that you know why we're here?"

"I'm fairly certain of it, aye."

When I'd first found the bandercoot's claw, my initial impression had been that he'd been one of the main culprits involved. But he was trapped behind glass, so how the bloody hells had his claw wound up in my crime scene?

"Tell me, Boris, when was the last time you left your mirror?"

He shook his head wildly, as did Hatter.

"The glass is merely a peek into the mad outer realms of Wonderland. Anything within the glass can never leave the glass," Hatter said.

I looked at him. "So how in the hells did his claw wind up at my crime scene?"

"Well, now," Boris squeaked, snagging my attention. "I can explain that, I can."

I raised a brow. "I'm waiting with bated breath."

Hatter cleared his throat, and I rolled my eyes, suddenly annoyed by all the silly rules of this place. Back home, if I had to interrogate a person of interest, I interrogated them as I wished, no kid gloves required. Bloody Wonderland.

Boris was again rubbing his strange little hands over his paunch, a nervous gesture of his, no doubt.

"The thing of it is that I canna leave, but those with access to the realms may enter."

I narrowed my eyes. "But you're in Wonderland, no? So couldn't anyone gain access to—"

"No. No." He shook a tiny clawed finger at me. "No, they can'nae. The outer realms are steeped in madness, ye ken, and only thems with warding spells may enter here. It's too dangerous for anyone else."

"He's telling the truth," Hatter said in his gravelly rumble.

I grinned, wishing I could stomp on Hatter's foot for not preparing me. "Instead of asking me whether I liked Wonderland, it might have been nice to, oh, I don't know, tell me all this to begin with," I said, turning on him with sugary venom dripping off my tongue.

At least he had the good graces to look contrite about it. Hooking a finger beneath his too-stiff collar, he dipped his head in agreement. "As you say," he mumbled.

It was all I could do not to scream. An officer of GPD would have had sense enough to brief me first. Bloody backwoods place.

I clenched my teeth together.

Hatter looked at Boris. "You know why we're here, old man. Tell us what you saw and how your claw wound up in a realm far separated from your own."

He nodded. "Aye. Aye. Anything." He held up his hands in a gesture of surrender. "Margo would no be too keen on springing me from the trapper today, I tells ya. She's an absolute bear this morning."

As if to punctuate his words, the hut behind him shook with several shrill voices screaming at one another.

He shuddered, causing his entire body to quake. But when he looked back at me, whatever must have been on my face caused him to straighten up and nod.

"Male came to me, many moons past now. A strange, furtive, fellow."

"What did he look like?" I asked, trying to hurry him on.

He shook his head. "Dinna ken. Was dressed all in robes, ye see, from his head to his toes. Heard the strangest sound whenever he walked though. And he reeked of sulfur. I mean, he stank, the poor bastard did. The missus could-nae get the rotten smell out of our home fer days."

He thinned his lips in obvious disgust.

My ears pricked at the description. I'd smelled sulfides at the crime scene myself, at mine and at Hatter's, which gave me an idea.

"Boris, by any chance did this man return just a few nights past?"

He frowned, thick, furry brows sinking so low he suddenly looked like the backside of a Shar-pei's head.

"Aye, weel, as me missus tells it, something were creeping round about the backside of our house just four nights past, muttering low to iself. Spooked me Margo, it did. She crept up behind it and took her claws to 'es face, she did. Lost a claw for her effort, poor dear. Don't grow back whens we lose 'em, ye ken."

His left hand twitched, and when I looked down, I noted that his pointer finger was clearly missing its claw—the claw that was evidence, buried in my pocket.

Hatter and I looked at one another, both of us clearly thinking the same thought.

"One final question, and then we'll let you get back to it," Hatter said politely. "I notice you've lost a claw yourself."

"Aye." He glanced down at his left hand mournfully. "Like I said, we've ten li'l ones now, and he were offering a year's worth of salary for it. Figgered I didnae have much choice in the matter."

"Why didn't you express the poison sack first?" I asked him curiously.

He frowned. "Ee said he were hunting big game and to leave it be. Gave me an extra fifty shilling for it, ee did." He shrugged, glancing between the two of us with a worried tilt to his lips. "I ken our claws have been banned, savin' for them black market deals, but it were all on the up and up. I swear it. He was just a hunter, was all."

Technically, we could book him. Hatter looked down at me, the question burning in his eyes. Willing or not, the bandercoot was an accessory to murder. In fact, I could even make the case that without him, none of the murders could have taken place. It was what Bo would want of me, I was sure. And yet...

I turned to look at the little beast and felt nothing but pity for him. The constant cries and screams emanating from within that tiny cottage were proof enough of his words. This was a desperate man trying to make ends meet as best he could for his substantially large and growing family.

I sighed. "Thank you, Boris. You've been very helpful."

"I'm no in trouble, then?" he asked, voice quivering as he glanced between Hatter and me.

"No, you're not," I assured him with a soft smile. "Go tend to your family. I'll be in touch again should any other questions arise."

"Aye. Aye. And thank ye, Miss Detective. I promise I'll no be selling me claws no more."

Not that it mattered now. I pursed my lips. I didn't know him, but I was pretty sure that if he knew the role he'd played in a triple homicide, the pitiful little bastard might actually suffer a shock. He was such a nervous wee thing.

Boris made as if to walk away, but I held up my finger. "Oh, Boris? One last question."

He nodded and waited patiently for me to continue.

"By chance, did you ever happen to find your wife's missing claw?"

"Nay. T'was like the damned thing sprouted wings and flew off. Never did find it again."

I nodded. "Thank you, Boris. That's all."

He vanished as quickly as he'd come, and I glanced at Hatter, who was tapping his finger to the glass again. This time, when the automated pathway moved, it sped with a swiftness that caused my hair to blow wildly behind me.

Only minutes later, we were walking back out the long pathway and into the heart of the city center. The air smelled clean, and the cobbled pathways were shiny with rain.

Hatter frowned. "Can you walk on it?"

"As long as I'm wearing my boots, I'll be fine. Boris won't disappear on us, will he?"

"No. He can't escape, neither him nor his missus. But they didn't do it. In fact, I doubt he even knows what he's caused."

I sighed, troubled by what I'd learned.

"Our cases are definitely linked. There can be no question about that."

I looked at Hatter, but his face was impassive, and his eyes looked troubled. "Aye. I reckon we ought to speak to Goose sooner rather than later."

I slipped my hands into my pockets, nodding slowly as we made our way back down the road.

"Constable," I whispered a second later.

He glanced at me. "Hmm?"

But I had no clue what I wanted to say, nor was I sure what I was feeling. Scratching the back of my head, I stared down at my feet as I thought about how different everything looked to me now than it had before. I'd thought this just a simple cold case, but it was looking more and more like a high-level conspiracy with Hatter and I at its unwitting center.

I needed to file my report, but who the hells could I trust now? I wasn't even sure, and that was a problem.

A big one.

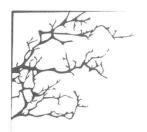

Chapter 11

Detective Elle

When we arrived at Goose's boot—literally, her house was in the shape of a giant, leather, and quite holey boot—we were greeted by a pack of dogs who looked as though they'd not eaten well in years. Their rib cages were clearly visible, and some didn't even have the energy to sniff our hand more than once.

Feeling pity for the poor beasts, I glanced around and spied a small pond a few meters away. I went to it and dipped my hand in the water, grinning when I felt the thrumming energy of life.

The pond was full of fish. I called them to me, pumping the water full of the siren's lure, and up they came. With a flick of my wrist, I shot the slippery little bastards toward their gruesome deaths. The dogs were rather pleased with me after that.

Hatter snorted.

"You're just full of surprises, Detective. You hate kids, and yet you melt at the sight of beasts. It's no wonder you chose not to arrest the bandercoot."

I rolled my eyes. "I could if you really wanted me to. We could always go back."

We stood nearly chest to chest, the heat between us feeling like fire the way it snapped and curled. He lowered his head, and my heart thumped wildly in my chest at the clean, masculine scent of him.

"I'm glad you didn't," he admitted softly. Then he stepped away from me and walked a perimeter around the boot. I turned and looked at the strange little house again, studying the layout.

There were miles of rolling green grass and neatly manicured garden patches as well. I saw the cabbage patch she'd been whinging about being destroyed by her neighbor's goats and wondered why in the two hells those goats had walked such a long distance to get here just for a few simple heads of cabbage. I saw the neighbor's paddock in the distance, but well in the distance, at least three miles as the crow flew. Quite a distance for a few heads of cruciferous veggies.

The place was lovingly tended... well, as lovingly as it could be considering the gaggle of children she kept as well. It was a wonder the dogs had any food at all to eat. The pathway that led to the boot was a winding, curvy, nonsensical thing lined with what must have once been pretty field flowers but were now nothing more than crushed and withered stems.

The goats had certainly done a number on her property, that was sure. But I wasn't at all certain why Pillar had sent us here. There was nothing about this place that seemed in any way connected to our crime scene.

"Nothing," Hatter said with a weary sigh when he came back around. "She's not here, and neither are any of her children. We'll have to come back."

I frowned. "My key card expires tonight at midnight. And unless I have something good to report back to the captain, the chances of me getting another are slim to none."

His dark eyes gleamed with worry. "You're going to need to talk with her, then?"

I tossed up my hands. "Only one problem. Who the hells can I trust there? What if she's in on this?"

He shook his head. "I could be wrong."

My look was skeptical. "How accurate are your visions, Constable?"

Licking his front teeth, he grudgingly admitted, "One hundred percent. They're never wrong."

"Well, there you bloody go. So I'm at an impasse. I know just enough to be in danger and not nearly enough to pin anything on anybody. Tell me, in my shoes, what would you do?"

"I'm a country investigator, Elle. I'm rather out of my comfort zone as well."

"Yes, but you have a crime scene now."

"Stripped from me."

I shrugged. "Be that as it may, there's no doubt our scenes are connected. I would assume you have just as much at stake in solving this as I do."

He scratched at his beard, and I noticed that he looked less neat and tidy than he had in days past. There were dark circles under his eyes, and I'd bet my eye teeth he'd not been sleeping well.

"I'd go back, present a case, enough to gain an extension, at least."

I had a bad feeling in the pit of my stomach. I didn't trust Pillar, and refused to go to her for another key card, not that she'd have given me one, anyway. Without the authority from Grimm PD, I was up excrement creek without a paddle. I could use the standard key cards, but the waystations in Wonderland were hazardous to reach, and I didn't want to find myself suddenly cut off from Grimm.

Ultimately, I had no choice. I would have to return to Grimm.

"Or," Hatter said, scrubbing at his jaw with his long fingers. "Or maybe I wouldn't go back."

"Come again?" I shook my head, staring at him blankly.

He rubbed at his beard with two long fingers. The movements seemed a type of anxious habit for him, like brushing his jacket was. "We've a wire at the station. Old as two hells and not very reliable, but Harry can get just about anything running with enough elbow grease. Ring her up, give her what you trust will grant you that extension, but just—"

"Keep the truth close to the vest. I can do that. But I'd no idea you had a wire here. That's why the Grimmers always have to drop by. The White Knight said—"

"His armor was white, Detective. But do not conflate that with the measure of his character, for you'd be sorely disappointed."

I grinned and shoved my hands into my pockets. "Hmm. Learn something new everyday. Well, then, lead the way, Constable." I gestured down the trail. "I've a report to file."

"I hope like the two hells this works," he muttered beneath his breath, and I knew that, for him, it was personal too.

"Me too, Constable. Me too."

Constable Maddox

HE SHOULD HAVE BEEN focused on the stacks and stacks of paperwork he still had to get in order. He'd not lied to her when he'd said that the White Knight had placed the station in a very precarious position. There were cases going back at least ten years that had been improperly filed, or even—to his great vexation—not filed at all. Nothing but a small note pinned to their insides to remember to do this or that, which clearly the Knight had never gotten around to doing.

How he'd managed to see his retirement with such a sterling reputation intact went beyond the pale for Hatter. It sickened him how badly matters had been handled.

Accidents and mistakes were one thing, but the deliberate choice of being too damned lazy to do it at all was another. Harry, who wasn't much of a filing clerk, or even much of a detective, for that matter, had been around during the Knight's tenure as head constable in Wonderland. And he was able to give Hatter at least some clue as to when and where. If it weren't for that and his genius with technology—a skill Hatter woefully lacked—he'd have sacked him on the spot and done the work himself, which he mostly was doing, at this point.

Dull, throbbing pain continued to spread like crawling feelers from the base of his skull, and he winced. He couldn't focus. With a loud sigh, he dropped the quill and rubbed his temples.

Leaning back on his seat, surrounded by an infinite mound of paperwork, he once again found himself glancing into the back office. The detective had left the door ajar just enough that every so often he could hear snatches of conversation.

Her words were breathless, rushed, and sometimes punctuated with emphatic bouts of anger.

"I understand, Chief," she snapped, "but I don't think you're hearing me. I'm telling you I'm close, damned close, to—"

Her words cut off, and he saw her shadow pacing back and forth as she tugged at the tips of her hair with obvious frustration.

"I see. I see," she said slowly. Quietly.

And his heart sank.

"Balls," he muttered. If she was getting yanked back to Grimm, he was out of options. Agent Crowley had cut him off at the knees. If they could just get back to that crime scene, he knew she'd find something. She'd been close as it was. He doubted anyone could dive as deep as she had. That pool was a known dumping spot for Wonderlandians. With its unplumbed depths, if you didn't want something found, that was the best place to dump it.

It was rare that a siren working on the side of the law and not against it came to town. In fact, it wasn't just rare. It simply didn't happen. But they didn't necessarily need that pool either. Yes, it might make solving the case quicker, but instinct told him they already had most of the clues. All they needed was to understand what it was they'd gathered. They were bloody close to cracking this thing wide open. He just knew it.

He tapped his fingers repetitively on his desk, that dull pain continuing its aggressive forward march.

"Yes," she muttered, and his gut clenched. He hadn't liked the tone of her voice.

If she left him now, that was it. Another unsolved case would turn cold and sit on a back shelf somewhere, growing thick with dust and forgotten by all. He didn't get into law enforcement to lose. He hadn't sacrificed everything just to back down when things got tough. That wasn't who he was.

Growling, he stood and marched over to the back bench, not even looking at what he grabbed as he filled his plate with pastries and made himself a quick spot of tea.

Butterflies flitted on canary yellow wings around his head, making him growl as he swatted at them. His place was a mess. It needed tending to. Taming. The gardens in the back were starting to grow wild, and more often than not, little furry beasties were scampering through his stacks of files, causing them to tumble into haphazard heaps that only made his job all the harder.

For the thousandth time, he wondered why he'd willingly taken on these duties. Until a year ago, he'd been content to be a beat cop, answerable to the White Knight, but free to handle cases as he saw fit and to leave at the end of his eight-hour shift.

After three months of sleeping, eating, and working at the office, he'd come to the conclusion that it was pointless to keep his home. So he'd broken his lease, sold off what he could, and now had only a bed and a few clothes to call his own.

Taking a sip of the orange-scented tea, he stared at the wooden walls, crumbling wallpaper in gaudy shades of lavender-green, and the pebbled scat from bunnies that'd scampered through his space, and felt that he was stuck more in a prison than an office.

This wasn't what he'd signed up for. Not even a little.

"Yes. Out," she said, and then he heard her replacing the receiver.

Jerking, he set his half-finished cup of tea down along with his untouched plate of sweets. He was just dusting off his hands when she walked out.

She had taken her jacket off, and with her tumble of blue hair, wispy coral shirt, and black leather pants, there was something young and almost innocent looking about her. She didn't look like the woman he knew her to be—a creature as fearsome as any boogeyman of legend.

"Well, I've got good news and bad news," she sighed, pulling Harry's chair out from his desk and plopping into it with a world-weary look about her.

He wet his lips. "Bad first, I suppose."

Her full lips thinned. "We didn't get the three-day extension."

"Dammit all to the two hells," he muttered before leaning against the tea bench, crossing his legs at the ankles and his arms on his chest. "Figured as much from the sound of things, though."

She thinned her lips. "Yeah, well. It's not all bad. I did get one more day."

He rolled his eyes, and she grimaced.

"I tried, Constable. And considering I couldn't tell her everything, I'm surprised I even got that. Bo's no one's dummy. I'm pretty sure she knew I wasn't telling her everything."

"What did she say?"

"Oh, you know." She laughed airily. "She'd bust my balls if I screwed her over and didn't give her something definitive by day's end. That she was sticking her neck out for me. That IA was up her arse to either poop or get off the pot. Yada, yada, yada... you know, same ol' spiel."

He snorted, understanding well enough.

Her mention of IA—short for Internal Affairs—caught his attention. "Why's IA there?"

Pursing her lips, she peered into the glass bowl on Harry's desk that he usually kept full of snacks. Flicking her fingers through the balls of truffles like she was looking for something in particular, she finally wrinkled her nose and sat back.

"It's Grimm. IA's always up our arses for something or other. I did hear a little chatter about a copycat, Slasher Gang-style robbery. No doubt IA's there about that. Been a year this case has gone unsolved, and I'm sure they'd like to see that stain against us handled sooner rather than later." She shrugged.

He knew a little of the Slasher Gang, a murder of shifter crows known for their ruthless and expert cunning when it came to robbing banks across several realms. The embarrassment was surely because their leader, Black Angus, had been held in the custody of Grimm PD, warded by level-ten witches and stones inscribed with runes of dark power. His escape had made him infamous, but it was the brazen robberies that'd begun only two days later that'd made him legend. It'd been in all the papers and the talk of Wonderlandians far and wide for several weeks afterward.

"So we've got only about thirty hours or so, give or take, to crack this thing wide. No pressure or anything," she said with an ironic snort.

Again, she riffled through Harry's bowl before growling beneath her breath.

Grinning because she looked like she was ready to crawl out of her skin with nerves, a trait he understood quite well, Maddox said, "What are you looking for, Detective?"

She twirled on him, the pupils of her eyes slitted as she grumped, "I'm bloody starving, and even this chocolate is sounding good right now."

Stepping away from the bench, he gestured toward a plate of lavender salmon sashimi, similar in succulence to the ruby-red salmon, but slightly sweeter in taste.

"Oh goddess," she moaned, unfurling her long legs from the chair as she almost ran to the plate. Reaching down, she took the whole platter in hand and grinned at him. "You don't mind, right?" Not that she gave him much of a chance to answer, as she was already shoveling the gelatinous slivers into her mouth and chomping happily.

"I'm disgusting when I eat. I'll own it," she said between bites, "so look away if it bothers you."

Chuckling, he rubbed at the back of his head, realizing it hurt less than it had just a while ago.

"No, Detective. It's rather refreshing to see a woman eating with such appreciation for her food. I'm rather a gourmand myself, you'll hear no complaints from me."

She mumbled around her bites of fish but didn't speak again until she'd demolished what had once been five pounds' worth of salmon meat. He had slipped the order for it onto Harry's desk before they'd left this morning.

When she was done, she leaned back in her seat and rubbed at her slightly distended belly, a look of ease on her face.

Taking his cup of tea in hand, he sipped the cooling liquid, not really tasting it as he said, "Considering we haven't much time, perhaps we should go back to Goose's—"

"No. Crane will be here soon with my new card. I'm on strict orders to wait."

"Of course."

She slapped her hands down on her knees and stood. "I'm going for a swim. My skin feels too tight."

He nodded. "Perhaps I'll join you."

"Pardon?" she asked with raised brow, and he chuckled, realizing how that had sounded.

"Rather, I'll tag along, as it were. I find that when I'm at a roadblock, it always helps to discuss what I know so far. Sometimes that helps jar the thoughts loose enough for me to make sense of the bigger picture."

He wet his lips, heart hammering as he realized he'd get to see her nude again. That thought hadn't entered his mind when he'd asked to tag along, but now he felt heat settling into his cheeks. He frowned.

"On second thought, Detective—"

"Fine." She flicked her wrist, looking unconcerned about him seeing her in the buff. "Come along, if it'll help." Then she turned on her heel and was already blazing a trail toward the fairy waters.

For just a second, and only in the privacy of his own mind, he admitted that he was a little put out that she'd not seemed to care. He wasn't sure he should follow her after all. He could just as easily talk things through with himself. The goddess knew he'd done it more than a few times in his years. And yet somehow, he found himself hard on her heels, pulse beating rapid-fire in his neck.

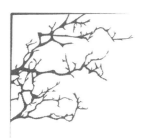

Chapter 12

I peeled off my clothes as soon I could. I'd only just been at my waters, so I shouldn't feel a need to swim so soon. And yet, it felt like I was covered in thousands of sharp, stinging ants.

I heard Hatter come up behind me, but I didn't care. I kicked the clothes to the side and, with a relieved sigh, dove into water. The quick flash of the change burned me, transforming my legs back into a tail, and I trembled.

I wished I could just live in my waters and never again have to leave them. I swallowed two quick gulps of the clean-tasting dew before reluctantly swimming to the surface.

I found Hatter easily. He sat still as a statue, staring straight ahead. His jacket was off and lying on a boulder beside him. His elbow rested on his nocked knee, his cravat was undone, and his white sleeves were rolled up, exposing the art on both arms.

I'd seen Cheshire grab hold of the demon, but I'd not known Hatter had an angel on the other arm. Her face was the same as the demon's, though, and I noticed what I hadn't back in the dimly lit chaos of the bar.

Cocking my head, I studied the sweeping brows, the sloping cheekbones, and the heart-shaped jaw. It was Alice. The face on both drawings was Alice's. I twisted my lips, and he finally seemed to notice me.

"There you are," he said with an easy, affable grin that made me feel queer flutterings in my nethers.

I coughed to hide the fact that I was attracted to Hatter. Well, attracted was too light a word. I was aroused, madly so.

With any other man, I'd just scratch the itch. Ich and I had done it on countless occasions. Ichabod was about as interested in a relationship as I was, which was to say, not at all. We had an understanding between us.

I swam slowly toward Hatter, watching him as he watched me like a hawk eyeing prey. I was glad he couldn't see the sudden ripple of bumps roll across my flesh at his visual caress. I swallowed hard.

"Balls," I muttered. I couldn't wait to get back home.

"Say again?"

I shook my head. "You wanted to discuss the case, so let's discuss," I said, voice sharper than I'd intended it to be.

He sighed, twisting a broken piece of tree bark between his fingers. "Where do we start? Crowley, for one, stripping me of the scene. Why? What was there that would make him—"

I thinned my lips. "There was nothing more in that pool, Constable. I'm sure of it," I said, holding up my hands as my tail flicked in the gentle undercurrents. "I found the only thing of true worth down there. What disturbs me more is that they must have known something was down there. Though good luck getting at it. Only another water elemental would have had the skills to do what I did."

His nostrils flared as he broke off chunks of bark and flicked them away. "But they closed down the entire scene. Why? What if there was more? Out of the water, perhaps? Something we didn't see?" He looked at me, and for once, both his eyes were just eyes. Neither of them glowed.

He looked tired.

I frowned. "You read the cold-case file, yes?" I asked.

The look he shot me said, "Clearly."

Grinning ruefully, I shrugged. "You can never be too sure. Anyway, what wasn't in the file but that I discovered—and was the very reason why I was sent to Wonderland to further this investigation—was part of what you'd seen in your vision."

I tapped my eye, and he nodded. "The ribbon and horse's head, yes. But I saw shears, too, and the woman with strange eyes. We've yet to find either of those."

"I'm sure we will, but whether we do or don't, I'm certain we can solve this case before my coach turns back into pumpkin."

He grinned at the reference, and I couldn't help but grin back. I liked his look. I wasn't shy when it came to my sexuality. No nymph was. And Hatter was undeniably attractive. So very tidy and proper, at least on the surface, anyway. But beneath that façade was a man who'd, for a time, made a life with a woman who ran the local sex shoppe.

"Your dichotomous nature intrigues me," I said, realizing I'd spoken my thoughts out loud as a hard look suddenly flashed over his features.

Wary was too fine a word for what Hatter was. This man was snake-bitten. He was like a feral animal, cornered and ready to snap if the hand that fed it got too close. It was a state I understood only too well.

I was about to mutter yet another apology when I saw his tense shoulders relax.

"I'm sure that I appear dichotomous, Detective. We all have our secrets, and the mask we show the world is rarely the truth."

I squirmed, understanding that his words weren't just about him, but me too.

"True enough. And I'm not trying to pry—"

"Aren't you?" he asked brusquely, his look flinty and intelligent.

I snorted. "Fine, I guess I am. But I've never worked so closely with anyone for such an extended period of time, so call me curious."

"You know what they say—curiosity killed the cat."

"Yes, but they also say curiosity is the lust of the mind. And to be frank, neither of us wound up in this profession because we aren't the curious types. Or am I wrong?"

At that, his dark eyes glinted, and a slow, curving grin pinched the corners of mouth.

"Indeed. Well, detective, we have time to kill. I'll answer a few of your questions, if you answer a few of mine."

Licking my front teeth, I shook my head. "I figured you'd say as much. You don't play fair, Constable."

"Neither do you, Detective. So, who goes first?"

I grinned, eyeing his markings. "Those." I pointed to his arms. "Why do you have them, and what do they do?"

He held his arms out in front of him, looking first at the devil and then at the angel. "I was marked years ago by an old sea witch. They... help me."

When he looked at me again, his eyes were blazing, one deepest green, the other luminescent blue. His eyes gazed sightlessly behind me as he saw not me, or even our surroundings, but a vision of both the past and the future.

Seconds later, it was over, and he turned his gaze my way. The angel on his arm now blazed the purest white.

"You saw something?" I asked.

"I saw you," he said simply, but I shivered, wondering what he'd seen and dreading knowing it too.

The way his jaw worked from side to side and the fact that he wouldn't quite meet my eyes let me know all I needed.

I knew if I latched on to the dimming glow of his tattoo, I would likely see what he had, just as Cheshire had done. But I shook my head.

"My past is my past, Maddox. And that's where it belongs."

A muscle in his jaw ticked.

"Must be terrible," I said softly, "knowing the darkest parts of everyone around you. Who can you trust when you see too much?"

He rolled down his sleeves, covering both his arms before rubbing his fingers lightly over the angel, which still glowed bright.

"I don't judge, Elle, if that's what you're worried about."

I scoffed. "My life is an open book. All anyone has to do is hear my name, and they know all there is to know about me."

Bitterness dripped off my tongue, and I had to look away as I scrubbed at my hot eyes with the back of my wrist.

"I know you were cast out long before you met your mate," he said, the words spoken haltingly, like he wasn't sure he should say them or that I'd want to hear them. "I know you weren't... sane."

I hissed, rising up on the water so that I was eye level with him. "You know nothing. Nothing! No one knows why I was cast out. That part was conveniently left out of my story."

The air between us grew thick with a sudden blanket of tension, and I shivered as his hot gaze looked me slowly up and down, resting on my breasts long enough to make me moan as I imagined it wasn't his eyes, but his hands that touched me now.

It had been so damned long.

"You're right, Detective. No one knows that part of the story. So, why were you cast out then?" His voice was an intoxicating, heated whisper that almost lulled my deepest, darkest secret out of me.

Not even Hook had known the real reason, though I sometimes thought, somewhere inside, he must have known why I was as messed up as I was, why I'd become what I'd become. Any time in my presence would make that fact abundantly clear, which was why I didn't get close to others and why I fought so bloody hard to keep myself apart from the rest of the world, only showing them the mask, the superficial parts of me.

Grabbing his collar, I fisted it tight and brought his face scant inches from mine. His strong hands braced themselves on my biceps, and all it would have taken to make his mouth mine would have been for me to close that last inch between us.

He wanted me too. I'd have had to have been blind not to recognize the lust in his eyes.

"You will never know my secrets, Constable. Not ever."

His jaw worked as he swallowed, but the way he looked at me made me feel cold and anxious.

"As you say, Detective."

I could hardly breathe, and I wondered all over again just what he had seen.

And that was how Harry found us when he came jogging up to us just seconds later.

"Detecti—ahh," he said quickly, turning on his heel as he looped back. "A thousand apologies," he said quickly.

Releasing Hatter's collar, I shook my head, more irritated than I had a right to be at the interruption. "It's fine."

I quickly sank beneath the waters just in case it was my nudity that'd embarrassed him.

Hatter stood. "What is it, Harry?"

He wrinkled his nose, making him look more like the rabbit he'd reminded me of the first night I'd arrived.

"There be a Grimmer here, says he's looking for the Detective."

"Crane!" I cried with a note of relief. "Send him back, please."

Rubbing the back of his neck, Harry bobbed an acknowledgement and turned. Hatter was yanking his jacket back on and dusting off his spotless coat as Ichabod, looking handsome in black, came through the gates.

"Elle. Constable," he said with a glance toward us both.

If he found it odd that I was swimming in front of the constable, it didn't show. What I did see was a harried expression pinching the corners of his eyes and mouth. Ichabod was the definition of cool under pressure, so this was different for him.

"Ich? Are you alright?"

He was reaching into his jacket pocket, walking past Hatter without sparring him a glance.

"What? Hmm? Yes. The key." He brandished the tiny golden key at me.

I pointed to the spot where my clothes lay. "Just set it there. Thank you. Are you sure you're okay?"

He dropped the key into my pile of clothes. "Yes. No." Then he turned on Hatter and nodded. "Might I have a word with my partner alone?"

For just a second, a look of confusion scrawled over Hatter's smooth forehead, but he was a master of disguising emotion, and in just moments was back to looking like an implacable and emotionless wall.

"I'll be in my office," he said to no one in particular and was gone just as quickly as Ichabod had appeared.

The second he was out of earshot I turned on Ich. "What the hells was that all about? And since when are we partners?"

He swatted at the air with his hand. "I just had to clear him out of here. Don't know who we can trust right now."

Ice zipped down my veins as I eyed my one and probably only friend at the precinct. "Come again?"

"Bo couldn't talk on the wire. We've got IA up our arses so high we can't even take a dump without them knowing about it."

"That has to hurt."

He snickered. "Aye, well, the worst of it is not only is IA shoving their noses into whatever the two hells pleases them, but BS is all over the fecking place."

I could probably count on one hand the number of times I'd seen Ichabod lose his cool this way, which was pretty much never.

"This reeks, and I don't mind saying so. Ever since ye left, nothing's been normal. Bo's up to her eyeballs in red tape and bureaucratic bullshit. Even now, that jackarse Crowley is taking over our cold-case files and has barred us from the evidence locker. Argh!" He growled as he took fistfuls of his hair and tugged.

Bo's sudden reluctance to let me stay in Wonderland made much more sense now. I shook my head. "But why?"

"Reports of improper handling and some other bull like that."

I swallowed, thinking about the key card Hatter and I'd recovered, the very one I'd not reported. But since no one knew about that, surely that wasn't the cause of the kerfuffle. Right?

I grew cold.

"Bo did report that I brought some evidence with me to Wonderland, no?"

"Aye. Thank the stars," he snapped and sank onto the rock that Hatter had recently vacated. "Dammit all to the two hells, Elle. Something's not right here. Add to that the stress of the Slasher Gang stepping up their robberies, and it's mad back there. But you're close, right?" He looked at me with his intelligent silver gaze. "With what Bo's going through right now, that she's even extended you a day tells me you're close."

I nodded, though I was hesitant to tell him much more than that. "You know I can't share the details of the case with you, Ich. Sorry."

He scrubbed a hand down his face and groaned. "I haven't bloody slept in two days. You told me the royals were crooked. Well, I'm telling you now, there's a cover-up, and you can be sure of it. Only someone with the kind of power the royals have could turn the precinct on its head this way. Find whatever the bloody hells you need to find, Elle, or we're all screwed."

I glanced over his shoulder to where Hatter would be waiting for me. The urgency to solve the case had just ratcheted up by several degrees.

"How long do you have until you need to go back?" I asked him slowly.

He looked at me from between his long fingers. "Bo didn't say, but I'm assuming sooner rather than later."

I nodded. "That's enough time."

"Time for what?"

I grinned. "You know we work best when we take the edge off. Scratch my back, I'll scratch yours?"

I was a siren. I had biological urges. And I couldn't bloody focus when I constantly wanted the constable. Ich was the next best thing.

He grinned. "Yeah, I think we've got enough time for that."

In seconds, he was nude and in the water with me. I laughed when he grabbed me up, and then there was no more laughing after that.

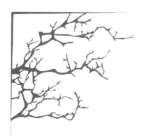

Chapter 13

Detective Elle

Walking from the gardens together, Ich and I were the definition of professional as we shook hands and nodded.

"Okay, and thank you, Ichabod. For everything," I added softly.

He nodded, dipped his head toward Hatter, and then, with a swipe of his key card, was gone.

Hatter looked me up and down, and for just one second, his eyes flashed. Grabbing his hat, he set it on his head and grunted. "Let's go."

I frowned and jogged after him. "Where?"

"Goose. She should be back now. I don't see any more reason to delay, do you?"

His voice was calm, but I sensed he wasn't happy. There was a sharp bite to his words that hadn't been there earlier.

I frowned.

Yanking open the door, he stepped to the side, as if waiting on me to pass through. But when I tried to smile a thank you at him, he refused to meet my gaze.

I scowled.

"If you have a problem with me, then just say it. Be a man and spit it out, Constable."

Looking down at me with hard eyes, he shrugged. "I've got nothing to say to you, Detective. Now, if you'd rather I visited Goose alone..."

"Whatever," I snapped, and walked through the door.

By the time he joined me outside, we were both quivering with quiet fury.

"Detective, if you would," he said with barely suppressed venom.

So angry I was starting to see black spots in my field of vision from clamping down on my tongue too hard, I yanked the key card out of my pocket and swiped the air.

Only once I'd done it did I realize how discombobulated we both were, since we hadn't technically needed to walk outside to do it.

In seconds, we were back in the hells that was the between. The quiet was smothering.

"I thought every second mattered," he snipped into the stillness.

And like a powder keg being lit, I turned on him, exploding with all the pent-up anger. "If you're talking about the fact that I had to—"

He scoffed, grinning cruelly, making him look far more sinister and deadly than normal. "Had to. That's rich. We're on the clock, Detective. Need I remind you—"

"No." I stabbed his chest with my finger, which he easily swatted away, looming large and intractable over me as he breathed like a bellows. "You don't get to judge me. You don't bloody get to look down your nose at me. You know what I am. And when I say I had to, I bloody had to, so bugger off!"

And dammit all to the two hells, my body burned. Ich had been great, but it was Hatter that'd lit this fuse inside me.

"Bugger off?" he roared. "Goddess dammit!"

Moving in a blink, he had me off my toes and shoved up against the tunnel walls. He wasn't just kissing me. He was claiming me, shoving his hot, delicious tongue down my mouth as he forced me to give him my own. My hands were in his hair, his hands were in mine, and though my eyes were closed, I felt the burning glow of light radiate against my flesh.

Fire raced through my bones, and memories, dark hated memories, came surging up of another man with hot, demanding hands and the devil's own charm. Madness and pain surged through me like a wave. I wasn't gentle as I clawed and nipped at him, dragging my long nails down his neck. But he took it and gave me back his own manic need.

His fingers were rough as they dug into my hips, grinding his cock hard against me. I hissed, curving into his hard strength as a warning bell rang out in my head that we had seconds before we were at Goose's, and that there was no way in hells we could afford to be caught like this.

"Dammit." I shoved him away. "Dammit," I said again, this time full of regret. My body burned like a sun flare, and my throat squeezed tight with the need to sing the siren's song.

I swallowed over and over, trying to shove it back down, that desperate desire and madness that this eccentric man had pulled out of me.

Hatter stood still as a statue beside me, hand planted on the tunnel wall as he hung his head and breathed deeply. His body trembled, and I bit my bottom lip.

"Maddox, I—"

"Don't," he breathed. "Just don't."

I closed my mouth, saying nothing.

A second later, we were out of the tunnel and standing on Goose's expansive front lawn. This time, it was littered with children. The sound of their squealing laughter grated on my shredded nerves, and I had to bite my teeth together to keep from snapping at them.

When I looked at the constable, he was dusting off his jacket and smiling broadly. At no point did I see the agitated beast he'd been back in the tunnel.

He started to walk up the trail, and I followed, not sure what to say or whether I should say anything at all.

After looking over the scene on the lawn, something felt off to me, different. I sniffed.

"I feel it too," Hatter said beneath his breath just as a gang of children ran up to him with their hands out, demanding sweets.

I curled my lips and watched as he dipped into his pocket and pulled out handfuls of Harry's truffles to give to the kids.

After receiving their treats, they ran off without a thanks to be had.

"What?" I asked once we were alone again.

"Something is wrong here, but I don't know what."

I nodded, glad at least that we could remain professional when it came to the case.

I stared at the worn shoe. The holes for windows. The kids calling and playing. The lines with clothes hanging out to dry on them. This place screamed domesticated hells to me.

The door was suddenly tossed open, and there she stood, the worn looking Goose of before. But there was a smile on her face now where none had been before.

"Oy, Detectives!" She said, gesturing with her hands. "Look at this, will ya's? Farmer Tom's made things square again. I'll no be filing a report after all."

She pointed at a massive basket full of perfect, beautiful cabbages the size of a horse's head. There were at least ten of them, more than enough to feed her gaggle for several days, at least.

Hatter looked at the basket with a worried scrawl. "I'm glad, Mother, very glad for you. But tell me," he said slowly, "when did Tom make this drop-off?"

"Oh, um..." Her smile slipped just a little, and her glance turned furtive as she said, "Why, last night. Left it on me doorstep, he did. What a nice man. You may go. Sorry for dragging yous all the way out 'ere over a simple misunderstanding. Shoo. Shoo. I've got dinner to get going now."

She waved at us, desperate to get us on our way. But her eyes glanced toward her garden then very deliberately back to me.

The vein in Hatter's neck throbbed as he clamped down on his jaw. She was lying, and we both knew it. But why? And what was she covering for? Suddenly, Pillar's clue didn't feel like such a waste of time after all.

"Are you sure?" Hatter asked slowly.

Her smile wavered. "Course I am, Constable. Course I am. All a giant misunderstanding, ye see."

Once more, her eyes traveled toward her garden and then back to me, giving me wide eyes. I knew that look, had seen it many times before when someone wanted to say something, but for whatever reason, they couldn't.

Hatter, though, wasn't looking at her. He was scanning the yard, so he missed her subtle hint. I frowned, and she didn't nod or look back, but her eyes reminded me of a pig's right before the big bad wolf took it down, and I knew there was something in that garden she wanted us to see.

I grinned and placed a hand over Hatter's forearm to gently move him back a step. He frowned, looking at me.

"Wonderful. Glad matters have been taken care of. Of course, we've come such a long way, and I'm just absolutely starving. Haven't eaten in days."

Hatter grunted, but I dug my fingernails into the back of his hand, and wise man that he was, he chose to stay silent. His look was wary but trusting.

"Ah! Well, not all was lost the day Tom's goats ate my flowers. I've a patch of berries just ripe for the plucking. Take as many as you'll be wanting, Detective."

And with that, she slammed the door in our faces.

Hatter and I looked at each other, understanding flowing between us. Without saying a word, we turned and headed directly to the garden.

At first, nothing looked out of the ordinary. The garden was still in a state of ruins, with a few patches of harvestable vegetables and fruits scattered around. My skin tingled like it did when I knew someone watched me. Glancing up, I saw that it was a cherubic, blue-eyed girl of no more than five, twirling a length of her curly blond hair around her finger.

"Yes?" I asked as Hatter walked up and down the rows.

"Bad people came here today," she said in a sweet voice.

Hatter whirled at that, looking at her and then at me. I dropped to my knees, taking the girl's hands into my own. "Really, sweetheart. And what did they do?"

"They told Mama they was gonna take us all away."

I blinked, feeling as though a rock had just settled in the pit of my stomach.

"They said they was watching her."

I looked back at Hatter. He was unnaturally still, every fiber of his being centered on the child and what she was saying.

I swallowed. "Why would they say that? Do you know?"

She shrugged, "Dunno." She spotted a flitting butterfly with magnificent magenta wings and pointed at it. "Oh!"

"Focus, honey," I said quietly. "Just a few more questions, and then my partner will give you a treat. How's that sound?"

I hoped to the goddess he had a few more of those chocolates in his pocket.

An ear-splitting grin stole across her features, and her little pink tongue poked out, licking her lips with obvious anticipation.

"Whatcha wanna know?" she asked, madly twirling a length of corn-silk-colored hair around her chubby little finger.

"What did these bad people look like?"

She shrugged again. "Dunno. They had big blankets on. All black. But they stunk, sure 'nuff. Mama made them stay outside."

She wrinkled her nose, clearly recalling that smell. Twice now, I'd heard of a smell.

"What's your name, honey?" I asked.

"Jeannette." She smiled, looking pure and innocent, and making me feel a tad bit bad for thinking of children as pests earlier. Maybe they weren't all little devils.

"Jeannette," I said with a nod, "just one last question, and then I'll get out of your hair, okay?"

"And then I'll gets my chocolates?" she asked hopefully.

"Mm-hmm." I crossed my fingers behind my back, hopeful that I wasn't about to see a child cry because I'd lied. "Did that bad smell make you think of rotten eggs?"

Her eyes went wide, and she gasped. "Just like it. Like when Gwenny lays too many, and mama can't cook 'em all up, and some just rot and stuff. Yeah, it were just like that."

Pulling her in for a tight squeeze, I said, "You did great, Jeannette. Just great."

Hatter, thank the goddess, had exactly two truffles left. Using sleight of hand so that none of the other children could see, he placed them in the center of her palm with a pat to her head.

Down the lane, I could hear a faint cry of police sirens.

"Bloody hells," Hatter whispered, and I stood.

Goose's home was high up on a hill, surrounded by little else, giving us the perfect vantage point from which to see the procession of clearly marked BS cars driving in a line directly for us.

They were coming here. Question was, why?

"We should go," I told him quickly. "The last thing we want is to be caught by them twice."

"Agreed."

I reached for my key card, and Jeannette, who now had a face full of chocolate, tugged on my hand.

"I found this," she said and proceeded to hand me a ribbon.

A blue ribbon.

A bloodstained blue ribbon.

Hatter sucked in a sharp breath. The mystic cross-stitch pattern was clearly evident to all but the blind.

"Where... where did you find this, honey?"

"We have to go now," Hatter snapped.

She smiled. "In the garden."

Then, twirling on her heels, she skipped away, taunting her siblings that she'd gotten extra chocolates and they had not.

Just before the agents could see us, Hatter snatched the key card out of my pocket and swiped the air. He yanked me through before the tunnel had even completely formed.

Only once we were safely ensconced in the tunnel did he lean against the wall, panting heavily and shaking his head.

"This can't be. It can't be."

"Hatter," I said softly.

When he looked at me, his eyes were hard as flint. "I'd have seen it, Elle! I'd have bloody seen it. Alice isn't who she once was, but she's not a bloody murderer. She's not—"

I shook my head. "Of course she's not. Think about it. Goose gets paid off by the goddess only knows who, told to shut up or her kids will get taken away. We were just here not an hour ago. That damn bloody ribbon wasn't in the garden. You want to know why I know that?"

He looked like a desperate man clinging to the last vestiges of hope. I knew it was because of Alice that he wasn't thinking right. He was too bloody brilliant not to see what was so obvious to me. We were getting close, too close, and whoever the hells was behind this was desperate enough to make mistakes.

"Why?" he rumbled.

Because I figured he might need it, I moved into the tense line of his body and hugged him. He was stiff as board, but he didn't push me away.

"Because this ribbon stinks like rotten eggs. It's coated in sulfide, the same sulfides that were at my scene and in the one Crowley stole from you. This is a frame job, Maddox, and Alice is their scapegoat."

With a desperate groan, he dropped his head into the crook of my neck, and for just a second, he hugged me back. Whatever their history, Hatter still cared for Alice. Deeply.

But now it was time for her to tell us why they'd chosen her. What did she know? What wasn't she telling us? I clenched my jaw and murmured nonsense into his ear, trying to get him back to some semblance of composure.

We were almost at the finish line, and those bastards were gonna pay for what they'd done.

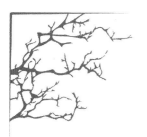

Chapter 14

Detective Elle

When we arrived back at the Crypt, Hatter was back to looking unflappable. No one but his closest associates would have been able to guess that he'd temporarily cracked as he had.

We stood just outside the door. I'd half expected agents to be swarming the place, but they weren't.

Maybe because I carried the ribbon the killer's associate had planted at the scene. But whether I'd delayed them or not, it was inevitable that all roads were going to lead the agents directly to Alice's doorstep, which meant our time together without interference was limited at best.

"You good?" I looked at him.

Handsome, but aloof, he nodded. Not that I didn't get it. I did, more than he might imagine.

"As I'll ever be. Let's just get this bloody over with."

We were about to enter a sex dungeon, a place that, twice now, had done unforeseen things to my body. I didn't want to breathe in that lust-laced air. He looked at me and, with a nod, quickly undid his cravat and handed it to me.

"It's not much, but it might help. Just enough to get us back to Alice's office."

Our fingers touched when I took it from him, and I gave him a jerky nod of thanks. I wasn't sure, though, which was worse—smelling the dungeon's pheromones or smelling Hatter's. Both seemed like a drug to my senses.

Sighing, I held the cravat to my face and breathed.

"Balls," I muttered as the powerful smell of him, dark nights and still waters, mainlined through my veins.

The bell above the door dinged when he pushed it open.

I was confronted by familiar sounds of desire and the heated whispers of lovers. Low, mood-setting music heightened the already-saturated carnality that lived and breathed in this too-tight space. I shifted on the balls of my heels, afraid to take a breath of air, remembering what this damned place had done to me once already. But thankfully, when I did, all I smelled was Hatter.

The Crypt was full of patrons tonight, bodies were spinning, dancing, laughing, and writhing. Large orgies were taking place out in the open for anyone to see.

There appeared to be a theme tonight. Everyone was dressed in white and gold only, with porcelain masks on their faces, painted with bold splashes of color. The memorable green fog curled densely around our ankles, casting everything in a sinister shadow.

Even Hatter looked more devilish, with the way the ambient light bounced off the hollows of his face, turning his features harsher, sharper, but no less sexy. He grunted, scanning the place, looking for Alice.

As Hatter looked around, I spotted a nude man, wearing only his mask and leather sandals that tied high up to his knees, break away from the group of moaning flesh parts and move unerringly in my direction. He stopped once he'd gotten my full attention.

I was a siren, and not prone to bouts of embarrassment, even less so now that I was a detective. I'd seen far worse than this in my day. The man was all gleaming brown skin with sinewy lines and rippling muscles. His chest was wide, his stomach flat but ridged tight. He stood unashamed before me, almost like one of my male counterparts would, letting me drink my fill of his smooth and graceful musculature.

He bowed, and I noticed he had dark curls cut tight to his head. He took his time coming up from the bow, but when he was once again erect, he crooked a finger, beckoning me to join him.

The hunger to do just that came alive like a tiny flame within me. Back in my day, I'd never suffered a shortage of men to meet my needs. As not only a siren, but a princess, I'd had my pick of the very best.

I sighed. I'd been a different person then. Opening my shirt, I flashed my badge, feeling just the tiniest squelch of disappointment. Shrugging, he turned and sauntered back toward his writhing group, athletic buttocks flexing with each beautiful step.

There wasn't much in the realms I liked to look at quite so much as tight male flesh.

Hatter looked at me with pinched lips.

I shrugged. "What?"

Giving his head a slight shake, as if to say, "Sirens," he turned and headed in the direction of Alice's office.

"Are you sure she'll be back there?"

"If she's not in the front, she's always in her office," he said, his normally hidden Adam's apple flexing with his words.

We walked down the long, sterile white halls, passing door after door, from behind which more carnal sounds emanated.

"Goddess above," I muttered. "I'll be happy when I don't need to come back to this place."

He snorted, keeping his eyes trained ahead. "Be around it long enough, and soon, even it fails to inspire. You can trust me on that, Detective."

The sounds of two women and one man crying out made my blood boil, and I shook my head. "Sex must be a chore for you, Constable, if this does nothing to you."

He glanced over his shoulder at me. "Screwing is just that, Detective. Screwing. Two bodies, or more, scratching an itch. Once you've tried it all, that's all it is; just an itch, and quickly forgotten. But sex with the right partner... well, there's nothing quite like it in all the realms, is there? That kind of union can drive even the best of men insane."

His words reverberated with a deep-seated knowing that made my flesh run cold. I shivered, thinking of another man and how sex had done just that to me. To us both, really.

I looked into Hatter's eyes, but they were guileless, as if he had no idea what his words had done to me. I was pretty sure he knew, though. I thought Hatter knew a lot more about me than he let on.

I clenched my jaw.

He stopped in front of Alice's door, knocked once, and then stepped to the side and gestured that I should enter first.

"Come in," she called from behind the door at the same moment I turned the knob and walked in.

Alice was at her desk. She barely spared us a glance before frowning back down at her open ledgers. I instantly noted a white bandage wrapped around her left hand.

"I'm sure you did not expect to see us again so soon," Hatter drawled in his throaty and cultured Wonderlandian accent.

She waved her hand. "Close the door behind you, and no, I thought you were someone else. Isa," she said by way of explanation, and Hatter nodded.

"Ah, she's here again?" he asked as he kicked the door shut behind us. We both took the available seats.

"Mmm." Alice, who looked less polished than normal, was tapping a pen against her open books, staring at us both with an obvious question in her eyes. "Said the pregnancy was ailing her, asked me to... well, you know," she said, glancing furtively at me before looking away and biting her full bottom lip.

She wasn't in a gown tonight. In fact, she was dressed in a sweet-looking baby-blue sweater stitched through with champagne-colored pearls that made her look young and almost innocent. Her hair was still that icy blonde, but pulled back into a high ponytail, only furthering the illusion of youthfulness.

"I'm sorry." She shook her head, worry lines scrawling over her smooth forehead. "Why are you both here? I'd assumed my part in this investigation was over. And I'm very busy. If you've come to use the rooms, be my guests. On the house." She sighed.

I cocked my head. Did she know? She looked worried enough, which got my feelers up, but she wasn't exactly acting like someone who was hiding something, or at least, not a murder.

I glanced at Hatter, wondering how to proceed. He cleared his throat and crossed his legs, but he flicked his fingers at me, a silent gesture that I should be the one to start.

I squared my shoulders and finally pulled his cravat off my nose, taking a tester sniff of the air just to be sure. It was clean. I sighed.

"Alice, I'm just going to get to the point here. We don't have much time, so I'd like you to listen," I said in a voice that conveyed the seriousness of the situation. I liked to call it "cop voice." Whenever a perp heard it, they knew we'd gotten to the real deal and generally reacted in one of two ways—either with fear or aggression.

And regardless of the reaction, I always learned a lot.

She stilled, becoming alert, eyes looking from me to Hatter and back again. "What?"

This was pure fear laced with confusion.

I frowned. "You already know why I'm in Wonderland—to investigate two homicides. You also know your ribbon was found at my crime scene."

She snorted, sounding heavily exasperated. "And I also told you that I had nothing to do with it. I cannot cross realms, or have you forgotten that, Detective? It would be impossible for me to do as you're suggesting."

Hatter scrubbed at his jaw, long fingers rubbing at his bottom lip in agitation. I frowned, getting the sense that he knew something she wasn't saying.

I shook my head. "I might have been inclined to believe you, Alice, except we've just found another one of your ribbons at our latest crime scene. Here. In Wonderland. Now, what have you got to say?"

Her jaw dropped, and a look of sheer disbelief blanketed her features. "Mad... dox?" She turned to him with a stutter. "What is this? She lies, surely."

His nostrils flared, but he shook his head. "She doesn't lie. It's laced with blood, Alice. You have to tell me why it was there."

She jumped to her feet, causing her chair to tip back on its hind legs precariously. "I didn't do that. I swear, I didn't do that!" She shook her head, the shock transforming into vehement denial. "You know who I am, Maddox. You know me."

His jaw clenched tight. She was acting exactly like someone who was innocent might. But every perp claimed to be innocent, right up until they weren't; that moment when *they* knew *we* knew, and they could no longer lie their way out of it. Some of them were such incredibly talented liars that, on occasion, even I'd been fooled, which was exceedingly rare indeed.

My brows drew into a sharp V as I continued to study her.

"Then if it wasn't you, Alice, why are your ribbons showing up all over the goddess's green earths?" I demanded, standing so that I was level to her.

She shook her head. Reaching down, she pulled open her desk drawer. Inside were what looked to be hundreds of blue ribbons with the same mystic cross-stitch pattern on them.

"Literally anyone who knows me at all knows where I store these. And when I play in the romp rooms, I routinely lose the ones in my hair. It's not a big deal, I swear it. My customers pay top dollar to lie with me. If they want a souvenir, I let them have a bloody souvenir."

I thinned my lips. "You're saying you've been framed?"

"Hells yes, that's what I'm saying," she snapped. "I lose my bloody ribbons all the time. Maddox, tell her. You know how scatterbrained I am about them. Tell her."

She gestured wildly at him, her look imploring and panicked.

He looked up at me, shoulders slumping as he quietly murmured, "It's true. I'd find the bloody things all over the place when we lived together."

My nostrils flared, and I shook my head.

Alice slammed her drawer shut. "I don't give two damns if you think I've done this. The evidence will prove otherwise. I'm innocent. When did this murder happen?"

I clamped my mouth shut, not sure I should hand her that information. But Hatter leaned forward and said, "Almost three nights hence."

I glowered at him, but he sat frozen in his seat, never taking his eyes off her. His nostrils were flared and his brows lowered. He desperately wanted to believe her, wanted to discover something to help exonerate her.

Maybe he shouldn't be involved in the case anymore. If he couldn't be unbiased, he could compromise everything. I worried my bottom lip between my teeth, wondering just what in the hells I should do. The constable had proven himself a worthy ally, so I'd ride this out just a little bit longer and hope for the best. But I'd pull the plug on his assistance if he couldn't keep his wits about him.

Shaking her head, Alice scooted around her desk and walked toward a section of wall that was jagged and rough, like it had been hewn out of quarry, with a miniature waterfall tumbling down in a hypnotic circle. Her hand passed through the rocks and water, and I recognized the handiwork of a high-level illusion spell as she gently tugged on an invisible item.

When she pulled her hand back, she held a ledger and was riffling through it quickly.

"It's in here. It's bloody in here," she mumbled, biting her full bottom lip. "I swear it to the thrice-faced witch, it's in here."

But as she turned the pages, a frantic gleam began to glitter in her bright-blue eyes. She gasped. "No. No."

Hatter stood. "What is that, Alice?"

"It's my personal ledger. In it, I make all my notations when I'm entertaining. I was with the Deedles. It's right here!" She smacked her hand down hard and hiccupped. "Except it's not. It's not, now."

Her eyes were large and shimmering with tears, her chin quivering, and I saw all I needed to see. Hatter took the ledger from her limp hands and, moving over to a bit of light from a wall sconce, traced his finger up and down the pages as he turned them, stopping only a minute later.

"A page has been ripped out," he said, glancing up.

Alice, who'd looked lost not a minute ago, ran over to him. "Let me see that." She snatched the ledger back and held the book up to her face. "Goddess dammit. What is this? Who'd do this?"

There was a knock at the door, and it opened a second later. A beautiful woman poked her head inside. She wore a large smile on her face that began to slip as she finally noticed us.

"Oh, excuse me," she whispered. "I... this is probably not a good time. I'll come back."

Alice shook her head, flipped the closed ledger at Hatter, and walked back to her desk, slumping onto it.

"Isa," she said, "I'm sorry. No, I'll give you the treatment. Give me a moment."

Isa walked into the office. She was a tall, statuesque woman, clearly of nymph heritage, with long seafoam-colored tresses that reached nearly to her ankles. She was dressed in a diaphanous gown of nearly translucent blue silk. Her eyes gleamed like clear amethyst, and her body was ripe with pending child. But even so, as all nymphs were, there was something enticing about her lush form.

Hatter dipped his head and walked over to her, taking her hand as he guided her toward the chair he'd just vacated.

"It's good to see you again, Isa. It's been a while. How is the family?"

Her pretty doe eyes widened as she chuckled and rubbed her large belly. "Growing."

Hatter chuckled in return. "I can certainly see why. Your husband is a very lucky man."

She grinned before glancing over toward me.

"This is Detective Elle from Grimm," he said by way of introduction.

She held out her hand to me, but her skin, which had gleamed like freshly cracked mother-of-pearl just a second ago, suddenly blanched, and she moaned, clutching her belly.

"Sorry, dear, sorry," Alice chirped. She yanked a glass vial out of her desk drawer and, with a snap of her fingers, manifested a cup of piping-hot amber-colored tea. Uncorking the vial, she poured a generous dollop of the clear liquid into the tea, stirred it, and pushed it toward Isa.

I cocked my head as I watched the nymph reach for it with greedy hands and take a large sip. Immediately, the color returned to her cheeks, and she sighed. "Oh goddess, the pains are terrible now."

The nymph looked up at me, smiling sweetly, but I didn't return the smile. There was something about her... I couldn't place my finger on what, though. It just felt like I'd seen her before, or I knew her somehow.

Water elementals weren't often found so deep inland. It was what made me so rare.

"Just a few more days now, and you'll feel right as rain," Alice said soothingly as she rubbed her friend's back, trying to comfort the nymph, even though I heard the tightness of her words. Her worry was palpable.

Isa grabbed Alice's hand and brought her palm to her lips, kissing it intimately as a lover would. In response, Alice leaned over and kissed Isa's plump lips, telling me all I needed to know about their relationship.

The nymph sighed, rubbing her belly.

I shoved my hands into my pockets, uneasy to my bones.

"Hatter, I think we need to ta—"

Suddenly, there was a loud commotion coming from down the hall, shouts of "Stand down," mingled with cries of alarm from those in the shoppe. Alice ran back over to the illusion wall and tapped out something that I couldn't see.

"Go, Maddox. See what it is," she said quickly. "I've turned off the pheromones. Isa, come with me. You need to get out of here now."

She wrapped an arm around her lover's waist, helping her to stand. Isa, looking panicked and worried, clutched at Alice's elbow.

"What's the matter, Alice? What's happening?"

But just as Alice was heading toward the door, it was kicked open, and at least ten BS agents, dressed all in black, with weapons out and pointed at Alice, filed into the room like a line of marching ants.

Without hesitation, I pulled my own Glock. "What in the two hells is this?" I snapped.

Hatter, who didn't walk around armed, was sidling closer to Alice and Isa, using his body as best he could to shield them.

The mood was electric, the air tense.

"Alice Blue, you're under arrest and charged with the crimes of conspiracy, murder, and treason. You have the right to remain silent." The lead agent, who I did not recognize, rambled on in a monotone. "You have the right to council. If you cannot afford council, one will be provided to—"

"Like bloody hells!" thundered Hatter. His hands were balled into tight fists, and his spine taut with anger. "What evidence have you?"

He and I knew damned well they didn't have the ribbon because it was currently burning a hole in my pocket.

"You cannot just waltz in here and—"

"Oh, but I can." That voice, deep and sinister, made my skin crawl and my nails lengthen into claws.

"Crowley," I growled just as the Big Bad himself pushed through the men, wearing a smirk as he glanced at us.

"I should have known you'd be here, Detective. Thought I said you were off the case. You know I could have you both arrested for obstruction—"

"We were just here visiting Hatter's ex." I shrugged, still aiming my weapon dead at his chest. So long as the men had their weapons up, there was no way in two hells I was lowering mine. "No crime against that, as far as I've heard." I smiled venomously.

Taking off his mirrored sunglasses, he stared at me for several long heartbeats. He was still wearing that pompous smirk, but his eyes burned with fury. He wanted to book us. That I could see. But thanks to Hatter's connection to Alice, there wasn't a damned thing he could do to us.

"I want to see the order," Hatter demanded, holding out his hand imperiously.

"Lower your weapons," Crowley said with a weary sigh.

As one, the BS agents lowered their guns, forcing me to finally lower mine. But I felt the prickling of my skin and knew that my siren's markings were glowing bright. Adrenaline made me look like a walking glowworm. I gritted my teeth.

Reaching into his vest, Crowley pulled out a folded sheet of paper and passed it over to Hatter, who snatched it up and quickly began scanning its contents. As he did so, his face looked more and more crestfallen.

"What the bloody hells is this?" he snapped and waved the paper.

"It's an arrest warrant, as you can see, Constable." Crowley's smirk was arrogant. I would have loved to kick the smug prick in the jewels, just once.

"On superficial evidence at best. Hearsay. Complete and utter tittle tattle. This won't hold up in court."

"Not my concern." Crowley shrugged and pointed to the agent nearest him. "Place her in cuffs, Agent."

Hatter stood still, hands trembling, as the agents marched past him, unable to do a thing to stop them.

"Maddox?" Alice said with a quiver in her voice. "Maddox!" Her voice rose in pitch when the first agent reached for her elbow. "I didn't do this! Unhand me at once!" Alice screamed. "Maddox? Maddox!" she screamed again as they manhandled her arms behind her back.

"Please, Alice," I managed to say, "don't fight this. Relax. Right now, you must relax." I holstered my weapon, feeling as impotent as a baby and wishing like the two hells that I could stop this. But the order had been signed with the royal crest. There wasn't a damned thing either Hatter or I could do.

Isa gasped, trembling like a leaf, as she and the rest of us watched Alice get handcuffed with a pair of irons dipped in dragon's tears. The steam and sizzle of burning flesh wafted under our noses, making me wince in sympathy.

Alice jerked, but she'd stopped fighting them. One of the agents placed his hand on the center of her back.

"Move," he ordered.

"Eat balls and die, you fecking bastard."

Raising a hand, he slapped her right cheek so hard that the dull snap of flesh on flesh was a gruesome sound.

Hatter roared, dropping the order as he reached for the agent. "You bloody, goddessdamned—"

But I shoved him back, getting between them, even as I glared at Crowley. "Check your men, Agent, or I swear to the goddess, I'll unleash a hell the likes of which you've never known before."

And I let my siren glow burn, let them witness the monster just barely checked beneath the façade, and I exposed teeth that looked more like fangs.

Crowley growled, the sound deep and animalistic in the back of his throat. His own skin bristled, growing dark with the shadow of shifter fur ready to break through.

I shook my head. "You know the bloody rules, you arrogant prick. I dare you. I just bloody dare you." My voice was a terrible, sonorous thing that made the men closest to me, even the constable, moan as they swayed my way.

Crowley's nostrils flared, and his pupils were dark pinpricks. I'd split his head open, and he damn well knew it.

After a tense second, he snapped. "No touching. Move out, men."

Then, without looking back at us, he marched from the room. The agent that had smacked Alice shoved her from behind. She whimpered, and I said in a silky, deadly drawl, "If I find even a hair out of place on her pretty head, you won't live to see another sunrise, Agent."

I knew I was threatening an agent of the crown, but I wasn't just a simple Detective of Grimm. I had political connections the plebs could only dream of. I was as untouchable as he was, and he knew it.

I smirked, blowing him an air kiss. He growled but didn't touch her again. Instead he barked, "Move."

Alice started walking, and Hatter called out to her, "We'll make this right, Alice. I swear it."

She glanced at him, her cheek already blossoming with scarlet. "The tapes, Maddox. Find the tapes." Then she was gone.

Hatter and I stood there, both of us silent for a moment. Isa, who'd been a non-factor the entire time, didn't glance at either of us as she hugged her arms to her belly and moved with a quickness I'd not expected from one so heavily pregnant.

Hatter swallowed.

"We will fix this, Maddox," I promised him. "Now, where are those bloody tapes she's talking about?"

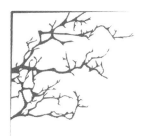

Chapter 15

Constable Maddox

They'd framed her, and it was bloody galling that even taking the ribbon hadn't been enough to stop the circus that had become their case.

But worse was that, not only had they framed Alice, but her trial was set to happen in less than two hours. Never in his life had he witnessed anything move with the quickness that this had.

He'd had no choice but to close the Crypt. He and the detective had taken all the tapes back to the station. They'd already gone through three hours of mind-numbing sex upon sex upon sex.

Neither of them spoke as they combed the grainy images for anything that would prove Alice had been telling him the truth.

That particular night had been a busy one, and Alice had been playing hostess through it all. His eyes were growing blurry from doing nothing but staring. He'd not slept in days, and the stress of this sudden arrest was too damn bloody much for him.

In the next room, he heard Harry's movements. The sun was just starting to rise.

"You need to sleep," Elle said softly, glancing at him with worried frown lines.

He looked at her, noting the pallor of her skin. What she'd done at the Crypt hadn't gone unnoticed by him. He blinked, knuckling the sleep-deprivation tears from his eyes. They burned like the bloody devil, and anytime he blinked, it felt like they were full of sand and grit.

He shook his head. "They're going to bloody nail her for a crime she didn't commit."

She sighed. "Maddox, have you stopped to think that maybe Alice—"

"No!" he barked.

At her startled look, he shook his head softer.

"Goddess, Elle. No. She didn't. She... she just didn't. I know her. Alice isn't capable of murder. She's ruthless and even cruel sometimes, but she's not a murderer. You saw her. What does your gut tell you?"

He held his breath, waiting, not sure what he was hoping for, only knowing that he needed to have Elle on his side for this one. He needed her to believe in him.

Sighing, she leaned her head back and stared up at the ceiling. "We've been going over these tapes for hours. They've pushed the hearing up so fast that it's made me dizzy. But Alice's ribbons have been found in two realms. That's a near impossibility, unless of course..."

He clenched his jaw and steepled his fingers.

"Alice has made her share of enemies. It goes with the territory, I suppose. There are many people with a vendetta against her."

"Such as?"

He flicked a glance back at the screens, keenly disappointed that all there was to see was bodies on bodies on bodies. The Deedles were rich bastards who could afford almost anything this realm had to offer. Balding and morbidly obese, the both of them, they were impossible to miss.

"Jilted lovers. Angry wives. Husbands. Partners. You name it. Discretion is the name of the game in this business, but sometimes a client's partner finds out, and they like to make Alice's life hell. She's been sued I don't know how many times. Threatened. Once, our house was even set on fire."

An image of his daughter flitted through his mind, and he squeezed his eyes shut as his throat spasmed with heat.

Maddox had to swallow several times before he trusted himself to speak.

"And there's been worse."

Elle sighed deeply, looking at the screen with a tight frown. "I'd imagine a business such as hers would attract a particular set of clients. I'll grant you that some of them might even have the means of traveling the realms. But this is a fine kettle of fish, and I'm not sure how we can save her from the guillotine. Whoever's behind this wants the case closed, and they want it closed now, to hells with who gets burned in the end."

He nodded. "If we can just find proof that she was where she said she was, then maybe—"

"Yes." She leaned forward and grabbed his hands. "But that only proves her innocence in your murder. Not in mine. No doubt the powers that be have found just enough to tie her to those as well. And as cold as my case is, it would be a miracle if I could get her off the hook."

Her hands were soft and silky, like the petal of a rose, and he turned their joined hands over, heart hammering violently in his chest.

He was exhausted. He was bloody tired of feeling like everything was spinning out of control. He needed a release. He needed... her.

But Alice's panicked eyes filled his thoughts, and he yanked his hands back, feeling scalded by Elle's touch.

She frowned, but set her hands on her knees, thinking, no doubt, that he didn't want her when he wanted her too damned much.

With a disgusted sigh, she stood up and stretched. "Look, I can't function this way. I need at least a swim to take the edge off. If we can't find the Deedles on the tapes, then at the very least, we can pay them a visit, no?"

He looked up at her.

"They're not always on the right side of the law, and if they suspect that they could hang for this, they'd let Alice burn before they told us the truth. We need to prove they were there, or it's done," Hatter said.

Weariness was etched into every line of her face. He wanted to apologize, but he didn't.

The door to Harry's room opened.

"Harry," Elle called.

A second later, the deputy popped his head into the office.

"Aye, Detective?"

"You've got fresh eyes," she said and pointed to the screen. "Watch the tapes, please, and tell us if you happen to spot Alice and the Deedles together."

"Aye, sounds good. Sorry I am 'bout Alice, Constable," he said with a sad glance at Hatter.

He shrugged, not knowing what in the two hells to say.

"You." Elle pointed at Hatter with a crooked finger. "Are going to bed. Even an hour of rest will do you good."

"I don't need—"

She glowered, and though her skin didn't glow with the siren's lure, and her eyes were the clear blue of lucidity and not madness, he caught a glimpse of the powerful woman she was.

"You'll get some bloody sleep, or I'll make you. You want to help Alice, then you'll get some damned rest. That's an order."

Technically, she outranked him. He stood, bristling, hands fisting open and shut.

But her peaked brows and no-nonsense demeanor let him know, in no uncertain terms, that this wasn't a battle he'd win.

"Dammit all to the twin hells!" he snapped, then pivoted on his feet and marched to his room, slamming the door behind him with a jarring rattle.

Detective Elle

I DIDN'T TAKE ANY OF what he'd done since Alice's arrest personally. If that had been Hook and not Alice, I'm sure I'd have been far worse. I swam the length of the miles-long fairy river in short, quick bursts of my flukes, powering through the water as I worked out the particulars in my head.

My gut told me Alice was innocent.

But my gut had lied to me before, and I'd paid dearly for it. I couldn't risk being wrong this time. Everything hinged on solving this case in less than twenty-four hours. It seemed impossible.

But here in Wonderland, it was easy to believe in the impossible, especially when I had a partner who could see the past and even sometimes, the future.

I paused, my head breaking the surface as I looked back at where Hatter's room would be. Was there some way, *any way*, to activate the sight and make him see exactly what we needed? Maybe the key to solving all of this was his madness.

Without thinking, I shoved from the water, transforming just before my feet hit land. I didn't bother with my pants, but I snatched up the shirt and slipped it on, breathing easier when I felt the press of my waters upon my flesh.

I jogged down the garden path, glancing ahead toward the office. Harry was slouched in his seat, eating chocolate truffles, but dutifully watching. He might not be the world's best detective, but the deputy had his uses.

Moving toward Hatter's clock-face door, I didn't bother knocking. Just pushed it open.

There he was, in the center of the large bed, clothes still on, eyes closed, and mouth open, gone to the world. But even in sleep, his brows were pinched, the furrows of worry evident in every line.

He'd been without sleep far too long, and I hated to wake him. I didn't suffer as Hatter did, mainly because swimming was almost as good as sleep for me. I wasn't completely rested, but I was alert.

The room was long with shadows, and moonlight spilled softly through its windowless space. This wasn't natural moonlight. It was already morning outside the cottage. But nothing had to make much sense in Wonderland.

Hatter had kicked off his shoes and removed his cravat. His hair was a dark, shadowy spill over his olive-toned skin.

My fingers curled. I couldn't solve this case without him, but I'd never seen him so unguarded before, either. I should go, give him an opportunity to catch whatever rest he could while we still had a few minutes to burn, but my feet were rooted to the floor. I couldn't seem to move.

Wetting my lips, I glanced over my shoulder, eyeing the door and debating internally with myself. But then I heard a small puff of air, and once again, I was staring down at him, confused by my own emotions and unsure why I was even still there. Sure, I couldn't just traipse through Wonderland alone, but at the moment, I could be in the office with Harry. I could still be doing something.

His chest rose and fell in steady intervals. He had to be tired to be so unaware of my presence. I saw the way Hatter looked at things when we were together. He was always wary, cautious, and exceedingly aware of his surroundings. I highly doubted that he was normally this relaxed. I really, really should go.

I glanced at the end table beside his bed and noticed an empty bottle of brandy. I remembered that bottle and thought it had been full. How much of the stuff had he drunk? And why? What demons had plagued him to make him resort to a drugged sleep?

I suspected it had something to do with Alice, more specifically, with what had happened to her tonight. It was funny that, in all the years I'd worked with Ichabod, I'd never really wondered about his personal life. But I wondered about Hatter's far more than I should.

I frowned. This job was hard, and regardless of which realm we detectives hailed from, over time, we each developed our own vices to deal with the stressors of the occupation. It was just that some of our vices were worse for us than others. Some of them could actually kill us quicker than the job could.

Biting the inside of my cheek as my pulse thumped unsteadily in my chest, I leaned back on my heels, determined this time to leave him to his rest.

But that was when the board beneath my foot squealed in loud protest. Wincing and knowing I'd woken him up for sure, I murmured an apology. Sure enough, his eyes fluttered open just a second later, and I felt like a bloody fool.

"Elle?" he asked in a rasping voice, looking at me in confusion, eyes slightly glazed over with sleep.

I shook my head. "Sorry. Sorry."

He waved off my words and shimmied up to a sitting position, leaning against the headboard as he scrubbed a hand down his face. He had a full six o' clock shadow.

"I slept." He sounded shocked by that. "Did Harry find—"

"No," I whispered. Glancing over my shoulder, I tiptoed in, gently closing the door behind me. "No, I just..." I shrugged, feeling a little stupid. "I just had a thought, was all. But you know what, you need sleep, and I really should not have come in like this. It was rude and—"

Nocking his leg, he wrapped an arm around it and gestured for me to come to him. "No, come here. Sit. Tell me what you were thinking."

His collar was open, exposing the hollow of his throat. He looked disheveled and rumpled and far sexier than I'd ever seen him. This wasn't an uptight constable staring back at me, but a man. My stomach feathered with nerves, and I realized I'd made a colossal mistake in coming here.

The silence between us was palpable.

"Detective," he grumped, "you've woken me. The least you can do is tell me why." He cleared his throat loudly.

"No, you're right. I just... well, I got to thinking about what you said back in the office, and I agree with you. Alice didn't do this. It makes no sense. She had no reason to kill my folk, and the little I know of your Jane Doe, I'd say the same would apply there too. But she is connected. She absolutely is."

His brows dipped, and his lips pursed. He didn't look pleased, and I couldn't say I blamed him.

Walking over to the edge of his bed, I took a seat and crossed my legs at the ankles in front of me.

His eyes raked like hot coals down their naked lengths, making my skin feel tight and hot. My stomach was flooded with thousands of razor-tipped butterfly wings. The way he looked at me sometimes... goddess, it was enough to make me spontaneously combust.

"Go on," he drawled before standing up and stretching his long, lean body, like a cat leisurely waking up from a nap.

As he stretched his arms above his head, the sleeves rolled down just a bit, exposing the tattoos. Those mysterious markings had done things for Cheshire that I now wanted to experience for myself. I wet my lips.

He padded on sock feet to the adjacent wall, which suddenly opened wide like stage curtains sliding back, revealing a clamshell stand with a basin of water in it that literally stood inside a strangely beguiling garden of dancing bug lights and shrubbery. As far as the eye could see, it was a garden of meticulously maintained topiaries, spread out like an emerald sea of green before me. They were all strange, wondrous shapes. A queen with a crown of red thorns twisted upon her head. A girl child holding a bottle. Birds dressed in suits and walking upright. Strange, but picturesque too.

I wondered if he made them in his spare time. Whoever made them took great care with their creations. Wonderland was a peculiar and dizzying place. It was no wonder everyone who lived here had a touch of the madness to them.

Flying all around were glow-in-the-dark butterflies with electric wings of blue and pink. There were even lightning bugs discharging miniature but brilliant volts as they danced through the navy midnight sky.

I watched Hatter splash some water from the basin on his face and wondered why he no longer seemed as enchanted and mesmerized by Wonderland as I was. Did there come a point where the madness simply became commonplace? I couldn't imagine ever viewing Wonderland as anything but bizarre, but he was brushing his teeth and taking care of his ablutions like he wasn't standing inside a room inside an outdoor garden with unusual flying beasties winging all around him.

Drying his face with a hand towel that seemed to have appeared from nowhere, he eyed me. The silence between us was electric and heavy, and I felt his look like a brand. I sensed he wanted me to say something or do something. I'd been the one to come in here, after all, seeking an audience.

But I was tongue-tied.

I was never tongue-tied. I thinned my lips.

After a second, when I failed to speak, he sighed. Maybe I was tired, but all I could seem to focus on was the shape of his broad and nicely toned body, the smell of the air right after a rain, and the soft lulling song of crickets. When I'd spent the night here before, under the White Knight's charge, I'd never imagined the wonders that waited on the other side of these sterile white walls.

"Detective?" Hatter asked brusquely as he folded the towel and laid it back on the basin.

I jerked, shaking my head slowly. What the hells? I'd slept with Ich. That should have been enough to see me through this investigation until I got home. I sighed a trembly breath.

"Right. Um, where was I?"

He grinned as he reached for a razor and shaving cream. "She's connected. Seems I'm not the only one that needs rest, Detective."

I rolled my eyes but didn't give him the satisfaction of answering. "She is. Her ribbons were there."

"Planted," he muttered even as he brushed the cream onto his face.

I frowned, not sure I wanted to see him remove the shadow of the beard. It gave him a rugged look I shockingly found appealing.

"Likely," I murmured.

Leaning over the sink, he maneuvered the blade deftly over the sharp angles of his face. His strokes were smooth and sure, and in next to no time, he was clean-shaven once again. Rinsing off the razor, he set it down on the sink. Taking up the hand towel once more, he patted his face dry.

"Definitely. What's your point, Elle?"

My toes tingled whenever he called me by name. Hatter wasn't at all like the detectives of my realm. There was a level of intimacy and familiarity that existed between us and had almost since our first meeting. I understood that things worked differently in other realms, but I'd never felt this ease with one of my peers before.

He moved like a sleek panther back toward me, leaning down on one leg on the mattress as he curled the other beneath him and took a seat.

It would be so easy to imagine that we were lovers in such an intimate setting. I fanned my fingers open on his rumpled coverlet. The air smelled of brandy and of him.

I forced myself to think of the case. "My point is that I think Alice knows the killer. And I think she knows him or her well enough that they could easily get their hands on her ribbon stash. Who is Isa?"

He wrinkled his nose, shaking my words off as nonsense. "I've known Isa for years."

The corners of his eyes crinkled as they took on a faraway look. He'd just thought of something, I was sure of it. So I waited for him to tell me more, if he wanted to. His eyes darted from his lap to mine and then back again, his reluctance to speak obvious.

I raised a brow, and he stared at me unflinchingly before his lips twisted and he leaned his head back with a weary sigh.

"Fine. When Alice and I were together, she required... well, to put it succinctly, more than I could give her." He shrugged. "I had no problem with it. I was busy with my duties, and there were times when I sought to release my needs elsewhere too. We had an understanding, and it worked for us. Isa was one of those understandings."

I nodded. "That's very forward thinking of you. Most human males aren't exactly keen on sharing their partner."

He grinned. "Sexuality isn't black and white to me. More than that, sex is simply one part of a relationship. The real bond lies in what happens beyond the sheets. Alice and I were strong in that department. Men and women came and went, but Isa was a constant, and over time, she and I developed our own relationship, mostly out of convenience. But she's harmless and cares deeply for Alice. On that, I'd stake my life. When I... left..." He swallowed, like the words were hard to say. "Isa remained and has been a true companion and friend to Alice, and for that, I'm grateful."

"I don't mean to pry"—he grinned, and I knew exactly what he was thinking—"but what do you know of Isa, really?"

He shrugged. "She's a nymph."

"That much I gathered. Judging by her coloration, I'd say her genus was water."

He grinned. "Correct. Though, she's landlocked now and has been for a great many years. She's married to a pan."

"Nymphs and satyrs—not exactly an uncommon pairing. And her partner, does he know of you?"

Hatter held up his hands. "You've no reason to worry on that account. Alice and I were always discerning. We would never engage in an affair, ever, unless our partners were willing. If they were mated, their partners not only knew but had to agree to our arrangement. If they didn't, if there was even the slightest whiff of hesitation, that was as far as we'd take things. It kept matters less complicated that way."

I grinned. "You are just full of surprises, Constable. I'd never have taken you for the type, to be honest."

"What's that?"

I shrugged. "The sharing type. Men of my realm, well... our sexuality is very fluid both ways, so to me, none of what you say is all that scandalous. But I've found few humans who feel the same. And yet you seem to have found a happy stable of lovers."

He glanced to his left, staring at the water basin. "Maybe I shouldn't say this, but you give me far too much credit. Alice meant a lot to me. Beneath the silks and the trappings of lust, she has a good heart. She was also the mother of my child."

The muscle in his jaw twitched as he grew silent, and I twisted my lips, wishing I'd not brought this up.

Painting on a fake smile, he turned to me and shrugged. "And for that, at least, I will always fight for her. Our history matters to me, whether we're together or not. But I had my own secrets. Our relationship fractured for many reasons. She fought for us, but there are some things you just can't fight, no matter how hard you wish to."

Plucking at the rumpled sheet with my nails, I shook my head. "Well, if not Isa. Then someone. Somebody. Somewhere. Alice is tied to the killer."

"Yes, but how? And the more I think about it, how in the two hells is she tied to Goose? Why did they even attempt to plant her ribbon in that garden?"

I shook my head. "I thought you'd know that."

He shrugged. "Alice and I haven't been together in years, so it's possible that she and Goose have knowledge of one another. If I'd been thinking more clearly, I might have asked her about the connection. I can't place them together, and that's problematic for me. Why Goose?"

"Hmm." I sniffed. It was a problem only insofar as linking motive to the crime, but a court didn't need to have motive to convict. The connection was obviously there for the perp to have planted Alice's ribbons. Of that, I was certain.

"To that, I have no answer. But I'm sure that if we had more time to dig, we could find the connection somehow." I shrugged, and he propped his chin up with his hand. "But that's not why I've come."

He cocked his head and frowned in question.

"I was hoping there might be a way to activate your sight. I don't know. Is there?" I looked at him hopefully.

His lips thinned.

"I saw you do it with Cheshire. I mean, that's what it looked like to me."

Sighing deeply, he riffled his fingers through his hair. "Goddess, Elle."

The way he said my name, with such an empty and forlorn sound, made me shiver. I could hear his pain and loneliness.

He held himself aloof from others, buttoned up and fastidious. But inside, he was a raging, ravenous animal. I could see it. I could sense it, that bristling serpent inside of him that he kept so tightly in-check but that sometimes escaped with fangs and claws and snapping teeth, just as it had with Crowley earlier.

"What I showed Cheshire was nothing more than a vision I'd seen before. That was it. It was nothing I could conjure up on my own. Sorry."

I bit the inside of my cheek, telling myself not to ask, but damning myself ten types of a fool because I knew I would. "And what did you show him? What wasn't he supposed to see?"

Hatter tensed, and his eyes began to burn both green and blue. I wet my lips, my own dark lure responding to the rise of his power.

"Sometimes," he chewed out, "I can't control what spills through. It's why I don't like to channel my markings that way. Sometimes others see too much."

I nodded, and hopped to my knees, knowing I was playing with fire, but not scared enough to stop. If there was even the remotest possibility that we could solve both our cases and absolve Alice of any wrongdoing, we had to try.

"Have you seen me before, Maddox?" I asked, suspecting I already knew the answer.

His nostrils flared, but he said nothing.

My insides quivered.

"Because maybe, if you have, you can show me, and then maybe something else might just spill through." I held my breath, tense and expecting him to deny me but hoping he wouldn't.

Shock rolled through me when he tipped his head back and laughed. The sound was dark and heavy and full of terrible, terrible pain.

But still he said nothing.

I pressed my flattened palm to my throat.

His breathing inched up, growing deeper, heavier.

I felt breathless myself. Jittery, like I couldn't catch a proper breath.

Nervous, because he still wasn't speaking, I said, "It's not like we can do anything else right now. It's worth trying, right?"

He scowled, body bristling all over. The air between us was as taut as a strained bowstring. But he was slowly moving toward me. For just a second, I felt not like the predator, but the prey.

It was how he looked at me, his eyes burning with madness and magick, his strong body so controlled, so exacting.

"Leave my room, Detective. This is the only warning you'll get." He said it softly, but with gritted urgency.

"And if I don't?" I breathed, feeling my skin begin to tingle and burn with the soft glow of my rising lure.

The devil's light filled his eyes. "Don't play coy. It's not becoming."

I grinned. "Fine. I won't. I want you, dammit. You've driven me bloody mad, and I'm not used to this. I don't like this. I haven't felt like this since..."

I trailed off, squeezing my eyes shut, fighting that desperate pull to slide into my own darkness.

"Then you decide, once and for all," he said. He grabbed my hands and laid them on his chest.

I sucked in a sharp breath, feeling the chained strength of him, like a dragon on a leash. I could leave, walk away before I got burned. Or...

I grinned, and just like that, it was over for me.

My hands were frantic as I tore at his shirt, throwing the buttons off in a thousand different directions. When I shoved his shirt back, his skin was gleaming, his markings burning both white and red. The demon and the angel glowed under my touch.

His hands were just as frantic on me. He reached for my shirt, but I had to shove his hands away. "Don't. I can't do without it."

Sucking in a sharp growl, he bunched the fabric in his fist and shoved it up just enough to reveal the underside of my breasts. His mouth was on me, sucking, teasing. His hands fondled my sensitive nipples.

I keened, the sound piercing and almost too painful for a human. But his growls only grew deeper, like it didn't bother him, but rather, excited him.

I wasn't sure when it had happened, but suddenly I was pinned beneath him, his big body cradled between my arms and legs as he rubbed his clothed and heavy center on my aching wetness. Moaning, I arched my spine and ran my hands down his flesh. Our scents grew fuller and deeper in the stillness of the room.

He bit down hard on the vein at the side of my neck, so damn hard that I nearly came off the bed. But it was wonderful too. The pain spiraled into something bigger, greater, better.

"Gah," I moaned, and even as I latched my teeth on to his bottom lip, I shoved that shirt off him. He helped me, wiggling madly to kick off not only his shirt, but his pants too. He was covered in tattoos all over, broad swirling designs that were both intricate and delicate. Butterflies, so lifelike in their design, looked to be taking flight each time he moved.

I gasped when I felt his naked length press against my inner thigh. "Now, now, now," I moaned incoherently.

"You want me?" He growled low, teasing my center with just the tip of his rigid thickness.

"Goddess." I knocked my head back against the pillow, squeezing my eyes shut so hard I saw stars.

"Tell me!" he demanded with a vicious-sounding bark to his words.

When I opened my eyes, I saw not a man, but a devil moving over me. My heart leapt in its cage.

"Yes. Yes!"

Slowly, he entered me, just the once, running his exquisite cock deep into my aching center. I groaned and cried out as more and more of my lure glowed from deep within me.

Sirens could kill. But we could also give life, a gift rarely given because we did not usually care enough to bother.

As I glowed, he began to make noises, moans that rolled and rolled like an endless wave upon a shore.

"Say my name. Say it, Elle. Not Constable. Not Hatter. Say—"

"Maddox!" I cried, and he thrust in so deep that he hit the very back of my womb and made me scream from the pain and pleasure of it. Our joining was quick, fiery, and tempestuous, all madness and fury.

He took my hands, using his strength to pin them above my head as he owned me. But I wasn't a simple human woman. My strength was as fierce as his. Even more so.

With a grin, I hooked my leg around him and reversed our positions, pinning his arms above his head. He grunted in surprise, but then his mouth tipped into a feral grin, and he undulated as I rode him harder and harder and harder.

He moved like he wanted to take back the dominant position, but I wasn't giving it up. I latched on to his wrists, curving my fingers around his thick forearms. The tip of my pinky landed on the burning red glow of his demon, and suddenly, I was no longer in that bed with him.

I was no longer smelling us.

No longer in that room.

I was on a beach. My beach. The moon was full and dancing over the waves. And there I was as I'd once been—a mad siren, screaming obscenely at it, vowing pain and torture and retribution for what had been done to me. I was slashing at my wrists with my claws as I bled black into the waters, wanting to kill and wanting to die.

I went cold all over. I was seeing the night of Hook's death, the night I'd very nearly lost my way and had temporarily forgotten all I'd learned about who I was.

I'd never shared this story with anyone save for Bo. It was why I'd been sent to Neverland. It was the reason for my temporary exile.

I'd gone mad. Completely. Absolutely.

And she'd had only two choices—banish me to seek out help, or terminate me.

I screamed as every terrible, horrible memory came lurching up like hot vomit. The yawning chasm of betrayal and desolation. The emptiness of losing the only thing I'd ever truly cared about.

It all came back in a heavy rush. The madness that'd driven me out to the exact spot where Hook had been the night we'd first met. The love that had suddenly turned into a nightmare of never-ending blood and gore and death and curses.

But soon, the scene shifted, and I wasn't on a beach, but standing outside of a ruined, blackened building with great curls of fire still belching out of its desiccated form. Standing over the body of a small child, burned over every inch of its perfect little body. Only its hair remained untouched, and it was a beautiful snow white.

Again, I screamed and screamed and screamed. The pain so deep, so all-consuming that I felt like I died as my voice flew out of my mouth, deep and raw. I dropped to my knees, reaching for the little butterfly.

"Butterfly. My little butterfly," I drawled in a guttural voice that wasn't my own. It was deep and masculine. I saw myself in a puddle of water, and it wasn't my eyes that I saw reflected back at me, but one burning blue and one burning green. There were wails and screams, feminine ones.

Heart thundering in my chest, I turned to my right and saw Alice, dressed in blue, staring down at the figure at my feet with horror, the worst sounds imaginable pouring from her lips.

Hate burned in her eyes when she looked on me.

"It's your fault! It's all your fault! You bloody bastard! I told you to hide it. I told you to keep her safe!"

"My love," I croaked, reaching for her, fingers outstretched, needing someone to share the burden of this all-consuming pain. But she would not come to me. She would not come...

Everything shifted again, and I saw myself stabbing. Stabbing. Stabbing a body with a pair of lethal silver cutting shears until blood spewed from the woman's mouth as she fought me off. She was dressed in a blue day dress, with pins in her hair and a blue ribbon clutched tight in her fists. Chilling words in the echoes of a man's voice escaped my lips. "I told ye to shut up, Mary. I told ye. It's all yer fault. All yer fault..." I sobbed as I stabbed...

When I blinked, I was me again, back in that room, not moving, barely breathing, and cold all over.

I looked up at Hatter. He looked as shocked as I felt. Shaking his head softly, his fingers spasmed as he reached for me then paused and pulled his hand back. The second vision had been him, reaching for Alice. She'd not taken his hand, and now I couldn't take his hand either.

Hatter was on his knees, his tattoos no longer glowing bright, and there was a bottomless pool of pain reflected in his dull blue and green eyes.

He shook his head, worry etched on his face.

Pain sliced through my heart as I felt it all over again. The child. My pain. The murder.

I swallowed, eyeing him warily, feeling betrayed and furious but mostly sorrowful. My eyes brimmed with tears, and my voice cracked as I said, "Your Jane Doe was named Mary, and the killer knew her."

The door was flung open, and Harry came racing in.

I jumped, scrabbling off the bed, holding my shirt to my chest in a protective stance, feeling numb and startled all at the same time.

"I founds it. I did it. I done saw'd her. I saw Alice with them Deedles. Tape was blanked out after tha', but thems didn't scrub it all off. I founds them! I'd bet me soul on it. C'mon," he cried then raced back out the door, so drunk on his findings that he'd not sensed the tension between Hatter and I.

"Elle, I'm—" Hatter started, but I had suddenly found my ability to move again and stalked toward the door.

"Don't. Just don't," I said, too raw to listen to another word, so full of pain and sorrow and heartache that I felt I might burst from it if he so much as spoke another word to me.

"As you wish," I heard him mumble, but I couldn't look back. I just couldn't look back.

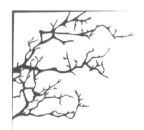

Chapter 16

Constable Maddox

S he wouldn't talk to him.

But they had a case to finish, and now wasn't the time. Now wasn't the time for any of it.

After hastily dressing, he made his way to the office, where they awaited him. His cravat was askew and his buttons only half done, and he didn't have any shoes on—those he carried in his hand. He sat in the only vacant chair as Harry rewound the tape and loudly proclaimed, "Ye's gots ta focus, but there's no denying them big bastards nor Alice."

Harry glanced quickly at them, his large buckteeth looking prodigiously prominent as he grinned with pride. Swallowing hard, Hatter nodded at Harry, giving his deputy whatever dregs of encouragement he still had left to give.

Hatter slipped on his shoes and made himself presentable as he waited.

Figures walked backward on the screen as the tape reset. Harry pressed Play again, and the tiny, grainy figures once more moved forward. Maddox scanned the dimly lit club. There was a strobing light pattern that made things difficult to see, but after half a second, he saw Alice, dressed in black silk and knee-high boots, holding a crop in her leather-clad hands and smiling broadly as two massively rotund men in dark suits nodded at her in greeting.

Then there was nothing but snow on the screen. The tapes had been scrubbed clean. They'd tried to hide the truth, but whoever had done it hadn't done a good enough job.

Alice had been with the Deedles that night, and this was proof that she'd not lied. The question was how long had she been with them? Long enough to prevent her from committing Mary's murder? Hatter's gut said yes, but they needed a hells of a lot more evidence to go on than merely his gut.

He looked at Elle to gage her reaction. She sat stiff as a board on the seat beside him, not looking at him. But he knew she was aware of him by the tense lines of her body and the way she clutched at the armrests with nails that looked more like claws. Her face was an unreadable, beautiful mask. He realized she wasn't fully dressed. Her long, lean legs were naked and crossed, the top one bouncing rhythmically.

Her nails dug into the leather armrests, leaving crescent-shaped markings behind.

"Elle?" he asked.

She whirled on him, sea-colored eyes flaring with fury, before she composed herself and said in a monotone, "Give me five minutes to dress. We have to speak with the Deedles."

Then she was gone, and he sat there, looking after her.

"Don't know what da hells ye did to that chit, but I'd wear ear plugs were I you, Constable. Just to be on the safe side."

Thinning his lips, he turned to his deputy and nodded. "I don't suppose you have any on you?"

"As a matter of course, I do," he grinned.

Detective Elle

I COULD BARELY LOOK at him. In fact, I didn't even want to be in the same sphere as him, breathing the same air. I wanted to leave, to return to Grimm and never see him again. Never again have to remember what it was that he'd shown me.

He'd told me he couldn't always control what came out of him, and I wished like hells I'd listened. I wished I'd not seen any of that.

I had my hands balled into fists and shoved deep into my pants pockets. I said not a word as we traveled through the between.

I'd not asked the constable where we were headed. I was loath to admit that he was still necessary for me to solve this case. I had to go on trusting that he'd do his job.

But I wasn't sure I could ever trust him again.

I knew my reaction was over the top and ridiculous. I knew it. Up until a few days ago, he'd not known who I was. How could it possibly be his fault that he'd seen what he'd seen. I got that. But the shame of what he knew and had deliberately kept hidden from me made me want to hate him because he'd seen me at my very lowest, seen me on the brink of complete and total insanity.

Just when I thought I couldn't hate him anymore, I recalled what he'd seen—the body of a broken, shattered little beauty—and my eyes burned with tears I could not shed.

It didn't take a genius to figure out who she'd been. The agony on Alice's face, the brokenness in Hatter's own... That had been their daughter, Mariposa.

I shuddered, wishing I could scrub that memory clean, wishing I'd never seen it.

"At some point, you'll have to talk with me," Hatter said, voice low and full of grit.

My nostrils flared. I squeezed my eyes shut, trying like the two hells to scrub that image from out of my head, trying to forget the smell of charred flesh and the wails of a shattered heart.

I wanted to hate him.

But all I felt was pity. And I wasn't sure which was worse.

"I'll speak to you about the case, and only the case. We have less than—"

"Elle." He stepped forward, reaching out a hand toward me.

But I hissed and jumped back as though scalded. "Don't you bloody dare, you hear me! Don't you touch me. Don't you dare."

His face crumpled, his eyes tightened, and his jaw set into a hard line of emotions I refused to name. I would not feel bad for how I felt. I refused. He'd lied to me. This was on him, not me.

My body trembled as I wrapped my arms around myself, staving off the panic as best I could. He'd *seen* me. Seen me as a monster. As a maniac. And I'd seen him. Hate and pity and pain—it was all there, and it hurt too much at the moment. Too damned much.

"As you wish, Detective," he said in that smooth urbane drawl of his, and I hated that my heart squeezed with regret. Hated that I cared so much. I didn't know him. What I'd seen was proof of that. He'd held all the cards, and I'd held none. He'd had me at a disadvantage, and though rationally I understood what he'd seen wasn't a topic of conversation easily broached between strangers, I hated him with an irrational passion that burned like ten thousand suns for knowing the depths of my pain.

I clipped a hard nod at him. We turned, looking straight ahead as we waited for the tunnel to deposit us wherever the hells the Deedles called home.

Blessedly, it did just a scant few seconds later. Stepping out of the between, I glanced around to get my bearings.

We were surrounded by towering trees that reached up with their infinitely long branches to the heavens. Leaves of burning blue and gold surrounded us. These were fire oaks at the peak of their blooming.

The roadways were dust-packed earthen trails with vendors pushing large, wooden carts as they rattled off the wares they were selling. The people were dressed in clothes that were riddled with holes, looking ten years out of season. They were all gaunt, cheeks hollowed out, bones poking out—women, men, and children.

Even the animals looked sickly. Cows were grazing nearby, barely mooing as they desperately ate at the earth, looking for whatever lone blades of grass they could find. Ducks and chickens marched by, looking little better, honking and quacking angrily at anything that dared come too close.

There was a small gaggle of children standing on a stone bridge, staring hungrily at a particularly fat green-and-black duck as it waddled past. Each of them held a small stone as they licked their little lips.

The houses and buildings scattered about were built of dried mud and clay and listing dangerously, crumbling at their corners. This was a dying city, stripped of nearly all its resources save one—the glittering jewels that were the trees.

"What is this place?" I asked. "Is this still Wonderland?"

I glanced at Hatter, wondering if he'd bother to answer. But he glanced in my direction and nodded quickly.

"Aye. This is one of the outer realms, once a thriving lumber district, now a city in its death throes."

He started walking forward.

I followed.

One of the kids tossed their stone at the duck, clopping it on its head. The bird gave a loud, angry honk and turned beady red eyes on them. But soon, another child threw her stone, and then another one after that. A loud, hellacious cry of desperation rang out from each of them, and the bird no longer had the upper hand.

I grimaced, turning away as the children pounced on the befuddled bird and feathers began flying. The sound of rending and screaming made me feel physically ill.

"Do not judge them harshly, Detective. Most here starve. Desperation makes animals of us all."

I whipped my head around, staring at him with hard eyes and wondering just what in the hells he meant by that. I was certain that those words hadn't just been about the children.

But Hatter was turning down a narrow alleyway, and the dirt paths gave way to slick gold-plated stones.

I frowned, noticing that even the buildings looked better tended here. The people walking down these roads were dressed in gaudy, silly clothing crafted of the finest silks, tulles, and laces. Men and women wore hats, and it seemed the sillier, the better. They gradually got bigger and bigger and more and more elaborate, progressing from standard hats toward fantastical works of art the farther we walked down the street—boats that seemed to sail upon oceanic waters; mountains brimming over with hidden oases filled with singing sirens bathing in their streams; airy, fantastical, whimsical clouds of wonder full of breathing, flying dragons.

And those were only the hats.

The gowns and dress clothes became even more luxurious, as did the homes. At the start of the street, the homes had been beautiful, but somewhat modest two-story Victorians. Farther in, they were sprawling estates with lawns full of the most bizarre looking creatures I'd ever seen. There was an elephant, dressed in jewels from head to toe and sporting grand golden wings, who preened in a placid pool. Giant cats with zebra-like markings in burning neon green and pinks hissed at us from inside massive golden cages. Little winged beasts with claws for legs and human-like eyes chittered as we walked past.

The people, too, were changing the farther we walked. They had started off looking normal but transformed into walking monstrous amalgams of both man and beast. Men with tiger stripes on their faces and fanged silver teeth smiled back at me with a lascivious wink. Women with scales like a goldenrod adder stared eerily in our direction, their serpent mouths set in tight lines of displeasure.

"One street over there is waste, filth, and starvation. Here there is—"

"—waste, filth, and starvation of a different kind," Hatter said.

I closed my mouth as I stared around at the wasteful opulence of this little oasis of hubris and greed amid the terrible suffering of just one street over.

Soon, we were marching up to a massive set of wrought-iron gates with twin Ds emblazoned upon them.

"The Deedles?"

He nodded. "Mmm. It behooves me to warn you, Detective, that the Deedles are quite out of their minds on hallucinogens, but do not mistake their silliness for stupidity. That would be a terrible folly. Stay on your guard and do not let them bait you."

A fissure of worry spread through my gut. Just who the bloody blazes were these Deedles?

Theirs was the last home on the street and easily the largest and most stately of the bunch. The sheer opulent wealth on display was nauseating and would make even the Charmings's castle seem like a peasant's hut by comparison.

There were flowers everywhere—cherry blossoms, bleeding hearts, birds of paradise, and dahlia blooms as big as my face. There were more, so many more, spreading out as far as my eyes could see. This was a sign of great wealth in Wonderland since to plant true flowers and not the killing kind cost more than an arm and a leg.

Peacocks with scaly crimson tales and monkeys with faces like terrapins clung to massive tree branches, staring at me with beady black eyes. There was a whirring sound from above, and when I glanced up, I noticed a flower turning its blossomy head to look down at us. There was a face at its center with two large, dead eyes. The petals were an electric shade of deadly blue, and my heart squeezed with panic.

I yelped, stepping backward as I covered my face and eyes. "Maddox, there's a... a—"

He whirled to look at me, looking tense and terrified. Then he looked up and blew out a steadying breath, shaking his head. His shoulders slumped in obvious relief. "It's not a flower, Detective. It's a monitoring system."

As if to punctuate his words, there was a click and a whirring sound, and then the gates swung open on silent, heavy hinges. The trail winding through the impressive garden was made of crushed diamond and glittering gold.

Feeling stupid, I squeezed my eyes shut. Nearly all inhabited places in Wonderland had cleared out the killing flowers ages ago. I should have known better.

"Are you coming, Detective?" Hatter's rhythmic voice cut through my humiliation.

Swallowing once, staring up at the blossom that had looked so eerily like an electric jeweled orchid, I shook my head and nodded.

"Yeah, I'm bloody coming," I gritted out, frowning heavily as I followed him down the jeweled path.

The trail wound without rhyme or reason through the massive gardens. As I walked, staring at trees with bark that glittered like polished tiger's eye and leaves of purest amethyst, I thought there really was such a thing as having far too much scratch and not knowing what in the two hells to do with it. The Deedles and my father would have gotten along just swimmingly.

By the time we reached the entrance to the gothic-style castle of spires and turrets, I was grumpy. The façade was built of veined snow-white marble. There were gargoyles perched all over the place, cruel mouths open and elongated, their clawed hands curved and looking deadly. Their stone cages breathed, telling me they weren't merely decorative but very, very real.

I glanced over my shoulder at the hour or so of sunlight left to this realm and shivered.

"I'd like to leave before the demons fly." The stone bastards, and I had a long and not so pretty history.

Hatter nodded. "Then let's make this quick."

As we walked up the steps, we were greeted by two nude guards holding massive broadswords before them. Not with their tips resting on the ground, either, but literally holding the massive things out before them. Their arms bulged and flexed with the action. They had to be exhausted, but they didn't move an inch.

They wore feathered masks of such brilliant colors that it made them look surreal and alien. Their bodies were honed as though from granite, strong and implacable, like walls of thick steel.

Standing at the entryway was a woman dressed in sheer pink silk that did nothing to hide the curves of her body. She was pale as milk in moonlight, with hair of raven's wing that spilled long and full down her back. The tips of it brushed against the white marble floor as she moved.

"Constable Hatter, the Deedles are expecting you," she said with just the slightest trace of a Wonderlandian accent. Her nipples pointed out at us like little needles.

I looked at Hatter, but he barely even spared her a glance. I frowned. Why did I care if he looked or not? He was free to do whatever he wished.

"Thank you," he said in that deep voice of his. Her smile was soft but encouraging. She was highly skilled because without even a word spoken, her body language had said it all. If he wished to, he could have her.

He looked back at me, his face calm and expressionless, but even so, I sensed exactly what he'd just done. He was also highly skilled because he'd denied her, telling her without words he was here with me.

Her spine stiffened, and her smile slipped. I swallowed, not sure how I felt about anything at the moment. All the pain and humiliation I was feeling was mixed in with other emotions I wasn't prepared to feel again for anyone. I hated it.

The woman gestured for us to follow, and we did, neither of us speaking as we walked down a long hall dripping with the richest and very finest of everything, from the diamond chandeliers sparkling above us to the Turkinish rugs beneath our feet. As we walked, there wasn't even an echo of our passage. Nothing but eerie, unnatural silence greeted my ears.

At spaced intervals, there were large glass cases full of taxidermies—dragons resting upon their golden coins; witches posed with fingers extended and madness on their faces; sea monsters so rare as to be nearly extinct, with their long necks twisted into hunting poses; beasts of the land so large they were like giants, with skins of fur and scales and feathers. On and on and on it went until one case made me pause and made all the blood in my veins crystallize.

Inside a rocky cavern full of placid water, with stalactites and stalagmites coming from above and beneath, sat a woman with a gleaming tail of ebony.

Her skin was pale, her hands and neck long, her breasts high and perky. She was covered in the markings of a river siren. Her eyes were boldly black, and her lips were tinged blue. Her hair was a cascade of wild, crystalline curls. Her mouth was open as though she sang.

I felt a tear slide down my cheek. They'd killed all these magnificent creatures for no other reason than because they could.

I placed my palm upon the glass.

"Oh no, you mustn't tou—" the woman cried, rushing over to me.

I hissed, raising my hand as a fury I'd rarely known crowded my bones. I felt the lure of my dark siren's magick begin to make itself manifest.

Hatter grabbed my hand and yanked it down hard, pressing his face in so close to mine that I felt the wash of his breath on my mouth.

"Elle, don't."

Just those two words was all he said, but it was the power behind them, the strength of his body, and the way that he looked at me that snapped me out of the killing haze and squelched the song in my throat that desperately wanted to break loose.

His fingers curled just a little bit tighter around my waist, making me hiss with pain, but also giving me desperately needed clarity.

Swallowing one last time, I blinked and nodded.

"You good?" he asked, the words spoken just for me, with tenderness, like a caress.

I trembled. I still hated him, and yet... I didn't at all.

Then I remembered what he'd accidentally shown me this morning, and I yanked my hand away.

"Yes," I hissed. "I'm fine."

He didn't look put off. He just dusted off his jacket and turned around, following the woman again. I didn't look at any more cases after that.

The female came to a stop at a door just a few more steps down the hall. She knocked once on the ornate gold door and then, with a nod to us, turned and melted back into shadow.

"Come in, Constable," said two deeply masculine voices, sounding like crushed gravel.

Hatter turned the knob, looked at me intently, and waited. I nodded. I was ready. I was fine. "After you." He spoke softly, moving to the side and gesturing at me to enter first.

I did and was met with the sight of two men more unusual than anything else I'd come across in the entire time I'd been in Wonderland. The images on the security tapes had not done them justice.

Unlike the woman and the two guards, the men were dressed in immaculate steel-gray suits and ties. I stared at them, offended by the very sight of the monstrous twins.

They were bald, both of them, with tiny dark eyes and high flushed cheeks. They had three sets of jowls each and hands the size of hams with fingers as thick as sausages, dripping in gold and jewels. They had to have been at least a half ton each and a good deal taller than Hatter by at least a foot.

They were half giants, both of them, which meant their girth belied the ferocity of their strength.

I was instantly on guard, hand creeping closer to my holster.

One Deedle, the one on the left, smirked. "Brother, does she think she can hurt us?"

The other Deedle, Righty, smirked back. "Try it, siren. We could certainly use a prize such as you in our zoo."

Together they guffawed, and my throat swelled as my body began to burn with the glow.

But Hatter was shoving me behind him and shaking his head. "Challenge the arm of the law, or in any other way attempt to derail our case, and I promise you, I will destroy you."

Such a weak threat would have gone nowhere for most people, but when Hatter said it, there was power in his words, power that the Deedles immediately sensed.

"Constable, of course," Lefty said.

"We've no bone to pick," Righty said.

"We're here to serve," they said together.

I gritted my front teeth, wishing like hells I could ram my claws through their soft meat and play with their viscera as I would have done long ago.

"Sit. Sit," they said, "the both of you, and let's talk."

Hatter sat beside me, keeping close as I trembled with barely checked rage. And though I wanted to hate him, I was grateful he was here.

The Deedles grabbed four tumblers and poured a pretty amber liquid into three of the cups, then a black thick fluid into the fourth.

Lefty handed Hatter the amber fluid, and Righty handed me the black sludge. I didn't have to sniff it to know it was demon-squid ambrosia. My mouth watered, but I shoved his hand back.

Hatter looked over at me and very pointedly tipped his head back and downed his liquid amber. I knew what that meant. While in Wonderland, do as the Wonderlandians do.

The Deedles stared at me, challenge burning in their beady eyes.

I stared at the thick fingers and fought the urge to slash Righty into ribbons of bloody meat. Keeping my claws sheathed, I gave him a tight-lipped nod of thanks, took the damned brew, and chugged it.

It went down like hell fire and warmed my gullet through. It was the most delicious bit of demon's ink I'd ever had. But I'd be damned if I thanked him for it.

I slammed the tumbler down on the desk in front of me so hard that I heard the crystal crack.

They grinned. "We've got more."

I just bet they did, the slimy bastards.

"Now." Lefty steepled his fat fingers together and turned to Hatter. "We've shared drink, so we are friends. Let us speak with honesty."

"Aye, brother. Honesty." Righty's folds quivered as he grinned.

My stomach heaved, and the ink that'd settled so sweetly just a second ago wanted to come right back up at the mere thought of Alice with these two. How had they not broken her? What in the devil had she actually done with them? And how could she stomach it?

I didn't give a flying rip that her profession of choice was frowned upon by polite society. I rather thought her brave for it. What did bother me was the disgusting beasts standing in front of me swimming in so much goddess-damned wealth, while the rest of their realm slowly starved to death.

"Where were you on the night of the seventh at ten thirty-two—"

Their eyes lit up with devilish glee, and Lefty smirked.

"Pounding flesh into your ex."

"Of course," Righty finished for his brother.

Then, as one, their eyes turned on me, and a look of pure, unadulterated lust scrawled over their corpulent features.

"Every Wednesday night," they said together, then both licked their lips before flicking their tongues out at me in a lewd, suggestive manner.

Hatter, who'd been deathly still just seconds ago, stood to his feet and slammed both his hands down on the desk, rattling the papers, cups, and a crystalline depiction of the realms.

"What do you know? Because I know you know, you filthy bastards," I hissed, vibrating with the tension of holding back my natural inclination to gut them like the fish they were.

"The girl is smart, she is," Lefty muttered.

Righty grinned. "Use her, brother?"

They clasped hands.

Hatter was so still it was almost like he was made of stone. His words were harsh, nothing but the grit of barely checked violence. "What do you know?"

"Alice will hang." They smiled and spoke as one. "Swing back and forth. Bye-bye, Alice."

"You filthy, arrogant, bastards! What did you do?" Hatter yelled.

Realizing he was losing his composure, it was my turn to hold him back. I got up from my seat and wiggled my way in front of him, pressing my back tight to his front. He didn't move, simply continued to vibrate. Every muscle in his body felt as if it were hammering against me. But he stood there, letting me take the lead.

I grinned, not holding my siren's charms back any longer. They flooded through me, spilling through my blood, my sinew, and my flesh until I gleamed blue.

The brothers gasped, lust dripping from them in waves. Hatter's shakes grew stronger.

When I spoke, my voice rang out with the echoes of the ancient power. "You will tell us what I want to know, and then I shall gift you with a song."

The brothers spasmed, orgasming from my voice alone. Their faces twisted into repellent looks of violent bliss, and the air reeked with the stench of their seed. I bit down on my tongue to keep from sneering with disgust.

Hatter breathed like a bellows behind me, his hands on my elbows, gripping so tight that I felt the circulation starting to cut off. My charms were affecting him, too, and I was sorry for that. But the Deedles didn't play fair, so neither could I.

I grinned, shoving lure into my throat so that, as I spoke, my words rang out like song. I'd yet to tap into the depths of my powers. I'd barely even given them a taste.

"Tell me, boys. Tell me what you've done."

They reached for me with their free hands, fingers flexing against their will as words spilled out their throats as one.

"Foxes and roses. Secrets and lies. Princes and kisses. All in due time."

None of their words made sense to me. I shoved more and more lure into my throat.

Their eyes widened, and the scent of seed grew stronger. Hatter moaned, dropping his head to my neck and breathing in slowly and steadily, but not with lust. He was fighting my lure with all of his might.

"Who stole the ribbon?"

"Not I." Lefty smirked.

"Nor I." Righty smirked back.

"Who!" I thundered, letting my words roll with the electricity of my power, fighting the urge to kill them, to end them, to destroy them as they'd done to so many others.

Lightning and thunder flared throughout the old-world-style room, cracking and banging like cymbals, rattling the ancient, leather-bound books on their mahogany shelves. Antiques and priceless artifacts trembled violently. The ground rocked at our feet and a strange wind howled through the windowless room. My hair rose, electrified by my lure. I felt my markings blossom and start to glow.

The brothers swallowed, finally having the sense to look nervous, but still they reached for me. My lure was too strong for them to deny.

"The cursed princess," they said as one, licking thick lips and spasming as long, rolling moans of orgasmic delight took them over and over.

I grinned, even as Hatter's fingers dug in tighter and tighter.

"The ribbon," I snapped.

"Ask Mary," they breathed, bodies jerking as they held onto one another, clinging like drowning men to a life raft.

That name pricked at my mind. I knew Hatter had warned me not to give too much away, but we had to know more. We were at a dead end. We had to know more.

"Mary's dead."

They laughed, tipping their heads back as their massive bellies rolled. "We know. Dead men tell no tales, or so they say. But she can. Oh, she can. Witch!"

They hissed. "Witch! Witch! Witch!"

And then they were on me. I hadn't seen it coming, hadn't been prepared for them to shake off my lure so easily. But their hands were on my face and their mouths were open. I screamed as I saw the yawning chasm of infinite eternity stretch forth from their parted lips. It was a whirling vortex of destruction that sucked and sucked and sucked and pulled the lure out of me. I screamed as they consumed me like ravenous vampires.

My heart was stopping, my skin was growing cold and my blood was turning to ice. And still I could not stop the screaming as they stole from me.

Darkness teased at me, whispering at me to enter into its eternal embrace.

Hook was there. In that darkness.

Hook.

My Hook.

And then my Hook was with me. Gorgeous. Dressed all in black. Smiling at me, and holding out his hand with that curved, silver appendage of his I'd adored so well.

Come to me, Elle. Oh, my Elle. My Elle. His words were a ghostly whisper in my mind, and I choked on tears as I held my hand out to him. But we were separated by lashing waves of father's waters, and anytime that water touched me, It tore flesh, making me bleed.

I screamed.

And then there were shouts, but they were not my own. Terrible, horrible shouts full of terror. I choked as the darkness receded from me, as the colors spilled back into my world, and the cold began to drift away again.

Hook was gone. And tears spilled unchecked down my cheeks.

I was on the ground, and I felt wetness on my forehead. When I reached up, my fingers were tacky with blood, and I knew I'd hit my head on the desk on the way down.

Dizzy, and not sure what was happening, I saw Hatter standing over them both. There were dark, black lights pressing down on their heads, singeing the flesh and making the air reek with the cloying, fatty smells of cooking meat. They writhed, moaning in agony, as they pleaded to be released.

I clutched at my throat, remembering the pull of that vortex of madness. The dread. The cold. That terrible, terrible cold that'd made me feel hopeless, without life, and so bloody empty.

My head hurt. My ears rang.

Hatter wouldn't look at me, but there was rage in the lines of his tense shoulders. His movements were jerky and without mercy as he cuffed the brothers.

Then he was pulling on the key card in his pocket. With an angry jerk, he swiped it through the air. The doorway opened, beckoning to us.

Snatching them up in his hands as though they were nothing, he shoved the brothers inside. And looking at me with fury burning in his dual-colored eyes like hell flame, he said, "Let's leave this goddessforsaken place now, Detective."

When I got to my feet, I immediately threw up. I'd hit my head harder than I'd thought. I swayed, gripping tight to the chair in front of me, terrified I'd fall on my face as the world whirled.

Hatter was there a second later, his body tense, but his hands infinitely gentle as he pulled me slowly into the between.

I vomited again as the starlight rolled around us.

And he just held me tight, pushing my hair off my forehead and whispering that I would soon be alright.

When we got back to his cottage, he told Harry to take me to the waters. Hatter didn't look at me as he took the brothers and booked them in separate cells.

"Ye look like ye swallowed one ta many halo-shrooms, Detective," Harry muttered, "and ye reek like it too."

Swaying on my feet, wishing like hells it was Maddox and not Harry helping me now, I moaned and gritted out, "Shut up, Harry. Just shut the hells up."

He chuckled, but wisely didn't say another word.

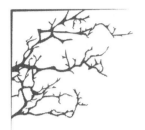

Chapter 17

Constable Maddox

"Goddess dammit!" He snapped into the looking glass, gripping the pane with a white-knuckled grip.

The White Queen stared down at him with a haughty frown.

He inhaled. It was easy to forget sometimes that though she was the Chief of Constables, she was also his queen.

"Forgive me."

Her nod was imperious. Dragonflies zipped around her crown of thorns, blazing gem-colored trails that heightened her allure. Her hair was white as snow, her eyes as well, but her lips were the red of freshly drawn blood.

She was a woman of stunning beauty and fierce intellect.

"You have been a good Constable. And you've given me much to consider," she said in that lazy, imperious drawl of hers.

"You can stop this, Chief," he pleaded one more time. "Alice didn't—"

Thin nostrils flared with displeasure. And a dragonfly with broad confectioner-pink wings was suddenly burned up in the release of her sometimes-uncontrollable powers.

Her eyes burned with lambent fire.

"I do this once, then I set a precedent. A precedent I cannot set. You are a favorite, Maddox, but not even for you," she hissed, exposing the sharp curves of her sickle-shaped fangs.

The queen was eternal. But only because she lived off the life force of others. It was a cannibalistic way to be, but she was a good and honest queen for all that. Better the devil you knew than the devil you didn't. It was why there'd never been a coup to try and overthrow her. It was either her or her sister, the bloody Red Queen. Queen Arabella fed off the life force of the condemned only. Her sister was far less discerning in her tastes.

It was a terrible, gruesome death for any. But the death penalty was reserved only for the worst and lowest of Wonderland.

And Alice, his once beloved Alice had just been sentenced to death.

"But how could they have tried her this fast? Does this not seem suspicious to you, Chief? I'm telling you, I'm this close to solving the case. Please. Please, if our past means anything at all—"

She hissed, causing even more dragonflies to fry in the face of her ire as her hair shone with the power of her rage.

"You've used far too many favors with me, Constable! I will give you two hours, and two hours only. Solve the case, or Alice dies."

The looking glass went dead and Hatter roared. Picking up a lamp, he slammed it against the wall. And then he picked up the receiver and did the same. Trashing his office as the panic and fear and rage of the last few hours washed over him.

He wasn't sure how long he'd lost himself to the madness, except the door was suddenly opened and there she stood, a lovely silhouette in the shadows, staring at him with her large woebegone eyes.

"Maddox," Elle said simply.

And this time when he roared, he felt the beast stir.

Detective Elle

I'D OFTEN WONDERED what the constable would look like if he turned off the tightly checked power of his. Now I knew.

My heart raced as I watched him burn, not just with the glow of his lights, but fire. Literal fire. He was a pillar of it, looking like Lucifer himself the way it embraced and curled around him.

"Go away," he roared, snatching up a cookie, of all things, and tossing it at me.

I swatted it away easily.

The destruction of his office was near total. He'd broken his own desk, and how the hells he'd done that, I'd never know. But there was a giant crack down the middle, and papers all over the bloody place.

But his fire did not touch any of it. I felt the unbelievable heat of it wash against me, felt it sizzling the precious waters from my shirt. But even so, I stared at him in wonder.

He was so much more than I'd ever imagined.

"What are you?" I breathed.

His handsome face curled. "You shut me out! Without even giving me a chance to explain. I owe you nothing! Nothing!"

He pointed to the door behind me. But I shook my head.

"You saw my secrets. My very private, very personal secrets. You should have told me," I yelled back, unleashing the pent up anger.

"Told you what?" he shot back. "How the hells was I supposed to tell you that? How the hells do you even start a conversation like that, Elle? Hmm? Oh, by the by, I saw you slit your wrists, siren. Sorry. Didn't mean to."

Then he pivoted on his heel and literally shoved his fist through the wall, the wall caved in with no great effort, and I stood in awe of him.

"I... I was ashamed." I squeezed the words out.

"You were ashamed! Ha!" He tipped his head back, looking manic and furious as his dual-colored eyes burned with their own strange fire. "You saw mine too! Damn you! And I could just kill you for it!"

As he said it, he practically ran toward me, and I gasped, holding my hands up, but unable to move away. I was drawn to him. Pulled in despite the clear and obvious signs that the man was impossibly dangerous.

He didn't carry a weapon, but then why would he need to? An image of his little girl lying at his feet, dead and burned all, over gave me pause and turned me cold and scared.

I didn't know what had happened that night, and I wanted to believe the best. But he could conjure fire. He could kill. I'd seen him with Deedles tonight. Had he hurt his daughter by accident? Had it been him?

It would explain Alice's resentment and hatred, but it would not explain his being a man of the law. If he'd killed her, he'd have hung for it. I wanted to ask him because I desperately wanted to know what had happened that night, but I'd felt his pain, and I knew we did not have the time for this.

I could feel my flesh tingling, feel it burning, feel the water evaporating. It was growing harder to breathe as his flames licked and curled closer and closer toward me.

I was a creature of water. He was a thing of fire.

I shivered. "It burns, Maddox."

Instantly his fire extinguished, as his tortured gaze roved my face.

"She's been sentenced to death, Elle. Death." His voice cracked and his pain bled through.

And I watched, as one of the most powerful men I'd ever come across completely shattered in front of me. His knees gave out, and I had to catch him and hold him to me as he trembled with violent, silent sobs.

His fingers dug into my back as his face slipped into the curve of my neck, bathing me in the salt of his tears.

I rocked him, holding him to me tight.

"It's okay, Maddox. It's okay."

He gulped but couldn't speak. All he could do was make the most heart-wrenching sounds I'd ever heard in my life. We rocked, holding tight to each other.

I was scared. So bloody scared because I knew what was happening between us, and it couldn't happen. This couldn't be.

But it was happening.

Want it or not, it was happening to us both.

I nuzzled his neck and continued to whisper words I couldn't know were true.

"We'll save her. I know we will. You're unstoppable, Maddox. You're so bloody brilliant, I promise we'll—"

Then his knuckles were on my cheeks, and he was turning my face toward his. There was a look burning in his eyes. A question. Hope. Fear.

I nodded once as a single tear slid off my nose.

He kissed me. This was nothing like what we'd done on the bed. It was only a sharing of breath, saliva, and the taste of one another.

But I felt my world tremble, felt everything shift out of focus, felt myself falling as a scream built in my throat. But he was there. He was right there.

Holding me.

Saving me right back.

We were so bloody broken.

I framed his face in my hands. "How many hours have we left?"

He closed his eyes, touching his forehead to mine as he whispered with grit in his lungs. "Two. Only two."

"Then we haven't a minute to lose. We have to find Mary's ghost."

"I know where she is," he said in a hushed tone.

"Where?"

"The Fox and the Rose. It's the pub where she was killed. She haunts the grounds."

"Bloody hells. Crowley closed it off to us." I remembered the pub that'd been just behind the trail we'd followed to the endless pool that day.

He shook his head. "Just the grounds, but not the ghost."

"Then we have to go to her. We have to—"

"Are you well enough to go there? Truth."

His gaze was frank, assessing. The waters had eased some of the pain, but I was still queasy. Still dizzy. My head swam like I'd been driven head first into a mound of bedrock. I still wasn't sure what the Deedles had done to me, and I wasn't sure I wanted to know, either.

"I'm fine. I'm fine."

His nostrils flared, and his eyes flashed with concern. He knew I had lied.

"Good," he said. "I'm glad."

Taking the key card out of his jacket, he swiped at the air, calling forth the between. I didn't want to go in there, but I did. We had a case to solve and an innocent woman to save.

Hatter gripped my fingers tight as we moved with dizzying speed through the tunnel of light, pulling my head to his chest and whispering in my ear as he lightly rubbed circles on my back. "Just breathe, little siren. Just breathe."

And I did just that.

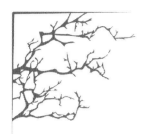

Chapter 18

Detective Elle

We were back in central Wonderland, and my steps were wobbly. I was fighting the urge to throw up with every step I took. The pain in my head hadn't gone away at all. It'd gotten a little better after the dip in the river, but I was still weak and queasy.

He gripped my fingers tight, giving me his strength as best he could.

I swallowed the bile rising in my throat and gave him a weak grin. "I'm fine."

His look was slow and measured. "I know."

I grinned because I was far from fine and he knew it, but he was letting me do my job, and for that, I respected the hells out of him. I needed my waters, but Alice needed her head more.

"For what it's worth, Elle, no matter what happens tonight, I wouldn't have wanted to make this journey with anyone else. If I ever had a partner, it would be you." His words were softly spoken, and I shivered.

I pulled my lip between my teeth, thinking I should say something, but not really sure what. I'd seen his memories. He'd seen mine. He was fire. I was water. I was still in love with the ghost of my dead lover. And Hatter was a mystery I was sure I shouldn't poke at. But for all that, I'd miss him. His sense of calm in the face of danger. His focus. His mind.

He moved me as fast as he dared, but though our walk was short, each step had me feeling worse and worse. I wasn't sure it was just hitting the desk, but whatever the hells the Deedles had done to me surely wasn't helping.

When we rounded the corner, I saw a stone façade with patrons moving in and out, some singing, others chatting, a few throwing up by the wall, and some even taking a piss. The noxious combination of odors was making my already-topsy-turvy stomach even worse.

We were back at the scene of the crime, the very one Hatter and Harry had found themselves at the day I'd arrived. I'd thought then it was the pool tucked behind the pub in the forest that had been important. But I saw everything with a new light.

I squeezed my eyes shut as I was blasted with another whiff of human filth.

"Oh Goddess," I moaned and slapped a palm onto the nearest wall, cringing at the slickness of slime beneath my touch, praying to the goddess I wasn't clinging to waste.

He moved around me, gripping my elbow tight. I looked at him, and he looked back at me. Not saying a word, not calling me out on my life. I swallowed reflexively, over and over and over until I shoved the sickness back down.

We had less than two hours. Everything hinged on Mary the ghost. Everything.

I should have just let Hatter come on his own. I was only slowing him down. And yet, when I opened my mouth to say the words, something inside of me wouldn't let me.

I was supposed to be here.

I wasn't sure how I knew that. I just did.

"What if you drank your water?" he asked slowly.

I cracked open one eye, absorbing his handsome, serious features. "What?"

"The water. In your shell," he pointed.

My thoughts felt cloudy and a little fuzzy. I had to stop and think about what he was actually saying, but my mind was disjointed, and I was starting to feel cold again. All over.

His thumb brushed hot against my bare back, and I was frowning, wondering how his hand had gotten underneath my shirt, but his touch felt good, made me feel connected, tethered, helped me to think again.

"I... I need it for—"

"No." He brushed hair out of my eyes. "No you don't. You go back to Grimm tonight, Elle. You go back to your waters soon. Will it help if you drink it?"

I couldn't even remember how many days of water I had left in this shirt. I might be condemning myself to a fate worse than death, but the thought of that sweet water sliding down my throat made me ache and feel dry, desiccated. I swallowed compulsively, and then I was frantic, feeling that if I didn't drink, I might die anyway.

He gently brushed my hand away and brought the shell to my lips.

I gasped at the first cool touch of its healing waters sliding down my throat, healing all the aches and pains, helping to erase some of the fuzz in my head, making the cold recede back, back, back.

I trembled, resting my cheek heavily against the foul-smelling, oozy wall. Hatter's warm hand still rubbed at my back.

"Elle. Elle?" he asked, worry inching through his words.

"Goddess, it smells worse than a pig's pen here," I muttered, moaning as I shoved off the door. It hadn't been much water, but I did feel a little better. Glancing down at my shell, I saw that it no longer glowed. I felt a little panic at how much harder it was now to breathe.

But I plastered on a smile and nodded. "I'm better, Maddox."

"You keep saying that, and I keep pretending—"

I planted my finger over his lips and nodded slowly. "I'm better."

His eyes closed as he breathed me in. I could feel his desperation to get to where we were going and the panic that ate at him, making him believe we wouldn't be able to save Alice in time. But he wouldn't push me, no matter how desperate he felt.

So I took a deep, fortifying breath, ignoring the countless aches and pains, and whispered, "Now, please. Let's go."

He took my hand, curling our fingers together and pulling me along. I was able to follow, and though I felt dizzy, I didn't feel like I was going to collapse.

When we reached the grounds behind the pub, I saw the abandoned crime scene tape fluttering like yellow bat's wings in the slight breeze. There were painted slash lines where MICE had marked points of interest and a spot where the ground was dark, scorched with death's stain.

Just a few feet over was a patch of wild halo-shrooms, the very ones Harry had fallen into the night we'd met, and the beginning of the dirt path that wound through the dark woods to the endless pool beyond. Behind us, I heard the revelry of drunkards and the plinking of a piano. The stench of filth and alcohol was heavy in my nostrils, and I had to fight to cling to my sanity. On the air, I felt the prickle of great and terrible energy. Angry energy. Malevolent energy.

Mary wasn't happy.

I nodded and dug my fingers into his vest, still forced to cling to him to remain upright.

"This is it. I feel her. I feel the presence of something otherworldly."

When I looked at him, Maddox was nodding too. "Aye. She's here."

We turned and stared at the patch of withered ground.

"Mary," I called softly. "Mary, are you here? Can you hear us?"

Green and blue lights glowed in the night. When I glanced at Maddox, I saw why. His eyes burned as he saw a vision.

"Did you see it? Do you know what's—"

His jaw clenched as he shook his head. "It was something else. Mary," he barked. "Mary, I know you're here. Mary, I—"

A powerful tempest came out of nowhere, shoving against Hatter and slamming him so hard against the bar wall that I heard the dull crack of skull on stone.

I gasped, covering my mouth with my hands as horror consumed me. Bobbing because I no longer had him to help balance me, I swung my arms out wildly to help right myself, but I dropped to my knees anyway.

I saw her, then. A dark, black blot of rage and terror was advancing on Hatter. He was moaning and shaking the stars from his head. She'd flung him so hard against the wall that his eyes looked glassy and glazed and there was blood sliding down his temple.

"Maddox," I cried out.

"Stay. Stay back, Elle," he groaned and held his hand out to me, telling me to keep away. Then he was gripping at the wall, trying to stand, but unable to. "You, you don't have to do this, Mary. I will not hurt—"

Again, that invisible wall cracked against his head, shoving him back into the wall.

I screamed. "Mary, stop! Just stop! Stop. Please Goddess, stop!" I couldn't see her for the tears blinding my eyes, but I saw him, his form, silent and slumped on the ground.

I felt the prickle of dark energy turning, felt the malevolence breathing down on me. My skin felt electrified, and my claws dropped, as did my fangs, though they were useless against the dead.

I squeezed my eyes shut but forced myself to keep talking. "We didn't come here to hurt you. I'm... I'm a detective and he's my partner. Mary, we know. We know. I know," I hissed.

She continued to advance, and I felt her hatred growing like a living flame, pressing against me, making my skin burn and my blood scream in my veins as my precious fluids began to sizzle.

I shook my head, digging my claws into the dirt and hanging my head.

"I saw him kill you."

The fog of revenge paused in its tracks, breathing like a flame down my neck, but not moving.

I was a siren. But I was also a woman. I knew what it was to fear men. And I knew what it was to want to hurt them all for it too.

Tears streamed down my face as I opened myself up to the hated, painful memories.

"I was raped, tortured, and nearly killed by the man to whom my father gave me. And I hated all men for it. Hated them all. Wanted them to burn. To die. And so I did it. I did it, Mary. I killed them. I wrecked them. Destroyed thousands of lives because what Lyre had done to me was a pain too great for me to bear. But then one day I met a man. A good man. A man no one wanted or liked. A man everyone said was the devil himself. He changed me, Mary. He made me better. Made me believe that they weren't all monsters. Please don't hurt Maddox. He wasn't the one who did this to you. In fact, he's trying to punish the man who did. Another woman is about to hang, Mary."

Realizing that Mary was listening to me, I opened my eyes and saw the fog hovering still and silent before me, swirling with impossible and terrifying power, but listening.

"She's a good woman, Mary. A good woman. I know she didn't do this to you, and you know it too. All I'm asking is that you please, please help us to find out who did this. Help us before its too late."

"Elle!" Hatter's voice pierced my thoughts. "Watch out!"

Confusion pinched me, made me go still. And that was all it took. The black fog moved, pouring down my throat. My body went stiff as a board as the fires of hell consumed me.

Constable Maddox

HE GROANED AS HE HEARD the low, heated whispering and realized in a small corner of his mind that it was Elle.

Terrified for her, but sick and disoriented, he tried to push up from where he lay sprawled on the garbage-strewn ground.

She spoke of her darkness, a darkness he hadn't seen, hadn't known. His heart bled, sliced open by thousands of razor blades. He understood Elle's darkness, why she would hurt, why she had killed so many. Her banishment from her peoples and realm, the destruction she'd heaped upon those she'd counted as her enemy. It all made sense to him now.

Through bleary eyes he saw the black shadow listening, drawing slowly and slowly closer. Elle was on her knees, looking small and frail but so brave in the face of the dark witch's wrath.

And then she spoke Alice's name, and when the shadow twitched, he knew what was coming.

"Elle, watch out!" He reached out for her, trying in vain to warn her.

But it was too late. Too damned late.

Detective Elle

THE DISORIENTATION I'd felt when I'd touched Maddox's tattoos was exactly like what I felt now. I was me, but I wasn't.

I was a figure in a cowl, running amongst streets and alleyways as I headed toward the Crypt. I had a baby to feed. I didn't want to do this, but I was poor, and I had nothing else I could do.

So I ran, knowing I was about to frame her. She'd been kind to me once. I hated myself, but what was I to do?

When I arrived, I was ushered to the back door.

A woman with flowing seafoam-green hair and large, innocent eyes looked grim as she handed me a ribbon.

"You know what to do."

My nostrils flared. "I don't want none of this business."

The siren hissed, her innocent-looking features transforming into cold beauty.

"You don't do it, and my husband will see you hanged. If you want your baby to see its twentieth birthday, then you'll damn well do it. Or he pins it all on you. Your choice, Mary."

"I... I don't think I can." I gulped.

She laughed, and the sound was cruel and vicious. "Fine. I don't care. Even now, the estate has reached out to Crowley. He comes, and if I were you, I'd plant the ribbon or..." She walked up to me, pregnant belly pressing against my own, and I hated the bitch for it, hated her. She laughed, flitting her long fingers around, "Well, dear, I'm sure you're smart enough to figure out what would happen."

"You bitch!" I seethed, gripping tight to the ribbon that felt like death in my hands.

Her laughter was unpleasant, and her eyes flashed. "You should have never stolen that apple, Mary, or slept with my husband, you adulterous bitch. He thinks I don't know who sired your bastard, but I know. I've always known."

She shoved her fist into my stomach, knocking me back on my heels.

"Isa! Where are you, sweetheart," a soft, feminine voice called from inside.

Isa startled and turned to glance over her shoulder. "Just a second, Alice. I'll be just a moment longer." Then she turned back to me with a snarl and said, "Do it. Or I tell Snow what you've done. It's a hanging crime, you know, to steal from the Queen."

"He gave it to me. He gave me the apple for our—"

She scoffed. "Like they'll ever believe you, a lowly filthy whore, over me."

I stomped my foot in hopeless fear. "You said I was done the last time. You can't keep hanging this over my head. You said if I helped you the last time, I would be done. I helped you. I killed them just like you told me to. I've done everything you said!"

Isa laughed. The sound was beautiful and made my blood turn to ice in my veins. "I see why he's taken you. Pretty face, but oh so stupid. Did you honestly believe me? More fool you. You'll never be done with me, Mary. Not ever. I own you."

"He told me you were supposed to be the one who—"

She slapped me so hard that my ears rang and my cheek blazed with heat. I gasped, covering my throbbing cheek with my hand. Her eyes narrowed to thin, dangerous slits.

"Hang for him? You're even more a fool than I'd imagined. If they catch him, they'll never tie this to me. But you..." She grinned, revealing sharp, tiny fangs. "Well... you'd better stay on my good side dear, because the same cannot be said for you."

Trembling with panic and fear that she was right, I felt shameful tears slide down my cheeks. My baby. My beautiful, beautiful child. Pain twisted my soul in two as I realized I had no hope of ever getting out from under her thumb. I was doomed, and my child would pay for my crime of loving a monster.

"I hope you burn in the twin hells for this." My voice quivered.

Isa sneered. "You first, whore."

Then she turned and slammed the door in my face.

Suddenly, I was me again and not Mary. I was me, and I was flying through time. I saw myself planting the ribbon in Goose's garden, saw a man with hooves plowing through her roses and azaleas, leering at me with sharp, wide teeth.

Then I was back in Mary's head.

I was seeing the man I'd once thought myself in love with. He was a stranger to me now. A hateful, hurtful monster. Mama had always warned me of my bad taste in men, but I'd thought this one was different. I'd thought he was so, so different. A man of the law. He was supposed to be good. He was supposed to be the one.

"Do it now, ye fecking whore," he snapped. "Now!"

His hair was brown. His eyes too. He wore a badge, a Grimm PD badge. There was nothing all that memorable about him, except the hate that emanated off him in waves.

Except that.

I knew little of forensics. I wasn't a bright woman. I was a poor woman. A desperate woman. But I knew this ribbon was the only key to my salvation, the only way I might make it out of here alive.

The only way I might be able to help my child.

So I whispered a hex, a small hex, into it. Just a little thing. A little one only. It was a call to the one who would help me most. The one who would make it right. And I dropped it in the Goose's garden.

"May the goddess forgive me," I breathed.

And then my one-time lover was grabbing me and grinning evilly. "Now ye come with me."

And we were traveling, flying through stars. And then we were here. At a pub. On the grass. With millions of jeweled stars twinkling in the sky.

And his face was no longer cruel but set and determined. He reached into his pocket and pulled out a wickedly curved claw and silver shears. I gasped, crying and pleading for mercy.

"I did what ye asked me to! I did it, I did—"

"Ye wee, filthy bitch!" he raged. "I told ye to never let Isa know of us. I told ye, and she found out anyway. You betrayed me, Mary. You betrayed us!"

I shook. "No! The... the baby was so hungry, and there was an apple there, and she saw our daughter. She saw our child, and she knew. I said nothing, Ta—"

He smacked me so hard that my teeth cut into the inside of my mouth, and I cried out. I sobbed, clutching at my face, looking at the man I'd thought my entire world. He shook his head, and the rage was gone. Now there was only pain on his face.

"Why? Why couldn't you love me enough?" he asked brokenly.

I didn't know what to say. I'd loved him more than he'd deserved, and I saw that now. I only wished I'd seen it then. He reached for me, and I hoped the beating was done. Hoped he would hold me now, make this all go away. Make this better.

I sniffed, face still ablaze from the sting of his slap, but I moved into his arms anyway. I was so terrified of the world that even a monster could bring me some relief.

He wrapped his arms around me, and for a second, it was good again. For a second, I thought that maybe it was finally over, that the madness had ended, and together, we could fix things so that me and my baby could be free.

I felt a searing, excruciating blossom of hurt flare through me. I gasped as I looked down at the claw just barely cutting into my gut. The bandercoot claw was pumping all its poison into me.

I gasped again, clutching at his arms. Soon I would be unable to move at all as the poison ate through me like acid. The death would be slow and painful.

He shook his head, brown eyes full of disappointment. "I loved you, Mary. I really thought you loved me too."

And then he stabbed me, ripping through my intestines with the pretty silver shears. The pain was dizzying, mind-stealing, but it was a quicker death than the bandercoot's claw.

"My baby," I cried and whimpered, closing my eyes as he stabbed me over and over, drowning me in his words of hate.

"Your fault," he said, "all your damned fault."

I was growing cold, stabbed so many times that I could no longer feel anything. I choked on the blood welling in my throat, still reaching for my invisible child. My beautiful Rose with clear, colorless irises. She was my hope, my love, my everything.

She was alone. All alone now...

"The house of blue. Please, Detective, take her to the shoe."

The ghostly voice rang like bells in my ears, and then the vision was gone and I was me again, on that grassy patch of dying earth, staring with crying eyes at nothing as I felt the cold and the terror and the pain.

Mary was gone.

She'd finished what she'd set out to do.

She'd saved her child, and now her soul could finally move on and find its eternal rest.

Hatter was on his knees in front of me, moving weakly as he grabbed my hand and squeezed.

"You saw her. You saw Mary, didn't you?" he asked, voice gravelly and full of grit.

I swallowed, nodding hard. "Yes. I know who did it, Maddox. I know who did it. And you were right. It was one of mine. It was Isa too."

He trembled, and tears spilled from the corners of his eyes as he latched on to my face with bloodstained fingers. There was so much pain in him that I felt it like a visceral blow to my stomach.

"I have to go now. And you do too. There is a child, Mary's child. She told me the baby waited in the house of blue. Her name is Rose."

He nodded. "I... I know where that is."

I nodded and clutched desperately at his wrist. "Save the baby, Maddox. Alice will be all right now. She'll be all right."

Reaching into his pocket with trembling fingers he pulled out the key card and handed it to me.

I went to take it, but his fingers refused to let go. He stared at me, a look of utter devastation scrawled in them.

I nodded, understanding, because I felt the same. Moving into him, I framed his face with my hand and kissed him softly. Gently.

It was our goodbye. And it was all we had left to give.

Then I snatched the key away from him and swiped, only letting myself cry as I sailed through a tunnel of dizzying stars.

When I arrived at Grimm PD headquarters, I knew I looked like hell. Everyone stared at me with mouths gaping and stunned, shocked looks on their faces. I could hardly walk, my stomach heaved, and I wanted to die.

In fact, I was sure I would. But not until I saw him cuffed first. That bastard. If I could, I'd kill him myself for what he'd done.

Crowley, who I could give two hells less about, was standing just inside the chief's office, wearing that arrogant, fecking smirk of his.

Bo, dressed all in white, looked harried, and her eyes were bloodshot. But when she caught sight of me, she ran, wrapping her arms around me and giving me her strength.

"You... you have to call the White Queen, Bo. I..." I coughed. "I know who did it. I know."

"What? What do you know, Elle?"

"What is this?" Crowley stood straight, glaring at us both.

White lights were starting to crowd my vision, and I was beginning to sway. I'd seen too much, felt too much, and that tiny bit of my waters was already weakening in my veins. I was a minute, maybe less, from collapse.

"Alice didn't do it. Tanner did. Touch me, Bo, and see for yourself!"

And just as she reached for the staff around her neck, just as the bit of metal began to burn white-hot, I sank into the oblivion of peaceful, black waves.

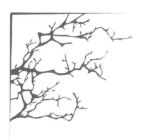

Epilogue

Detective Elle

One year later

"Wonder who he is?" Ichabod teased me, waggling his brows at me from behind my desk.

"Shut the hells up," I snapped, more than a bit pissed off at the thought that, against my will, the Chief had decided to give me a partner. I didn't want a damned partner, and she knew it.

They all knew it.

"Aw, c'mon, little princess," he teased. I bared my fangs, and he cringed and swallowed hard. "Erm, Elle, rather. It might not be so bad. He comes highly recommended. Said to have had the best scores in the history of the academy. I'd be damned glad if he were mine. Wish I could understand why all the bloody secrecy surrounding him, though. Bo's sure being oddly uncommunicative this time."

"Look." I threw a pen into my desk drawer and slammed it shut. "I wouldn't care if it was the queen of the bloody pantheon. I don't want a fecking, bloody part—"

"Hello, Elle."

I stopped speaking, skin tingling from head to toe. Hardly daring to breathe, I shot Ich a panicked look.

Ichabod sat behind his desk, mouth ajar, staring at the man behind me with wide, disbelieving eyes. "You? You beat my score?" he groused.

But then the male touched me on the back of my neck with his silky, callused hand, and I couldn't help but grunt. Not giving a rip who saw me, I jumped to my feet and then into his arms, squeezing Maddox so damned tight that I heard the air rush through his lungs.

He only chuckled, nuzzling my neck and breathing me in. "I dreamed about you every night, Elle. Every. Single. Night."

I sniffed, hating the tears, hating that everyone was witnessing what should be private.

"Oh sure. She snaps at everyone all goddessdamn year long, but you... you she hugs. Life, man," Ichabod bemoaned.

I took Hatter's hand in mine, ignoring Ich, ignoring them all, and raced for the back doors, not stopping until I was out the door and down the steps into the smoke pit.

There was only one fairy there, smoking her pipe. She never looked at us.

But I wouldn't have cared. I feasted my eyes on him, refamiliarizing myself with every line, every sharp curve. The peaked brows. The full lips. And the razor-sharp jaw. The green and blue eyes. The patrician nose. His top hat, coat, and cravat. Not a square inch of him had changed, he was exactly as he'd been. As he was every night in my dreams.

And I kissed him.

I shouldn't. We were on the job. But I kissed him like my bloody life depended on it. And he kissed me right back.

"Ugh. Get a fecking room," the fairy hissed, and we broke apart guiltily.

She turned over her pipe, dumping out her tobacco and stomping it out before shoving past us.

I laughed, and so did he. Then I punched his shoulder. Hard.

"Ow! Bloody hell, Elle. What did you do that for?"

He rubbed at his shoulder, and I almost whispered an apology, but I was pissed as twin hells.

"One year, and you never called me back! I sent you countless letters, you bastard. I hate you."

He grinned.

"No, you don't. And I didn't write you back, Elle, because I was at the Academy. I never got any of your letters."

He moved in just a step, reaching out to me slowly, like someone trying to tame a wild beast.

I bristled, even as I desperately ached for his touch.

"You could have called me. I was so—" I stopped talking, clamping my lips shut, refusing to tell him just how terribly bad I'd missed him, or how an ache had grown in my chest every day since I'd left him back in the alleyway.

He shook his head. "I... I couldn't, Elle. I had to breathe. I needed to see if maybe what had happened there was even real."

He smelled so bloody good. I sucked in air, dragging his scent of cool nights and clean soap deep into my lungs.

"I hate you," I said again, but this time with heat and trembly things behind it.

He grinned, and my stomach coiled into tight knots.

"Goddess, I missed you," he said. "So damn bad I thought I would die from it. I missed you, Elle."

My eyes closed, lashes fluttering as I absorbed his words and let them marinate in my heart. I'd been so sick with longing and pain, drowning my sorrows in man after man, sinking into misery all over again.

"My time in Wonderland scared me, Maddox. Ruined me. You brought up so many painful memories, and I cursed you every night. Every. Single. Night."

I couldn't stop the tears as I reached for his shirt and fisted it tight in my hands, rumpling his immaculately pressed self.

But he didn't seem to care at all. He moved into me, large frame making me feel safe and warm and protected. I felt the tremors coursing through him and knew I wasn't the only one. Something had happened to us both in Wonderland and it'd changed us, maybe forever.

His eyes were sad, haunted. "I'm sorry. Maybe I shouldn't have—"

I shook my head. "No, no, you should have. I never hated you. I couldn't have survived Wonderland without you, Maddox. But there is so much I don't know. So much that still doesn't make sense to me. And I don't know if I can be with someone that I don't trust."

My words were soft, barely even audible.

But his voice rumbled as he wrapped his arms around my waist and held me fast.

"Ask me anything, Elle. I'm an open book."

The one question I wanted to ask, I still wasn't sure I could. He was a man of flame. His child, his little butterfly still haunted my dreams. I sighed and squeezed my eyes shut as I laid my head against his chest and listened to the gentle rhythms of his heart.

"Did you find the girl?"

He nodded, grinning from ear to ear. "I visited with her recently. Goose adopted her. Did you know all those children are adoptions? Goose is a brilliant woman. Entire town has pitched in for her. She does a good thing, that woman. Oh, and I eventually learned of Alice's connection."

I raised my brows, waiting.

He brushed his knuckles lightly down my cheek. "She funded all the adoptions." His voice quivered, and I understood why. Alice and he had lost their child. Hatter had thrown himself into his work, and it seemed Alice had thrown herself into saving children. It made me like her even more than I already had.

I grinned, feeling stupidly happy about it. "I like kids."

He snorted. "This coming from you? Have I died?"

I slapped at his chest, scrubbing off the tears that still hadn't stopped with the back of my wrist. "Oh, shut up. I never said I wanted my own. I just said those little brats aren't so bad. Maybe." I shrugged.

He kissed me, and I melted.

It was always a bad idea to mix business with pleasure. Always. And yet I'd fight to the death to make sure Maddox stayed with me.

"Does Bo know?" I whispered. "And how the hells did you manage to convince her to let you work with me?"

"Bo knows. We had a long chat, she and I. She saw everything with her staff."

I cringed. I remembered so little of that day, other than I'd shoved into the office doors, decrying Tanner the Satyr the villain, and had promptly passed out like a fecking damsel in distress.

"I still can't believe it was him. I always thought he was a nice guy. And I can't believe I didn't recognize his wife earlier. But it's not like he'd ever really brought Isa around much. There was just a picture of her on his desk." I shook my head, scowling as I thought about the destruction they'd wreaked and the countless lives they'd destroyed.

"I can't understand why he did it at all," Hatter said. "There are still holes for me. Like why kill the gardener and maid at the Charming estate?"

I rolled my eyes, sighing, but not letting him go.

"All clear and justifiable evidence ends at Tanner. But I know he wasn't behind it all. He was the killer. He was not, however, the catalyst."

Taking my hand in his, Hatter led us toward a bench and sat. I joined him, still clinging to his hand.

"Who was?"

My lips thinned. Ichabod and I had had many alcohol-fueled late-night talks, and our best guess was something that could see us hanged for treason.

I worked my jaw from side to side.

"You know you can trust me."

I grinned weakly. "I know I can. That's not what's bothering me. What's bothering me is that my gut tells me, with the active participation of BS in all of this, all the bribes and the hustle that went on behind the scene, there could only be one reasonable culprit."

He frowned. "Who?"

"The very people now paying for Tanner's children to live out their lives in comfort and ease. The very goddessdamned people who live high up on a charmed hill with too many damned bloody apples growing on their trees. The very people who, until just two years ago, had been declared sterile by even the most high-ranking wizards around but then one day, have a miracle daughter. The maid had been pregnant, did you know that? If the child had been born to her and not cruelly ripped out of her womb, the child would be roughly the same age as the princess."

The confusion vanished from his face, and he gasped, glancing worriedly over my shoulder. To speak out against royals would be folly, so I wouldn't do it, but goddessdamn did I think it.

"Those people."

He pulled me into a tight hug, kissing the crown of my head with obvious worry. We'd come so close, but we hadn't come close enough. Not nearly close enough to expose the real monsters amongst us.

I shook my head. "Sometimes I wonder why we do this job day in and day out. The bad guys just keep getting away, no matter how damned hard we try."

"So we keep trying, and we keep trying, Elle. Because that's who we are. We have to keep pressing forward, believing that one day, we'll get them all. We'll catch every one of those sick bastards and make them pay. But until we can, all we can do is grind and press on."

I closed my eyes.

"The groundskeeper and the maid that had been found on their estate, did you know they were father and daughter?" I swallowed hard, feeling the tears pricking at my eyes. "He...he must have gone searching for his daughter, I doubt they'd have killed him otherwise. He must have stumbled on the scene and was just another casualty in a long list of them."

He sighed deeply. "I didn't know that."

I nodded with a sniff.

Hatter's jaw clenched, and his Adam's apple rolled. I knew he felt it too. The injustice. The absolute and wretched injustice that, at the end of the day, power and money had been all that was needed to see them free and still living their lives while so many others had been lost.

Hatter was right. There were parts of the crime still fuzzy and unclear, but it was a miracle we'd been able to uncover what we had with the cover-up that had gone on. Tanner, when he'd been taken in, never talked. Even up to the bitter end, he'd never cracked. Isa had spoken, but all she'd said was an apology to Alice. Tanner had been hung in the town square for his crimes. Isa had been allowed to deliver her child before being thrown in the eternal fiery pits of the Darkrealm, forever cast out of the universe of Grimm.

Cases like these were the hardest to swallow and the hardest to let go of. But it was the reality of the job. Sometimes there wasn't going to be a neat and tidy resolution. Sometimes it was as messy and confusing as the twin hells.

"Maybe someday, they'll see the hanging end of the rope. Maybe someday, Elle. But for right now, we at least brought the murderer and his accomplice to justice."

"How's Alice," I asked softly. "Isa was her—"

He sighed. "Better now, though I don't think Alice will ever trust anyone again. Not after me, and especially not after Isa."

"Was it you, Maddox?" I asked in a breathless rush, hating myself the moment the words escaped me, wishing like the two hells that he wouldn't understand what I meant.

But he went snake-bitten, so still he looked like stone.

His eyes blazed, and I knew he was seeing something. I watched him, pained in my soul for this good man, but desperately needing to know the truth. Desperately needing to be told he didn't cause the fire, couldn't have done that to his own child.

Letting me know in no uncertain terms that he'd understood what I was asking, he took my hands in his and stared deep into my eyes.

"Hear me now, Elle. Only you could ever make me say what I'm about to say. My butterfly is off limits to all but you. You ask me did I do this terrible thing, and I have just one question for you."

My nostrils flared, waiting with bated breath to hear what he'd say.

"If I tell you the truth, will you believe me?"

I blinked.

"Will you really?" he pressed.

"Yes, Maddox. Yes, I'll believe you."

"The short answer is no. I could never have done that to my precious child. But the long answer is that it's very complicated, and in a way, yes I did."

I sucked in a sharp breath.

"Will you leave now?" he asked slowly.

Chewing on the inside of my cheek, I shook my head. "I want to know you, Maddox. I want to know you. So no, I won't leave. But someday, you're going to tell me the full, complicated story."

His face was serious, and his eyes looked broken. "I know. But that's not all I came here for today, Elle. I... I saw something. And the last time I saw something and didn't tell you, I nearly ruined any chance for us. So I'm going to tell you something now that I don't want to tell you, and I'm pretty sure it will destroy our story completely. But I care for you too much to keep it hidden."

I frowned, a sick feeling worming through the pit of my stomach. "We haven't been together for a year, Maddox. What could you possibly have to tell me that's so dire?"

"He's alive, Elle." He squeezed my fingers so tight that I felt bone rub on bone.

I blinked, confused by what he was saying. "What? Who's alive?"

"Hook. He's alive. Hook's very much alive, and... he's not well."

I suddenly felt cold all over. Shocked. Numb. I was sure he was teasing, but I saw nothing but heartbreak in his eyes. It took a full minute before I was able to register what he was saying.

"What?" I shot to my feet, looking down at him, numbed to my very core. "What did you say?"

He closed his eyes and, looking like a man resigned to his fate, whispered, "Hook's alive, and I know where he is. So, now tell me, will you leave?"

He looked at me, green eye and blue glittering with profound pain.

I felt nothing as I said, "Yes. No. I don't know. Maybe?"

There was too much in my head, too much for me to process, to work through. Hook was alive. Alive? How was that even possible? I'd seen him die with my own eyes. I'd seen and felt his lifeless body. I'd kissed his blue-tinted lips, and then I'd let him sink into the depths of the sea he'd loved so well.

I shook all over.

Hatter's shoulders slumped, and he stood. "We need to talk with Bo, and if you've got leave, take it. I think I might know where to find him."

He was cool, calm, and collected, just like he'd been after I'd attacked him for witnessing the darkness of my past. He would work with me, stand beside me, but he'd gone cold. I knew him well enough to know what this was. He was hurting and protecting himself as best he knew how. Hatter turned on his heel and marched right back through the precinct doors, giving me my space.

I wanted to chase after him, to put him at ease. But I was rooted to the ground, cold, and staring up at the noonday sky with disbelief pinching my features. This wasn't possible. None of this was possible.

Hook was alive?

Alive...

All I could do was tip my head up and watch as a large, lone raven flew through the sky. I watched it until it became a dark speck on the horizon, and only once I was completely alone did I whisper, "Hook."

THE END IS ONLY THE BEGINNING...

There will definitely be more Elle and Hatter and who knows you might even learn a bit more about Hook in the future. In fact, should all go well I'll be releasing book 2, The Long Goodnight, in 2018. So keep your eyes peeled to my Jovee Winters FB page for further updates about the Grimm Files. And if you loved this book, I have plenty other UF titles to whet your whistle while you wait. If you're looking for something edgy and dark consider starting with my Night Series I wrote as RS Black. All 4 books have been released and deals with the physical manifestations of the 7 Deadly Sins. Or if Berserkers are more your speed check out Selene's Tempted Series. If you like Shifters and Vampires, then you might just love my Southern Vampire Chronicles. All 3 of those series are completed and published.

If you'd like to read a short preview to book 2, The Long Goodnight, then make sure to keep turning the page!

Remember keep an eye on my FB[1] page for further updates! Want to know when the next Grimm Files book releases? Make sure to sign up for my newsletter[2]!

---

1.   https://www.facebook.com/joveewintersauthor/

2.   http://eepurl.com/xo-bj

More Books!
The Night Series written as RS Black

The Night Series Collection, Book 1 and 2 (TOTALLY FREE)
Howler's Night, Book 3
Red Rain, Book 4
COMPLETED SERIES
Tempted Series by Selene Charles YA Urban Fantasy
Forbidden, Book 1
Reckless, Book 2
Possessed, Book 3
COMPLETED SERIES

The Southern Vampire Detective Series
Whiskey, Vamps, and Thieves, Book 1
Fae Bridge Over Troubled Waters, (short story) 1.5
Me and You and a Ghost Named Boo, Book 2
The Vampire Went Down to Georgia, Book 3
COMPLETED SERIES

SNEAK PEEK: THE LONG GOODNIGHT

G *rimm Reports*
      Cold Case File# 308: The Slasher Gang Heists
Detail of Events-

Seventh Robbery in one year. Traversing realms and dimensions. Each time the shifters get bolder. 16th of May they held a group of peaceful fae nuns from the Holy Tree of Immaculate Conception at gunpoint, escaping the vanguard of uniformed dispatch waiting out front with ease. 22nd of July they took it one step further and held a high-ranking wizard's gnome hostage, forcing him to draw on dark magick to release locks dipped in dragon's blood, narrowly evading capture. Golden grains of sand found at scene. Possible clue. 27th of August they committed their worst act of terrorism yet. Holly Thorn, daughter of high fae Lord Banyon and Lady Seraphina caught up in crosshairs of gunfight. M.I.C.E. on scene attempted to resuscitate but she was later pronounced DOA at Winged Seraph's Infirmary.

Actions Taken-

Working hand in hand with Bureau of Special Investigations. Profilers have determined they might have a possible inside man with some form of law enforcement. Slasher Gang top priority catch. Self-avowed ringleader is number one most wanted, goes by the moniker Sleepy. Considered armed and deadly.

Summary-

Task Force created. All active and retired investigators called to action.

Made in the USA
Middletown, DE
11 January 2024